make a deal: I'll help him to become heir to
…on Empire by pretending to be his mate, and
…nt for my sister. Then I'll take revenge on the
…who took her. My only problem…? He's my
…spect.

…ain longer than seven days in the underworld,
…can never leave. Yet caught in the prince's
…ut protective embrace, do I still want to?

CU00825621

MY
# DEMON OF FIRE

So, we
the De
he'll h
demon
main s

If I ren
then I
sinful

REBEL DEMONS B

**When a billionaire demon prin**
**case of mistaken identity, I ne**
**claim me as his mate...**

The hot-as-hell Shifter De
Deadly. *Sexy.* And on my birthda

When the arrogant but gorgeou
Demon of Fire, mistakes me fo
fated mate, he whisks me away
world. I need an escape from h
what if this leads to somethin
demon prince finds out the truth
to survive is to fake our Soul Bo

MY DEMON OF FIRE: REBEL DEMONS BOOK ONE ©
copyright 2022 Rosemary A Johns

www.rosemaryajohns.com

Copyright notice: All rights reserved under the International and Pan-American Copyright Conventions. No part of this book may be reproduced or transmitted in any form or by any means, electronic or mechanical, including photocopying, recording, or by any information storage and retrieval system, without permission in writing from the publisher.

This is a work of fiction. Names, places, characters and incidents are either the product of the author's imagination or are used fictitiously, and any resemblance to any actual persons, living or dead, organizations, events or locales is entirely coincidental.

Warning: the unauthorized reproduction or distribution of this copyrighted work is illegal. Criminal copyright infringement, including infringement without monetary gain, is investigated by the FBI and is punishable by up to 5 years in prison and a fine of $250,000.

Fantasy Rebel Limited

# CONTENTS

BOOKS IN THE REBEL VERSE

## RECOMMENDED READING ORDER

## ALL BOOKS ARE STANDALONE SERIES

### *REBEL GODS - COMPLETE SERIES*

**BAD LOKI**

**BAD HADES**

**BAD RA**

### *REBEL WEREWOLVES - COMPLETE SERIES*

**COMPLETE BOX SET**

**ONLY PERFECT OMEGAS**

**ONLY PRETTY BETAS**

**ONLY PROTECTOR ALPHAS**

### *REBEL ACADEMY - WICKEDLY CHARMED COMPLETE SERIES*

**COMPLETE BOX SET**

**CRAVE**

**CRUSH**

**CURSE**

# REBEL: HOUSE OF FAE - COMPLETE

## HOUSE OF FAE

# REBEL ANGELS - COMPLETE SERIES

**COMPLETE SERIES BOX SET: BOOKS 1-5**

**VAMPIRE HUNTRESS**

**VAMPIRE PRINCESS**

**VAMPIRE DEVIL**

**VAMPIRE MAGE**

**VAMPIRE GOD**

# REBEL DEMONS

**MY DEMON OF FIRE**

**MY DEMON OF AIR**

# REBEL VAMPIRES - COMPLETE SERIES

**COMPLETE SERIES BOX SET BOOKS 1-3**

**BLOOD DRAGONS**

**BLOOD SHACKLES**

**BLOOD RENEGADES**

**STANDALONE: BLOOD GODS**

BOOKS IN THE OXFORD VERSE

**RECOMMENDED READING ORDER**

# CHAPTER ONE

**Academy of Music, The Hill, England**

*BLUE*

"The demons are coming for us," Skye, my twin sister, whispers.

I startle in shock, hissing in a breath. "What? *Now*?"

Skye's cobalt blue eyes are wide and frantic. "I've been having nightmares…visions, I guess. They're going to take us away as human sacrifices just like they did Mum and Dad. Please, Blue, can't we run?"

Skye's shaking, even as her elegant fingers dance over the piano keys.

She's playing a jazzed up version of Little Mix's "Black Magic" because even when she's gigging at an elite ball like the one this evening, she still has a crappy taste in music.

We may be identical twins, but I'm the badass.

If *badass* means juggling three jobs and *still* being a term behind in payments for my sister's place at the Academy of Music.

*Or perhaps it means the dagger that I always wear around my waist for when the demons return.*

My dagger is called Light-bringer.

Light-bringer is short, sharp, and stabby. It's also the antique steel blade that has been passed down through my family, and which I always wear through a loop at my belt in a copper scabbard.

Skye sits with perfect posture at the piano. Her long, golden hair falls around her bronzed shoulders to the curve of her hips. Since this is the Heaven and Hell Ball to celebrate the start of the summer term at the academy, she's dressed in a glimmering white outfit with satin top and pants, along with a sweeping pair of angel wings and an aluminum halo that I spent all last night making, along with my own.

It's tradition that we dress the same way on our birthdays, and I'm not going to break it after twenty-one years.

*But I'll be damned if I'll be forced into a dress.*

Looking at my twin is like looking into a mirror. Except, I know that Skye's gold makeup is perfect, whereas mine's a hot mess.

On the other hand, I'm the one wearing a dagger, so who's truly winning?

*Right?*

"Fucking lies. No one in the Hill is sacrificed," I correct, more fiercely than I intended, "they're *stolen*."

My pulse is racing, and my mouth is dry.

*Shit.*

I can't do this. *Can't.*

Every couple of years, the demons rise out of the demon underworld and raid our English town, The Hill.

And the humans who are taken, never come back.

Dad told me that originally, the raids were about arranged bondings like marriage treaties. But now, The Hill's Council call those who are taken *Demon Sacrifices*, claiming that they're to be devoured or enslaved as the price of peace: *an honor.*

But that's bullshit. They're not really sacrifices. *They're Demon Stolen. A*nd I've sworn that I'll get them all back and save my town from the demons.

*Somehow.*

When I take a deep breath to calm myself, I'm flooded by the intoxicating, perfumed scent of the ballroom.

The glittering chandelier's light is too bright. The heat in the hall, which is high ceilinged, is suffocating. It's been decked out on one side in a version of heaven

3

with white walls that shimmer and fairy lights strung between the buffet tables, which are covered in trays of canapes, neat sandwiches, and dips and tortillas. Feathers are strewn across the floor.

On the other side, it's covered in blood-red velvets with piles of skulls in the corners. Flaming torches gutter on the walls, casting dancing shadows across the ballroom and the stage at the far end.

The piano is placed right in the middle, straddling the line between heaven and hell.

I clench my fists at my sides.

The crowds around me press too close. The swirl of the beautiful men and women of the academy, who are dressed in tailored suits with devil horns or elegant dresses with angel wings, makes me want to hurl.

They're displaying themselves like pretty baubles for the demons.

Hell, why don't they just smother themselves in syrup and bang the sacrificial gong to summon the demons for dinner?

See, I know three things for certain.

Never trust a demon.

Never trust a guy

And the only person in the world who I *do* trust is my sister.

I balance my golden serving tray, which glitters with crystal champagne flutes, on the top of the piano.

I'm working tonight at this ball for the elite brats

of The Hill because my sister asked me to, even though I've already spent all day cleaning their parents' houses.

Shadows smudge under my eyes, and my muscles ache with exhaustion. I sigh, shifting from one tired foot to the other. It doesn't help that Skye insisted on high leather boots with spiky killer heels.

Killer on my ankles too (although, probably useful to kill demons).

I try to hide my fear behind a smile, but it doesn't work because Skye knows me as well as I know myself. It's a twin thing like answering questions at the same time, being able to prank other people by pretending we're each other, and having to get used to being stared at…all…the…time.

After all, we're the only identical twins in The Hill.

When the elemental brand on my wrist tingles, I rub it, absentmindedly. The mark bears the symbols of fire, water, air and earth: the four elemental kingdoms of the demon underworld.

They're why we can't run or hide.

Everyone in The Hill is born with the brand, as if it's been burned onto us by hell's flame. It marks us out as belonging to the demons. They trap us within the bounds of the town, unable to tell the outside world the truth or risk losing our memories…or our minds.

"Sorry." Skye bites her lip. Her gentle gaze darts to mine. "I'm just scared."

Yet I'm *angry*, fuming. A red rage sears through me.

I never thought that I could hate anything as much as I hate the demons.

Skye and I are two halves of the same Soul, but we couldn't be more different.

"Scared doesn't survive," I reply. *"Hate, don't be hurt.* That's how we damned well survive, remember? And not by running and hiding. Even if your nightmares are visions, then we can't stop what's going to happen. But by the Stones, look around us..." I gesture at the dancers. "We're surrounded by the pretty elite." I cock my head. "If you were a demon, wouldn't you steal the Queen Bee?" I point at a woman in a scarlet dress, whose fiery curls cascade to her shoulders. She has such a haughty expression that she looks disappointed to be stepping her dainty foot on anything but a red carpet. "I've been reliably told that Lana can even get a guy off in less than a minute."

"Impressive, if she hadn't started that rumor herself."

I point at a guy with dirty blond curls and caramel skin, who's dressed in a gray suit and waistcoat. He's leaning against the far wall like he's bored.

"Then what about Maxton? His ass is so tight that

any female demon would be mesmerized by it. Maybe they won't even notice that he's a dick. Hmm, what if he's actually an incubus?"

A shadow chases across Skye's expression. "You pretend not to care, but we both know that you'd fight to stop Lana, Maxton, or *anyone* from being stolen."

My jaw clenches. "I'd fight any demon. Period."

I glance out of the high, domed windows. I can see the town's slanted roofs in the ghostly gray of dusk, and the church's spire in the distance. Beyond that, is the darkness of the Eternal Forest.

*And everyone knows to never step foot in there.*

Dad once warned Skye and me that the forest is in between worlds. It's neither dark nor light but a place of shadows. Then he leaned closer, pushing the hair from both our faces, before he added: *beware most, the demons who devour you.*

Then the demons *did* devour him.

Five years ago, they came to the Hill and...

My breath hitches, and I hug my arms around myself.

*Horns, fangs, and black eyes.*

*The sweet smell of roses.*

*Summer rain hitting the window.*

I shake my head, desperately trying to hold onto the present and not lose myself back in that moment from five summers ago.

7

My chest is tight. I can't breathe. Sweat slips down the back of my neck.

"Skye," I force out between gritted teeth. *Hell, I need her.* "Skye."

Skye leans against me because she knows… always knows…when I'm lost back in the moment that our parents were stolen. Only she can ground me in the present. Her touch is reassuring.

Mum told me that we played together, even in the womb.

Skye swallows. "This isn't the twenty-first birthday that we'd always planned, right?"

"Yeah, I'm disappointed. Where's the burlesque dancing, the Jell-o shot tower, or rave in the town square?"

"I was hoping for a naked bartender and a private cocktail lesson."

I let out a shocked laugh. "Is that a euphemism? I knew you had it in you. Your whole meek and sweet thing is all an act."

She cocks her brow at me. "You're the one with a crooked halo."

"Always."

"I mean, it's really crooked."

"Oh." I reach up, adjusting my costume. "But hey, there's vodka and a cupcake with a candle for each of us waiting at home. We just have to get through this thrice demon damned night."

8

"Chocolate and raspberry...?" Skye asks with a hopeful glint in her eye.

"Could it be anything else?" I tap my foot. "Although, I should've got you carrot cake, since you took my iPod again."

Skye looks outraged, and I fight to hide my grin. "You wouldn't be that cruel." Then she tries and fails to look innocent. Sometimes, she forgets that one of the negative, as well as the positive, things about being a twin is how well we know each other. "It must've been your other sister who *borrowed* it. You know, the one who isn't your favorite and that we keep hidden away in the attic, so her cries don't disturb the neighbors."

I stare at her. "Creepy."

Her fingers pause on the keys. "Actually, that joke went darker than I was expecting."

"I'm a bad influence."

"You should've come dressed as Lucifer then."

I gasp. "Hell, I *am* a bad influence. Get back to work before I have to gag you."

"If I was gagged, then I couldn't tell you that I have a surprise planned for you tonight. Your gift."

My expression lights up. "Clues...?"

"Nope. It's a secret. You'll have to wait and see."

I stroke her hair out of her face, and she begins playing again. She's the other half of me, and I love her. She's been with me from the moment that I was born, exactly three minutes after she was.

Mum named us Skye and Blue after the intense blueness of our eyes. Sometimes, I think it was more that Mum simply loved to sit outside our cottage and stare up at the skies and imagine that she — any of us on The Hill – were as free as the endlessly reaching skies, instead of trapped beneath them.

"Aren't you supposed to be working, Smurfette?" A bored voice demands. *Maxton.* "Pass me some more champagne, would you?"

Maxton strolls toward me through the crowds. His waistcoat is embroidered with red flames that match the flashing horns, which light up his curls.

He always loves tempting danger.

*Me.*

After all, why else is he still trying to be friends? He's been trying since we were five years old, so kudos for perseverance.

I growl, studying his outfit that mocks the real devils in the Eternal Forest.

Why doesn't he just wear a sign: **Demon Snack?**

*Idiot.*

I snatch a glass off my tray and pass it to him. The champagne sloshes over the edges, but he still sketches a bow as he takes the drink. "Thanks, Smurfette. I like to know that my father's money is being well spent."

I roll my eyes. "We get it. Your big, powerful father, the Mayor, owns this town, academy, and probably our asses too. Still, have you considered that you have daddy issues?"

Maxton's hazel eyes dance with amusement as they meet mine. "Obviously. Haven't you?"

I bristle. "You know, this is the perfect time for you to become a missing person."

"Harsh."

"But so fair. Your daddy's been prepping you as sacrifice material for years."

"Blue." Skye shoots me a warning glance.

Why is my hand on the hilt of my dagger?

Maxton's eyes are gleaming, and his tongue darts out to wet his lips.

Is he getting off on pushing my buttons or on the fantasy of what'll happen if I actually hold my blade to his throat?

To be fair, I've known some guys who are into that kink.

Maxton leans closer. "Then he can *go fuck himself.* I'm as fierce as a demon. I'm a bloody devil in bed and out of it. I won't be stolen by one."

I stare at him, shocked.

*WTF?*

Maxton's lips curl into a smile. "Surely I haven't shocked the cold as a blade Smurfette…? Go me. I won't bow down, shaking and scared, pretending that

11

the demons aren't our enemies. You're not the only one in this town who's a rebel."

I let my hand fall away from my dagger, scrutinizing Maxton so closely that he squirms (*go me*). "Then by the Stones, after this ball, let's talk. You're the second most powerful man in The Hill. I have more fire for this fight than anyone. If you plan on starting a secret scheme to save us, then I'll be there right alongside you." I meet Skye's gaze and I know how she's feeling, as if she's spoken out loud. "*We'll* be alongside you."

Skye smiles.

Fire sparks in Maxton's eyes, before his bored mask settles back into place. "Later then. It's too dangerous here. What we're talking about is treason." He adjusts his cufflinks, but it's a nervous tell. The Mayor also freaks the hell out of me, and I don't have to live with him. "He would, you know."

My brow furrows. "Would what?"

"Sacrifice me." Maxton's gaze is blank in a horrifying way, as he gazes out at the beautiful ballroom, which is paid for by his dad. "He's told me every night since I can remember that it's *an honor*. I remember sitting in the dark after he'd close the door to my bedroom, terrified that the demons would climb through my window to devour me. And then I'd feel so ashamed because I wasn't glowing with the honor of becoming a *sacrifice*." He snorts, shaking himself.

"If he finds out that we're doing this, then we'll be thrown into the Eternal Forest."

Skye gasps, and I shiver.

He's right.

That's the ultimate punishment: exile into the Eternal Forest.

It's worse than death.

I grasp Maxton by the chin, and his startled gaze meets mine. "Then he won't find out, right?"

Maxton nods.

"Who said that I wouldn't make our birthday exciting?" I tease. "Who needs naked bartenders, when I bring you a revolution?"

"Excuse me, but I believe that was *my* gift?" Maxton arches his brow.

All of a sudden, I catch movement close to the stage at the far end of the ballroom. There's a buzz of chatter and excitement.

What's happening?

Shit, are the demons here? Is Skye right about another raid tonight?

*Please, not already.* Let us have our birthday...*not now.*

My gift to Skye is still lying where I left it on her bed, waiting for me to present it to her: a silver and sapphire treble clef pendant.

*I'll fucking kill any demon who touches my twin.*

Adrenaline spikes through me, and my lips curl back into a snarl, as I spin to watch the commotion.

A sinfully beautiful man swaggers through the crowd, who are staring at him.

I'm frozen to the spot. My heart races, and my pupils dilate.

Who the hell is he?

The man is palely mesmerizing. His dark, shiny hair tumbles messily around his face, as if he's just tumbled out of bed or is too lazy to style it. But he has thick, black eyeliner under eyes that are large and so dark in his porcelain face that they're almost black.

I can't look away from them.

My chest tightens.

How haven't I noticed someone in The Hill, who's daring enough to pull off the hot rock god look that's always had me panting?

He's taller than anyone here, and his shoulders are broad. When he pulls himself up onto the stage, his strong muscles under his sheer black top that's scooped low at the front to reveal his translucent collarbones, bunch. His tight scarlet leather trousers that glitter like dragon hide cling to his muscled legs.

I've never wanted to lick a man all over so much in my life.

He has cute red horns that stick out of his lustrous hair (which would be perfect to wrench his head back by), and a matching fluffy tail hanging from the back of his pants.

I freeze.

*What the fuck is wrong with me?*

This is the first time that I've found a demon sexy, even a fake one. I must be coming down with something. I seriously hope that it's not love sickness.

The rock demon snatches up an acoustic guitar, which is balanced at the front of the stage. The guitar is emblazoned with flames, and he slips its leather strap over his shoulder. Then he flashes the crowd a wicked grin. His teeth are sharp and white.

I shiver.

He's not even looking at me but somehow, it's like every glance and smile are for me alone.

Lana whistles, and the crowd screams and cheers wildly, flocking around the stage.

My hands clench at my sides.

*I'm screwed.*

I have a revolution to plan. Real demons to freak out about.

What I don't have time for…? Impossibly gorgeous singers with hooded, bedroom eyes, indecently tight pants, and slinky hips.

I bite my lip. *Hard.*

"And *that* is my hot new music professor." Skye's lips turn up at the side.

"Your professor?" I splutter.

My heart beats even faster.

"Surprise!" Skye stops playing Little Mix and claps her hands in delight. There's something gleaming in her eyes that scares me: *she's hiding something*. We never keep secrets from each other. "You're going to love your gift. And *he'll* love *you.*"

# CHAPTER TWO

## Academy of Music, The Hill, England

Mesmerized, I'm unable to look away from the gorgeous guy on stage, who rocks the whole bad boy look without even trying but somehow, is my sister's professor.

Shit, if I'd known that professors came in sinful packages with tight asses like that, then I'd have worked harder to become a music prodigy like Skye.

Actually, that's a lie.

But I'd have offered to work more of the academy's events.

"How the hell is one of your professors my

surprise gift?" I breathe, hoping that I'm not as flushed as I feel.

Why is dread coiling in my stomach that this is the type of surprise with a sting in its tail?

Kind of like when Mum insisted on inviting Maxton, as the Mayor's son, to my tenth birthday party. When I opened my beautifully wrapped emerald box, which Maxton had handed to me with a wink, a snake slithered out onto my lap.

Maxton snickered, expecting me to scream. He stared at me in awed respect, however, when I joined him in his laughter, instead.

Unfortunately, his dad was less amused, and it was Maxton, who was left with a sting in his tail that day.

I scowl, remembering how frequently Maxon's dad has punished him for his wild spirit.

Maxton and I may be enemies as much as we're friends, but it works for us. Probably, because Maxton's one of the few people who's never tried to tame me either.

Plus, I adopted the snake and named it *Maxton*.

You need to be smart with your revenge.

Maxton crosses his arms. "That guy's nothing special. My horns are flashing. His look cheap."

My lips pinch. "Congratulations. You win the *overcompensating for something with fake horns* contest."

"Then he wins it with the way he's holding his

guitar like he's about to fuck it." Maxton waggles his eyebrows.

Hell, it's true. Why did Maxton have to put that image into my head?

I can't tear my gaze from the impossibly beautiful guy, who despite the fangirling (and fanboying) of the crowd, looks like he'd rather be anywhere but up on that stage. Probably, still snuggled under the blankets of his bed, between the legs of his lover, or slouched in a bar somewhere nursing his pint.

He only looks a couple of years older than me.

Despite teaching here, is he struggling to pay his bills like I am? Is this just another gig for extra cash?

Then I straighten in shock. What if he truly is *working for money* tonight?

Don't say that Skye's really bought or hired him…?

What if this whole thing is a fantasy treat for me?

I slam my hand onto the piano, and Skye squeaks. "What have you done? Okay, he's scorching-hot, exactly my type, and clever cover story with the whole *professor* line. But tell me that he's not an escort."

Is it bad that a part of me hopes that he is?

Skye's eyes widen in shock, before she covers her face with her hands. Her shoulders shake.

My stomach plummets.

I hate it when Skye cries. *Hate it.*

19

"I'm sorry. I swear on the Stolen that I didn't mean…" I stroke her shoulder, desperately.

When Maxton snorts behind me, I stiffen. Then Skye pulls away her hands, and I understand.

*She's laughing.*

I open and then shut my mouth in shock. "So, I'm not about to get my *Pretty Woman* moment in reverse…? You're breaking my heart here."

Maxton takes a long sip of champagne. "That would be a short film anyway, since your savings consist of a handful of ancient daggers and chocolate coins."

"And he really is a professor…?" Now would be a good time for the earth to open up and swallow me.

"That's Mr. Underwood." Skye grasps my hand, and as always it feels like the most natural and right thing for our fingers to entwine. Holding hands in the crib with Skye is one of my earliest memories. "He just started this term and is only teaching a few lessons. He's not really my professor, more like a star appointment to show the rest of us what a real prodigy looks like. I've only spoken to him once or twice. Half the campus is already in love."

*Of course, they are.*

"Still, teacher and student. That's hot," I say, just to see Skye blush.

She's still a virgin.

Losing our parents in such a traumatic way

affected us differently. Skye's too frightened to love, but I *love* pleasure.

I can't let myself fall in love, however, because that would mean the risk of grieving again: what if I lose them in a moment?

*What if they became the next Demon Stolen?*

Still, Underwood looks like he knows a lot about *pleasure.*

My brow creases. "I don't understand. He seems about our age. So, how haven't I seen him around?"

Skye's eyes gleam, as she stands up. "You know that mansion close to the forest, the one our parents told us never to go near?"

"The one my father forbade *everybody* from entering the grounds of," Maxton adds.

I nod. "Cardinal Hall."

Skye's gaze slides to Underwood, who's adjusting the microphone stand. "Well, *he* lives there. The gossip says that his family were all eccentric, reclusive billionaires. They homeschooled him; he's a genius. But they never let him out."

My chest tightens. "That sucks. Poor guy."

"You'd think he'd be able to afford better horns," Maxton smirks, "and a comb."

Except, I like how Underwood looks.

A mysterious reclusive billionaire who still wants to teach music…or is that simply his way of escaping as well?

I thought that I was trapped in The Hill, but what must it've been like to have been trapped in Cardinal Hall close to the Eternal Forest?

My heart aches.

"So, why'd the rumors say he finally left the mansion?" I ask.

Skye watches my face, carefully. "His parents were Demon Stolen."

I gasp, battling against the flood of emotions that threaten to pull me under.

My gaze shoots to the guy who's standing on the stage. He looks alone amidst the crowd, and I get it now.

*I felt like that for years.*

Suddenly, the lights dim, leaving behind the glittering of the fairy lights and the guttering of the torches. The crowd quietens to a hushed, excited chatter.

They're waiting for something.

Anticipating it, the magic.

I'm caught in the moment as well.

"Why is he my gift?" I murmur.

Skye edges past the piano stool to slip her arm around my shoulder. "Well, I got you here, and him as well. I can't do all the work."

*Wait, what?*

Is she playing matchmaker?

"The demons," I hiss. "Your visions and night-mares and—"

"Scared doesn't survive." Skye throws my own words back at me. Don't you just hate it when it's your own ass that needs spanking? "I still sense that they're coming, but you said that we can't run and hide. So, I won't. Anyway, I set this up, before I knew that."

"Set what up?"

"We both know that you're lonely," Skye says, quietly.

I bare my teeth, even as my stomach twists. "How can I be lonely with treason to plot, a town to save, and Maxton to torment?"

Maxton preens. "She wants my ass. She just won't admit it."

I roll my eyes. "We both know that if we got together, the only thing we'd do is kick each other's asses."

Maxton winks. "How'd you know that's not my kink?"

Skye turns my chin to make me look at the stage, which is now backlit with a light show of flickering flames; Underwood's finishing up his soundchecks. "Give him a chance. You have so much in common." I huff, unconvinced. "Did you think I wouldn't have done my research? He's into weird stuff like you: ancient weapons, crappy rock songs, and kinky stuff.

Well, that last one's a guess. But just look at him; he has to be, right?"

*Hell, yeah.*

"I get it. Hot kinky professor. But why'd you even think that he'd talk to me?" I demand.

Seriously, it'll kill me if he doesn't now.

Skye shoots me a sly smile. "Just listen to him sing. I'm going to dance."

Like the gentleman he isn't but pretends to be, Maxton holds out his arm to Skye. "Shall we?"

Protectively, I snatch at both of them, holding them back. "We shouldn't split up."

"We can't discuss our plans until after the ball, and your sister needs a distraction. Now, unhand me, Smurfette," Maxton commands, haughtily.

"I'll only be on the dance floor," Skye adds.

Reluctantly, I let go and watch as they weave out into the jostling crowd.

Then my gaze is drawn sharply back to the stage, as the room's main lights go down, leaving Underwood alone and lit only by the devilish flames.

And I'm screwed.

Totally and utterly.

*Screwed.*

Because the moment that he strums the first bluesy rock chords of Courtney Barn's "Hellfire", I'm lost, drawn into his performance like everybody else.

Underwood's voice is raspy, raw, and gritty. It's so

deep and filled with anguish that I'd guess he was centuries old and not barely older than me. His eyes flutter closed, as he sings, and the dancing light catches on his sinfully long, coal black eyelashes. His hand lashes down across his guitar in savage strokes.

I slide my hand down myself, teasing myself through the satin material. I struggle not to slip my hands down my pants.

If I could bottle his sexiness, I'd never have to work again.

I'm burning up inside and I can't look away from *my gift*.

His music winds around me: it's elemental.

*Magic.*

It's exhilarating.

But not even half as much as his performance.

Underwood's on fire up there. He no longer looks like he's just rolled out of bed. His eyes are burning, he's thrumming with energy, and he's striding around the stage like he owns the whole town.

And we're all in his thrall.

The crowd are wildly whooping and dancing up and down, caught in his spell too. My heart is beating so hard that I feel it'll burst out of my chest.

Underwood's tail sways along with his hips, and his dark eyes flash.

Right now, under the red haze of the lights, he's not a professor. He's the King of this Hell, and everyone here would willingly crawl at his feet as his slave.

*And that's power.*

For a moment, his gaze appears to pierce the darkness to meet mine.

I stop breathing.

He can't see me in the dark, right?

My knees buckle, and I sit heavily on the piano stool.

My hands clench in my lap. I hate that he can affect me like this.

Nobody should be able to. It's not safe.

But do I want *safe*? Have I ever?

I rub absentmindedly at the brand on my wrist, shuddering.

Let the music stop.

Stop. Stop. Stop.

*Don't let it ever stop.*

Finally, Underwood strums the final wild chords.

He leans closer to the microphone. "This song is dedicated to Blue, the special birthday girl, if you're out there. Have a wickedly fun evening, princess."

*WTF?*

I freeze.

There's an unsettled stirring in the crowd. It must be killing these elite brats that their hot professor, who they're in love with, is dedicating the song to *me*: their cleaner, server, and dog-walker.

*The servant.*

My grin is so wide that my cheeks hurt.

So, this dedication is Skye's secret gift.

*She's awesome.* Plus, her professor must be pretty awesome too because how many reclusive billionaires would take birthday requests from students that they hardly know?

Underwood hauls off his guitar and hurls it across the stage. He looks ready to fight a war, raging with energy and adrenaline. He leaps down from the stage, landing in a crouch that makes his muscles bulge.

*Diva.*

He straightens, and the students around him explode into applause.

When the lights rise, he appears to be scanning the ballroom for someone.

A curl is plastered to Underwood's forehead, and his hair looks even more tousled than before. His sheer top clings to his muscled chest, and after his active performance in the summer heat, I can see every outline, from his abs to the gorgeous V leading to his leather pants. Yet he looks even more handsome now than he did before.

When he swaggers through the fangirls, who are hanging around him, like they're not even there or he doesn't notice them, his intent gaze meets mine across the room.

I startle and draw back.

I'm shocked by the cool smile that breaks across his face. I'm even more surprised by the warmth that settles in my stomach.

Instantly, Underwood stalks toward me like he's the predator, and I'm the prey.

I'm used to it being the other way around, and it's unsettling.

My heart is in my throat, and I can't swallow, as he approaches me, but before he can reach my side, Lana snatches at his sleeve.

"You can steal me to the underworld anytime," Lana purrs. I hiss in a shocked breath. How can she say things like that as a pick-up line? *Like they mean nothing?* "That was literally the best. I mean, wow." Then she glares at me. "Don't bother with her. Maybe nobody's told you, but she's only the help."

Underwood blinks like he's just noticing Lana and she's of no more interest to him than an annoying bug.

"And you're only a brat." Underwood's voice is deep and as beautiful as his singing, but it's threaded with such cold danger that my hand instinctively slides to the hilt of my dagger.

Lana steps back in shock like he's slapped her, and he pushes past her, as if she doesn't exist and isn't actually a Duchess.

Lana's the most powerful, prestigious woman in The Hill. Guys beg to date her.

*For her to glance at them.*

Nobody in The Hill has ever stood up for me like that. This professor hasn't even met me, but he's already got my back.

I harden my expression.

*Hate, don't be hurt.*

It's my primary rule. Spellbinding dark eyes and plush, kissable lips can't tempt me to break it. And neither can being in my corner, no matter how rare that is.

I've already allowed myself to love Skye (Maxton too), and I can't let anyone else in.

Underwood's intent gaze never leaves mine, as he prowls across the dance floor toward me.

Shit, where's Skye or even Maxton? Why aren't they coming back?

I wish that my phone was as easy to loop onto this stupid costume as my dagger, then I could text her to get her ass back here.

*Too late.*

The feathers on my wings shake. Why do I sense that my pretend innocence is about to be corrupted?

Underwood slouches against the piano.

I clear my throat. "I feel like the start of a joke. An angel and a devil walk into a bar…"

He tilts his head, and his hair tumbles across his eyes. "I don't think you're telling it right. Isn't it: An angel walks into a bar….*oww*?"

I let out an undignified snort of laughter, and

Underwood's whole face lights up with a brilliant smile like he's the sun.

It's so different to the coldness, which made me shiver, as he dismissed Lana that I wonder if I imagined it.

Except, I didn't.

When he grabs a glass of champagne and holds it out to me (has any guy in The Hill *ever* been thoughtful enough to serve me, rather than the other way around?), I stare at his powerful fingers around the glass. His fingernails are painted blood-red.

When I accept the champagne, I immediately take a sip. It's the first alcohol that I've had this evening, and I damn well need it. I wrinkle my nose at the fruity aroma with a hint of honey, and choke (in an attractive way) on the bubbles.

When I glance over the lip of my champagne flute, I catch Underwood watching me. He looks away quickly. When I take another sip, his considering look is back on me.

I flush.

"Did your sister enjoy the song like you thought she would, sweetness?" Underwood drawls. "You're the first person to invite me...anywhere. Your request was the least I could do to repay you." He leans closer. "So, where is she? I'd love to meet her."

*Sweetness*, seriously?

My brain screams to a halt. My hand tightens so much around the glass that it squeaks like it'll shatter.

*Of course.* Underwood thinks that I'm Skye.

My stomach roils, and I battle not to roll my eyes.

This is vintage Skye. No wonder he calls her *sweetness*.

Skye is sweetly, blindly innocent. Yet she's still tricked both her professor and me into meeting up tonight on a blind date with a twist. She hasn't told him that her sister is actually *her twin,* and he's been hidden away as a recluse and one of the few who'd fall for her plan.

Yet all the time, she hasn't seen what's obvious: her professor thought that she was inviting *him* on a date.

Well, time to have some fun with both of them.

Revenge needs to be smart. So, this is payback. He can have a Skye who he's never met before.

*He can have me.*

"My sister's just dancing with some guy who she's been in a love-hate relationship with since kindergarten, when a prank war got out of hand."

He raises his eyebrow. "She sounds…interesting."

"She is, Mr. Underwood."

"It's Sol, remember?"

"Sol," I place down my glass by the side of the stool, and he follows even that movement like it's fascinating, "your music was badass. I bet it was the highlight of her monumentally crappy birthday."

Sol's brow furrows, before to my surprise, he dives toward me and sniffs my hair, scenting toward my neck.

I shove him back, pushing myself off the stool. "What the hell?"

"Problem, sweetness?"

"Fuck, yeah. Do you normally go around sniffing people?"

Sol looks unfazed, merely cocking his head. "You're welcome to smell me."

To be fair, he's standing so close to me now that I can smell him. And the scent is delicious: a masculine aroma of leather with a spicy hint of ginger. It makes me want to wrench him closer and truly nuzzle along his neck...or lick him all over...or both.

Instead, I try to calm the fast beat of my heart.

This reclusive billionaire has been trapped by himself for his entire life. I don't know why, but nothing is normal in The Hill. It's no wonder that he doesn't exactly get social conventions.

*Or is a sociopath.*

Wow, my sister can really pick them.

"Let's not spoil all of the mystery," I mutter.

"Have you changed something? Your hair or...you feel different."

*Kudos.* He's picked up on the whole twin swap

prank faster than those who know that we're twins normally do.

"Well, I have gone with the whole smudged makeup and exhausted under-eye shadow effect tonight," I reply. "Have you seen me as a hot mess before?"

When Sol laughs, it's deep and rumbling, and it makes warmth unfurl in my stomach.

I crave to make him sound like that again.

"I like it." He ducks his head. "I can be a little intense, I've been told."

"I would never have guessed."

He grasps his chest. "Slain by sarcasm. Sweetness, you wound me."

"Not yet."

He looks far too delighted with the threat of assault. Perhaps, he is kinky.

When he brushes his lustrous hair back from his face, I have to battle not to replace his hand with mine and pull him closer. Instead, I grab his red tail, stroking it. It's just as fluffy as it looks.

Sol's eyes widen, and he practically melts against me. "And I thought that we weren't at the intimate stage of sniffing, but here you are, stroking my tail."

I chuckle. "It's cute. And believe me, I've never thought that about a demon before, even a pretend one."

His lips curl up at one side. "Let this be the night

for firsts then." He taps the top of the piano. "Are you playing?"

*Uh-oh.*

Only if he wants a version of "Chopsticks" that'll make his ears bleed.

I swallow, shaking my head. "I played earlier. I need to give my magic fingers a rest."

*Magic fingers?* Somebody shoot me now.

And why the hell am I even waggling my fingers in demonstration?

To my surprise, Sol grasps my hand and massages it, in a way that makes me sigh.

"You rest," he says. What does he think I am: a delicate flower? Except, that's exactly how he sees Skye. *Damn this whole twin thing.* Why do I have to be enjoying this guy's company? Why couldn't he be a dick? "I know how hard you practice. Well, when you're not trying to convince me that I should be having my hair cut like Harry Styles or allowing you to play Ed Sheeran…"

I slap my palm over my mouth to smother my grin.

Yeah, that sounds like Skye.

"Come on, beneath your rock god exterior, I bet you fucking love drill, right?" I smirk.

Immediately, Sol freezes.

*Whoops.*

I bet he's never heard Skye cuss. He's in for a shock around me.

"I can imagine you now," I continue, "alone in your mansion, rapping at the top of your voice."

"How did you find out my secret?" He deadpans. "Why don't you come and visit Cardinal Hall and then you can discover how talented my mouth is...at rapping."

I gape at him, pinking.

Is he flirting with me?

Dirty talking?

*Did he just ask me on a second date?* Except, he thinks that he's talking to Skye.

Yet they've never met up outside a couple of classes. This is their first date (and I bet, first proper conversation), and he's spending it with *me*.

This is *our* date.

But what will happen when he discovers that I'm *Blue*?

My palms are sweaty, and I rub them down my pants. My guts churn with what feels suspiciously like guilt.

I like Sol. Genuinely like him.

It was Skye who set us up like this. I can't keep up the charade any longer. I want to tell him the truth, but will it get my sister in trouble with her professor?

I rip my hand out of his, and he stares at me with

wide, impossibly dark eyes. "This has all been... strange...but I've got to go and find my sister now."

Sol leans closer, and my breath hitches, as his hot breath gusts against my lips; I have to fight against the urge to kiss him. "You *are* different. Plus, broken. There's a fire burning in you. It's irresistible. I wish to consume it and feel it sear me. Don't you want to brand me with your anger?"

His words hurt in a way that twists me inside. *In a way that I didn't know I could still feel.*

Tears prick the back of my eyes.

*Hate, don't be hurt.*

"As I said," I hiss, "*strange.* I don't play without a hell of a lot of negotiation, including checklists and safe words. Is that poetically *broken* enough for you? Now get the fuck out of my way."

Sol's eyes blaze, and his smile is cold enough to make me tremble. "Oh, I am so happy that I accepted your invitation tonight. I've dreamed of meeting you. Haven't you dreamed of me?"

That's it. I'm telling the beautiful, dangerous asshole the truth.

"You don't get it," I bristle, "I'm not..."

Except, the confession's shocked out of me by the roar of wind that rushes through the ballroom.

Terror jolts through me.

It can't be happening. Not now.

*On the names of the Stolen, please, not now.*

But it is.

The earth rumbles, and the marble floor cracks open. Feathers and skulls are caught in the whirlwind, dragged up into the air in a crazy dance above the ballroom. I shiver in the sudden cold, wincing at the deafening noise of the hall being ripped apart. The students scream and tumble into each other, stampeding for the exit in terror.

But running won't help. It never does. It's too late.

The real demons.

Are.

Coming.

Someone has been selected as a sacrifice. Tonight, a human will be stolen.

*The demons are here.*

# CHAPTER THREE

**Academy of Music, The Hill, England**

Ashen, I draw my dagger. My knuckles are white around the hilt of Light-bringer, as I crouch in the devastation of the ballroom.

Students dressed as devils and angels flood out of the hall or huddle against the walls, weeping. The flaming torches are knocked from the walls and light fires around the room. The feathers smolder.

The hall has been transformed into hell.

A chasm gapes down the middle of the dance floor, cracking the stage at the far end in half. The hall has been broken like the night and my birthday.

*Like my whole fucking town.*

I don't want to let these assholes steal anyone else and destroy another family, as they wrecked mine.

My adrenaline spikes, and my breathing is ragged.

Tears burn my eyes.

All I wanted tonight was vodka and a cupcake.

Were my expectations truly too high?

My sister outdid herself with the song dedication, but a demon raid wasn't on my wish list.

*Skye.*

Hell, let Maxton have got her out of here. If he has, then I'll forgive him for inventing the nickname *Smurfette* and allow him to become an honorary sibling. I know he's lonely as the only child of the Mayor.

*As long as he's saved Skye.*

I catch the movement of real horns across the ballroom and dark eyes in the shadows.

They meet mine.

I scream, stumbling back.

*Horns, fangs, and black eyes.*

*The sweet smell of roses.*

*Summer rain hitting the window.*

Fiercely, I shake my head.

My fingers clutch even more tightly to Lightbringer.

I can't freak out.

*For Skye.*

When I take a step toward the smoking dance

floor, a hand snaps around the brand on my wrist, and I snarl.

"Stay with me," a deep voice rumbles. *Sol.* I glance to meet his dark gaze. He's no longer slouched and casual, but his muscles are coiled for a fight. He looks as dangerous as me. "I'll protect you."

*Seriously?* A pampered professor? Some rich… admittedly sexy as hell…recluse, who's probably never even handled a blade, is going to protect me?

I snort.

*Yeah, right.*

Wait, he still thinks I'm Skye. To be fair, she is the damsel in distress sort.

But I'm fucking not.

I pull my wrist away from Sol, and he lets me. My brand tingles. I force myself not to rub it.

"Come with me or not, but I'm looking for my sister," I reply. "You're weirdly possessive."

Sol smiles like it's a compliment. "I know."

He follows at my heels.

I scan the room for my mirror image: angel wings and golden hair. My heartbeat ratchets up.

Where the hell is Skye?

All of a sudden, there's a deafening creak above me like the entire room is being snapped in half by a giant. I pale, glancing up, only in time to see the chandelier hurtling down toward my upturned face.

Shit!

It's going to crush me.

Then I let out a startled *oomph*, as Sol barrels into me, shoving me face first into the ground but out of the path of the huge chandelier that smashes with a jangling crash that makes me wince.

I catch myself with my hands, scraping my palms along the floor.

Behind me, I hear Sol's groan.

My eyes widen. Did the chandelier hit him, instead?

I grit my teeth, pushing myself up. My palms are skinned and bloody. I pick feathers out of them, before levering myself onto my knees.

Plaster and dust rain down on my hair and shoulders. I must look like a ghost.

My breath stutters, when I look up to see Sol standing over me. His expression is shuttered and indecipherable in the shadows of the hall. His ebony eyes stare down at me from his ridiculous height.

Finally, he holds out his hand to me, and I let him help me to my feet.

Then his eyes crease with concern. "Is that blood?" Tenderly, he turns my hands over, and I watch in a daze, as he kisses at my scraped palms like each bead of blood is rare or precious. Maybe he's never seen someone else hurt before? "This is all wrong."

"I'm fine. I'll survive."

I regret it, when he casts me a dubious look but lets go.

"Okay, how about we protect each other?" I offer.

"Works for me, sweetness." He casually smears the blood off his bleeding lip.

Damn it, the chandelier must've caught him, as it fell. Why's he acting like it never happened?

He's the one who needs first aid.

Sol's cheek and eye are swelling purple. He's being too careful how he's standing on his right side. And his teeth are bloody.

He looks wild and savage.

I even love the way that his eyeliner is smudged.

How is he even more beautiful like this?

Uncomfortable, I look away. "Cheers for, you know, saving me."

He nods.

When I look around, the hall is almost empty now.

Skye must've escaped with Maxton, right?

I swallow, before prowling around the chandelier. Then my foot hits something, and I gasp.

A woman with fiery curls is lying like a broken doll behind the chandelier too close to one of the fires.

*Lana.*

Is she unconscious or dead?

I'm far from one of Lana's fans, but if The Hill's Duchess dies at this ball, then it'll destabilize not only my sister's academy but the whole town.

I bite my lip, as I crouch next to her.

The train of her long red dress is already smoldering. Before I can duck closer to check her pulse, the embers on her dress burst into flames.

"Shit, shit, shit." I point at Sol, urgently. "Grab something to roll her in and put out the fire."

Sol shrugs. "Why? She hates you."

Is he kidding?

I stare at his cool expression.

*He's not kidding.*

I freeze just for a moment.

*Recluse*, I remind myself, *fucking beautiful sociopath.*

My mouth falls open. "Are you screwing with me?" I kick at Lana's train, trying to keep it away from her delicate skin. "I don't, as a rule, let my enemies burn."

"Interesting policy." Sol cocks his head. "How's that working out for you?"

"Do you see me wearing the mayoral robe and gold Chain of Office?" I yell. "Put out the fire. *Now.*"

Sol slams his palms down over the flames, extinguishing them with his hands. "Don't let anyone convince you that I can't be obedient. For the right woman."

I'm shaking. It's possibly adrenaline or shock.

*Both.*

"What the hell?" I gasp.

Sol cradles his burned palms to his chest, but raises his eyebrow at me like I'm going to compliment him for putting out a fire with his bare hands simply because I ordered it.

Something tightens in my chest.

Has no one explained to him about toxic relationships?

I bite my lip. "We probably shouldn't move her, but the ceiling's about to cave in. Just grab under her arms gently, and I'll grab her feet."

I can't help thinking how much Lana would hate the indignity of being hauled like a sack of potatoes out of this ball, especially by *me*.

Sol's lips quirk. "I lied. I'm not obedient at all."

He snatches Lana up like she weighs nothing and drapes her over his shoulder in a fireman's lift.

*Asshole.*

To my great relief, Lana groans.

How many times have I wished that Lana would disappear out of my life? But in truth, I don't want anyone in The Hill to be taken.

*Demon Stolen.*

My mouth tightens, and I dart across the floor, leaping over cracks and piles of skulls toward the doorway out into the courtyard behind the hall.

It's dark now, and pale moonlight streams across the tiny courtyard, which is flanked by the grand, red-brick buildings of the academy. Students mill around in torn and bloodied finery. Some are sobbing, while others are slumped against the walls with their heads in their hands.

*What a start to the summer term.*

There's a collective gasp and squeals, when Sol appears with Lana. A crowd swarms around Sol. I hear hushed, revered whispers of *hero*, as Lana's friends take her from him.

He doesn't deny it.

I snort.

Knowing Lana, she'll dine out on the story of the night that the hot, heroic professor chose to save her in his arms after the demon raid because he was secretly in love with her.

Everyone in The Hill wants their own fairy tale.

*Fuck fairy tales.*

I spin in a circle, desperately searching for Skye. She'd never leave without me.

Where the hell is she?

I'm breathing too fast. I can barely suck in enough oxygen. My head is light; I'm dizzy.

I'm only partially aware of Sol dumping Lana with the students who are circling him, but the world has dimmed to the thump of my heart and the scream inside my head.

*Skye, Skye, Skye.*

Then Maxton launches himself into me, barreling us both into the wall. His arms are tight around me in the bone crushing type of hug that I only just realize I wish we'd always been brave enough to give each other.

*That Maxton always needed somebody to give him.*

Maxton's shaking. His fingers grip my shoulders hard enough to bruise.

Unexpectedly, Maxton lets out a yelp, as Sol rips him away from me by the scruff of his neck.

"Don't touch her," Sol growls. "No one hurts her. So, I'm going to bust your balls now."

Was that really the correct discipline procedure by professors or just him being kinky?

"Let. Go," I snarl. I'm flooded with white-hot rage. "If you hurt my friend, I'll cut off your balls."

One fake date and the guy is already acting possessive enough to threaten other men. And that's one red flag alert too many.

Maxton's eyes widen at my use of *friend.*

Sol hesitates like he's weighing up his options, before letting Maxton go with a shove. "As long as we have an understanding."

Maxton side-eyes Sol warily, running a shaky hand through his curls.

The moment that I clearly see Maxton's tear-streaked face, however, something inside me breaks because I know.

*I fucking know.*

"Where is she?" I whisper.

Maxton's expression crumples. "I'm s-sorry, s-so sorry. I tried to stop the demons, but there were m-more than... I tried. I did. I fought like you would..."

He clasps his hand to his chest, and his fingers become stained crimson with sticky blood.

It's Sol who catches me, when I sway. His arms are like steel around me, but his touch is soft, as he strokes my hair. I breathe deeply his scent of leather and ginger, which cocoons me.

Yet I can't look away from the raked lines of claw marks down Maxton's chest, which rip all the way through his suit, until a sickening realization hits me. Then I glance down and notice the crimson staining the front of my white top as well. I must've been dyed in Maxton's blood, when he hugged me.

"I believe you," I force myself to say.

Maxton collapses against the wall.

Tears well in his eyes, tracking down his cheeks. "Your sister was the sacrifice."

"You mean the Stolen! How the fuck can you still say *sacrifice*?" I pull away from Sol, vibrating with distress.

Maxton straightens, snatching the flashing horns off his head and smashing them against the wall — again and again — grinding them until they're shattered and broken. Then he hurls them across the courtyard.

Sol flinches.

The remaining students are watching Maxton with wide, frightened eyes.

"We'll get her back." Maxton's thrumming with as much fury as me. "We'll get all of them back. This is war. My bastard of a father should be fighting. Has he even looked for a way out of the contracts with the demons? Have any of our ancestors? We're not sacrificial animals, pegged out by the forest, waiting for the demons to come and devour us. We're not prey."

Sol's eyes flash. "Really?"

Maxton lets out an enraged howl, before he shoves Sol in the chest. "Fuck. Off." Pride blooms through me. If Maxton can stand up to the authority of a professor who's taller, stronger, and looks ready to rip off his head, then there's hope that he truly can take over from his dad and save The Hill. "I promise you, I'll take this town from Father."

When he turns back to me with his chest heaving, it's like I can finally see the man and not the boy who my friend has turned into.

He loves Skye too.

"And I promise you, I'm getting my sister back." I duck past both Sol and Maxton, darting across the courtyard.

Rage and grief burn through me.

I could slash and stab the world, but all I want is to kill those who've taken my remaining family.

The other half of my Soul.

I feel cold, *dead* inside.

Hollow.

Skye warned me that the demons would be coming tonight. Did she set me up with Sol because she thought she was leaving me?

A sob catches in my throat.

"Where are you going?" Maxton calls. "That's not possible."

He's right. No one's ever come back from the demon underworld. Yet there's one place that the stories say you can *summon* a demon, if your Soul screams loudly enough: The Stones. Then you can choose to be devoured and dragged into the underworld.

*If you're a fucking idiot.*

And right now, my Soul is screaming loudly enough, and I'm enough of an idiot to offer myself to be Stolen, so that I can find my sister and get revenge on the demon who took her.

Perhaps, I'll even be in time to save her from bonding with a demon.

*Because scared doesn't survive.*

"I'm coming with you," Sol insists. "Are you forgetting the whole part where we protect each other?"

"Not happening." I prowl to the archway at the end of the courtyard, drawing Light-bringer. "Stay here and terrorize students or practice your impossibly sexy just rolled out of bed look. I don't care. I'm protecting you by going alone. I'm sorry but…"

I make the mistake of glancing over my shoulder.

Maxon and Sol are standing next to each other, striking opposites of blond and dark hair; Maxton's head only comes up to Sol's shoulder, and Sol slouches against the wall like he's too much of a rock star to stand straight for long. Yet both their gazes are focused on me with the same intensity, and they're wearing matching expressions of concern.

I want to say goodbye to both of them. *Need to.* But I can't.

"I'm trusting you to do your duty and lead the revolution, Maxton." I swallow as I turn away. "You're my best friend. I know you can do this." I don't say anything to Sol because he thinks I'm Skye. What the hell do you say to a fake date who's saved your life? "And it's my duty to go to the Eternal Forest, summon a demon, and be devoured by the Stones."

# CHAPTER FOUR

## The Stones, The Hill, England

I sprint through the fields at the edge of town under the moonlight, which gilts the town in a cold light. I brush through the tall cornfields, stumbling in the black. The blades are sharp. They tear at the feathers of my fake wings, ruffling their perfect lines. I hold my arms over my face, and the leaves scratch my forearms.

Is The Hill trying to hold me back from the Stones, or protect the Stones from me?

By the time that I stumble out to the line of the dark forest on the other side, I'm a fallen angel:

smeared in blood, losing my feathers, with a crooked halo.

When did I ever claim that I could pull off angelic?

Somehow, this look suits me better.

Panting, I pause only to slit the satin loops with my dagger that hold on my wings to my costume, and they tumble into the grass.

I don't need wings where I'm going.

Then I stalk toward the hulking boulders like my chest isn't pumping with adrenaline, my pulse isn't thrashing in my ears, and a voice isn't screaming inside me to *run* back into the cornfield.

The Eternal Forest lies in front of me: vast, shadowy, and thrumming with ancient magic.

*Deadly.*

I shudder, convulsively tightening my hold on Light-bringer.

There's something dark and wicked in the Stones. I feel it, moving sickly in my gut.

The Stones loom above me, glowing faintly red under the cruel moonlight. The prehistoric megaliths are smooth and shining in a way that shouldn't be possible. The giant vertical stones are connected by horizontal lintel stones into a perfect circle in front of the forest.

*It's a magic circle.*

A long time ago, the demons created it here to

travel through to The Hill. There are other henges, like Stonehenge, dotted throughout the world, which are used by gods and demons to travel between veils, realms, and underworlds.

Never trust a magic circle

*A Stone Circle.*

That's why Mum and Dad warned us not to go near the Stones.

*The Stones will devour you*, Mum warned.

Except, when you tell a kid not to do something, that's like daring them to do it, right?

WHEN I WAS EIGHT, SKYE SIDLED INTO MY ROOM ONE summer morning. "I want to play sacrifices."

I glanced up at her from my place sitting cross-legged on the floor, shocked. "No way."

She pouted. "All the kids at school are playing it."

"Bet they're not."

"Okay, they're not. But Maxton said—"

I rolled my eyes. "*Maxton said.* Right. That brat."

She wrinkled her nose, plopping down on the floor next to me. "Well, he said that he'd seen a demon come through the Stones and eat somebody."

Of course he had.

*Liar.*

Maxton simply liked being the center of attention.

I snorted. "He only said that to scare you." I

slipped my arm around Skye's shoulders. "Don't worry. I'll protect you."

Skye's face lit up, and she clapped her hands. *What had I said?* "I knew you were brave. You wouldn't let me go by myself, right? Come on, let's play sacrifices."

Reluctantly, I sneaked after Skye out of the cottage. We held hands, as we unlatched the garden gate and then ran though the fields toward the Eternal Forest.

I was jittery. Everything felt wrong, as if I had bugs under my skin.

Going out without permission. Breaking the rules. Putting Skye in danger.

Why did Skye want this?

By the time that we reached the glowing stones, which glistened in a disturbing way like they were slicked in blood under the sunlight, I wanted to hurl.

Skye's hand tightened in mine.

Fascinated, we stood in the Stones' shadow, staring up at them.

"Wow, they're big," I breathed.

"Yeah," Skye looked away, troubled.

"So, how do we play this game?"

Skye scuffed her foot backward and forwards in the grass. "I don't know. Lana was talking about all this exciting stuff at the sleepover. You know, the special one last weekend. I overheard the other girls chatting about it in class: how if your Soul screams out loudly enough, then the demons will be summoned. We'd have known too, if we'd been at the sleepover."

*The sleepover that we didn't go to because Lana and her gang didn't invite us to anything.*

Rage surged through me like a fire at the same time as the desperate craving to cry.

"That meanie never invites us. No one does. So, what's new?" I demanded.

Skye looked down, biting her lip like she was trying not to cry as well. "She called us *scaredy-cat freaks*. It's all around school."

I wrenched away from Skye, and my eyes flashed. "What's this game then? Let's play it."

Lana and Maxton, the kids of the elite, could talk as big as they liked. But Skye and I didn't need them because we had each other. We were stronger and braver than everybody in this town.

*We'd show them.*

"I don't like it out here," Skye's voice was very small, as she backed away from the Stones. "I've changed my mind. I want to go home."

"Don't you want to test it out?" I didn't know what was possessing me but I edged even closer to the Stones. My fingers itched to reach out and stroke them. Were they throbbing with a heartbeat? "We can prove to them that we're not *scaredy-cat freaks*."

"You dare the Stones to devour you. Three times. Then you run, before the demons come." She took another step back. "But I don't want to play. *Please*, Blue."

My chest was tight, but I tilted up my chin as I faced the Stones.

I hated them.

*Dared them.*

"Devour me," I taunted.

Skye let out a hissed breath behind me. "Don't, don't, *please don't.*"

"Devour me."

Was something moving beyond the Stones in the shadows of the forest?

The trees were shaking. A wind struck up in the calm of the day.

Ancient magic was stirring.

*And something out there in the forest was watching.* I could sense it.

For a moment, I forgot how to breathe.

Then Skye's arms were around my waist, dragging me back.

I wanted to turn and run. But Lana had called us names. Skye would never forget the fear of this moment, I knew it — I'd never forget it either — and I was nothing without my mask of bravery.

"Devour me!" I screamed.

Strong arms encircled me from behind, and I screamed.

Dad pulled me against his chest. He was ashen and shaking. Mum was holding Skye and crying.

"We looked for you, but you were both gone." Dad's arms tightened around me; I'd never heard his voice raspy with tears before, and it frightened me. "We thought that we'd lost you."

Then my parents carried Skye and me away from the Stones, the Eternal Forest, and the creatures moving in the shadows.

NOW, MY CHEEKS ARE WET AT THE MEMORY, AND I violently wipe at them. Once again, I'm standing here before the Stones playing sacrifice.

Except, this time Skye has already been Stolen, and my parents are the ones who were lost.

Is it my fault? Did I mark my entire family to be Stolen that day?

The guilt that's haunted me for the last five years, since my parents were Stolen, burns into rage because then, I can hide behind it.

How did Sol understand that about me?

My hand's sweaty on the hilt of my dagger. I straighten my shoulders, lifting my head, as I pace to the base of the Stone Circle.

The Stones burn brighter, throbbing in time with my own heartbeat.

Are they alive?

*I can do this.*

For family, I can do anything.

"Devour me." *Once.* Rags of clouds veil the moon. The night becomes even blacker. "Devour me." *Twice.* The wind picks up, whipping my hair into my face and attempting to steal my voice. I blink against it, finding myself hollering now. "Devour me!"

*And something stirs in the Eternal Forest.*

I'm frozen with fear.

There's movement within the Stones themselves now.

My heart is hammering in my chest.

*Shit, shit, shit.*

Black eyes, fangs, and horns.

I've done it. I've summoned a demon.

*He's here.*

The demon steps in front of me but still within the circle of Stones. He's so tall that I need to crane my neck to see his face.

My eyes widen, and I gasp.

It can't be. *It fucking can't be.*

Except, it is.

*Sol, the professor.*

Sol's watching me with an inscrutable gaze from eyes that are like drops of the night sky. He's sinfully beautiful under the pale moonlight. More beautiful than he was before, and it makes me more furious than I've ever been.

Rage surges through me; it beats like a drum. I can hardly think through the red haze.

He's no longer wearing a devil costume because he's been transformed into a real demon or perhaps, it's simply that his magical glamor has been stripped away, revealing the true monster that was always hidden beneath.

I can't move. I want to scream, but it's my Soul's scream that summoned him.

This is what I wanted, right? A demon to steal me into the underworld.

I simply didn't think that I'd know him.

While Skye thought she was tricking Sol, he was tricking us both.

*Ironic.*

What sort of asshole wore a costume that revealed their true self and hid it at the same time?

This demon is either a twisted psycho or a genius.

Maybe he's both.

Sol's dressed now in a sweeping silk robe that's so black in the shadows it's like the void. Over his heart, there's a flame emblem: the symbol of a fire demon. A ruby leather belt, which is emblazoned with the same emblem, pulls the robe in at the middle. His horns are ruby and curved, and fire skitters across them: I hate that I find them as beautiful as the rest of him. Their tips glisten and are as sharp as Light-bringer's point.

He looks deadly and otherworldly.

In the academy, he'd been wearing a mortal disguise.

"Y-you-re a d-demon," I stutter.

Sol leans against a Stone, crossing his ankles. "So, I may not have told you everything about me. But since we've only had one date, it all adds to the mystery, right?"

"Who are you? I mean, really?"

He grins, and I flinch at the flash of brilliant, white fangs. "I'm Sol. I'm hurt that you've forgotten already."

"You're not some flirty professor with a tragic backstory. You're a fucking demon."

For a second, I catch hurt flashing across his expression but I must be wrong because just as quickly, it's gone. "And you're a *fucking human.* Impressive that you think we can change what we are." He waves his hand lazily at himself, and his grin is sharp. "I can merely camouflage myself to walk amongst you. It's a predator's trick. It wouldn't be nice of me to scare the *prey*, would it?"

*Asshole.*

I raise my dagger. "I never called myself prey."

His grin fades. "*Hmm*, I find that both sexy and scary."

"As long as you're smart enough to stop calling me *sweetness*, it can give you the hardon of your demonic life. I don't care. I'm in charge here." I seriously don't feel it. But I can't lose my nerve now. "You know why I'm here. I need to find my sister, and that's not changed because I have to deal with the dick who lied about being some reclusive billionaire."

He scowls. "I didn't lie."

"Poor Mr. Underwood, trapped in Cardinal Hall. All alone, until your parents were Demon Stolen just like mine."

"False sympathy. For a moment, I was expecting a hug." He winks. "Underwood's a pretty clever invention of mine, don't you reckon?"

I narrow my eyes. "To think I felt sorry for you."

"To be fair," Sol examines his blood-red fingernails, "I never told you any of that about my life. Gossip is a terrible thing."

"Fucking demons. You let everybody believe it. You're all liars and tricksters."

He blinks. Why do his eyelashes have to be so deliciously long? "Well, of course. But still, I truly *was* trapped at Cardinal Hall for decades, forbidden to leave, since demons live for centuries. My...demon father...wanted me to learn about mortals but from a distance, until I discovered my Soul Bond. It's my chance to impress him and become the Crown Prince of the Demon Empire. And my mortal guards *were* stolen." His expression becomes serious. "Now, don't we have somewhere to be?"

He taps on the boulder impatiently. "Step into the Stone Circle." He holds out his hand. "Come with me to the demon underworld."

*Why is his hand shaking?*

I take a step toward him, lifting my hand, before I even know what's happening.

It's the call of the Stones. They're winding in my head, summoning me, as surely as *I* summoned Sol.

I grit my teeth.

Dark, ancient magic thrums through me. Clutching my arm around myself, I hesitate.

Hell, this feels wrong.

*The Stones will devour you*, Mum warned.

I remember the rags of clouds veiling the moon. The night becoming even blacker. *Devour me*, said thrice. And something with horns stirring in the Eternal Forest.

Sol snarls, and I jump.

Did his gorgeous eyes just flash red?

But then, they clear again, and his expression smooths. "Don't you wish to find your sister?"

"Where is she?" I forget my fear, pacing forward.

Sol's eyes light with hope. His dark waves of hair tumble around his face, but it's his glinting red horns that curve from his head, which I can't look away from.

Are they as delicious to lick as they look? Every inch of him appears created to tempt.

All of a sudden, something predatory shifts in Sol's gaze, and I startle. My pulse races, and my mouth is dry. I can't swallow.

It's time to leave behind the Hill, my life, and everything that I've ever known.

Should I trust this demon?

*Hell no.*

But still, I must let him steal me away, if I have any chance of finding Skye.

I take a deep breath, before I straighten my shoulders and reach across the Stones. Sol shivers, as our fingertips graze. Then I place my smaller hand into Sol's larger one.

*There's no going back now.*

Sol's hot fingers close around mine, and his lips curl into a devilish smile. Then he yanks me into a close embrace and inside the Stone Circle.

Instantly, the Stone's magic hits me in a powerful, agonizing wave.

And I scream.

# CHAPTER FIVE

**The Stones, The Hill, England**

T he Stones are devouring me.

I scream and shudder. The ancient magic scours my insides as if with acid. The Stones are greedily hollowing away my humanity.

*Eating my Soul.*

I struggle, howling.

By the Hill, am I dying?

Then I stumble out into a night-time forest on the other side of the Stones, unsteady on my feet.

I'm no longer in the world of humans but the paranormal; a savagery prickles in the air. I can taste it.

*The Eternal Forest.*

I choke, coughing. I clutch at my throat, bending over like somehow I can force my mortal Soul back inside me.

I knew...*I fucking knew*...what the Stones would do.

Why didn't I believe that the myth was real, after everything I've seen?

Yet these things are meant to be metaphors, right?

I pale.

Does this mean that the demons will truly eat me or only my Soul?

Seriously, which is worse?

The tales say that the Eternal Forest is the meeting place of the godly realms, where the veils meet the Other Worlds and the underworlds. It's the deadliest place in England, and the spirits and gods here are equally deadly.

*But not as bad as the demons.*

"The Stones devoured my Soul," I gasp.

"Only the mortal part that you'll need if you return to your world." I startle at how close Sol is at my side all of a sudden; his spicy, masculine scent winds around me. "You'll get it back. Well, if you return to the Hill."

I don't miss the *if.*

I also don't expect to be pulled against his hard chest and get a snuggly, *purring* armful of demon. "Are you cold?"

I'm shivering.

It's freezing. What's happened to the warm summer night? More importantly, *demons purr?*

Surprised, I glance around at the gloomy grove of yew trees. Vines hang between them. I don't recognize what species the vines are, or the violet tree growing next to them. I don't think that they come from the human realm. They're beautiful in the same way that Sol is: wild and toxic. They frighten and fascinate me in equal measure. The thick canopy of branches blocks out the moonlight.

I stare down at my heels, which are sinking into a bed of curling, fiery leaves that crackle like paper. I wrinkle my nose at the scent of damp moss.

A cold wind whistles through the grove, and I'm chilled.

What happened to summer? How has it transformed to autumn already?

"The Eternal Forest is a rebel like me." Sol pats the violet trunk next to me fondly. Briefly, I wonder if it'll poison him, and whether I want it to. "She doesn't have natural seasons but adapts to the moods of those around her. So, knock it off because this is a happy occasion. *Joyous.*"

For a moment, nothing happens.

Then Sol narrows his eyes warningly, and finally, the wind drops, and leaves sprout on the trees like spring is approaching.

Sol smiles, kissing me on the forehead. "By my horns, you're truly here. I've dreamed of this. Longed for it, my sweetness."

My gut roils.

I snarl, pushing away from him. "I'm not who you think I am."

His lips twitch. "Isn't that my line?"

"There's been a mistake."

"I don't think so."

If he truly knew me, he should be thanking me for having the patience not to kill him.

*Wait, too late...*

I draw Light-bringer and hold it under Sol's throat. His eyes widen, and his back hits the trunk with a satisfying *crack*.

*No more being scared...at least, for me.*

"Fucking listen." I don't lean in close enough to do more than hold Sol in place; I've never hurt anyone before and demon or not, I don't want to start now.

*Except for the bastard who took Skye.*

Unless...Sol took her?

I shake away that thought as fast as I can because despite knowing that Sol's a demon, he's also the mesmerizingly hot professor who won my attention by rocking out on the stage earlier tonight, stood up for me to Lana, and made me laugh with corny jokes.

He's the first guy, who's sent sparks through me and at the same time, succeeded in making me lower my guard and wish that I could truly get to know him better, which is messed-up.

My breathing becomes ragged, and Sol's eyes crease in concern.

Light-bringer is more than a weapon. It's a stabby security blanket. The type that reminds me of my parents.

It's belonged to my family for generations and was Mum's before becoming mine.

The copper hilt has the four elements on it in high relief, which match the brand on my wrist. The scabbard is decorated on one side with dancing other-worldly men, who are more beautiful than any human, and on the other, with horned demons. The demons are dressed like warriors before a battle.

As a kid, I was endlessly drawn to it. Both Sky and I were. We'd lie in front of the fire, passing that scabbard between us, tracing over the decorations. Only, the difference was that I'd linger over the other-worldly beauties, while Skye would turn it over, mesmerized by the darkness of the warrior demons.

Sol taps the blade with his nail. "Would you mind putting that sharp thing away? You're making me feel like you may use it."

"What gave me away?" I raise my boot, resting it with deliberate care between Sol's spread thighs. His breathing picks up, and his cheeks pink. "Of course, I could use my sharp heel instead."

When I catch the way that Sol's dick is tenting his pants, I bite my lip not to react.

So, he is kinky...and we are well-matched.

I meant it as a threat, however, and not a promise. I'm clearly not cut out for the whole mafia thing.

I may as well have just called Sol a *bad boy*, before telling him that he was in for a *spanking*, by the way he's smirking at me.

Sol melts against the tree, casually stretching and holding his hands above his head like my knife isn't at his throat. "Are you going to punish me then? You're the only human I'd allow to. Are you so eager to put me over your knee?" He licks his lips. *And hell, I wish that image wasn't so hot.* His eyes become half-lidded. "You're playing with fire, sweetness."

I bristle. "So are you."

"Still, it's hardly fair, when you're the one who summoned me. You screamed for your Soul Bond, and here I am."

Shocked, I step away.

Why's he looking disappointed?

"Soul Bond...?" Instantly, I feel lost and confused. *Wrecked.* "This is about my sister. You're meant to be taking me to her."

"And I will, if I can," Sol corrects. "I don't know who took her. I wasn't involved with that. But I'm an elemental demon. The Demon Empire is divided into four kingdoms: fire, air, earth, and water. I'm a

Demon of Fire and the Emperor Anwealda's adopted son, along with my brothers. And my father, Anwealda, insisted that I find my Soul Bond amongst the humans or…well, the consequences will be severe. They always are." His gaze is intense, adoring. I shrink away from the hope in it that I don't understand. And *a need to be loved,* which I understand better than anyone. "It's always only been you."

Fury rolls through me like thunder. My sister has been stolen, and now Sol intends to steal me as well…?

*No. Fucking. Way.*

"This is romantic to you?" I twirl around wildly. "Cruelly abducting people and then claiming them as your wife?"

Sol runs his hand nervously through his hair. "*Ehm*, yes. Demon here." His eyes flash red. *Uh-oh, that's a definite warning sign.* "And I didn't steal you like whoever took your sister. I don't do that. You came willingly into the underworld."

My lip curls up. "Wow, is that how you justify it to yourself? Trick me here to find my sister and then dump the whole *you're my Soul Bond thing* on me?"

"Exactly." Sol smiles like he's delighted that I'm getting with the program. "Look, I really didn't take your sister. I had no idea until you asked me to sing for her that you had one. *Trapped in Cardinal Hall,* remember? I only knew your name and that you were a student at the academy." My heart flips. *Shit, he still thinks I'm Skye.* I'm an idiot. *Of course he does.* I swallow. If I tell him the truth now, will he leave me here with my Soul partially devoured? Will he abandon me to be slaughtered by the spirits in the Eternal Forest? "I hoped to court you and that we'd be allowed to…"

"Fall in love?" I ask with sickly sweetness.

Is he lying? Surely demons don't care about romantic stuff like that, right? They just take what they want.

Sol's cheeks flush. "I simply hoped that you'd want me. Well, too late for that."

He falls to his knees on the forest floor, and I'm shocked, as a bed of red roses that have petals of flame blossom around him and up the surrounding trees in a bower.

The roses are spellbinding. Like Sol.

All of a sudden, something whips out and wraps around my wrist.

I yelp and glance down. A long, ruby tail is coiled around my forearm with a soft, fluffy fork at the end.

*Sol has a thrice damned tail?*

A *gorgeous* tail that tightens and yanks me closer like it has a mind of its own, even as Sol's flush deepens.

"At least I can do this properly." His midnight

71

eyes stare intently into mine. "I, Prince Sol and Demon of Fire, claim you as my Soul Bond."

He holds his breath, and the soft end of his tail twitches nervously against my skin.

He's a prince.

*A fucking demon prince.*

"Does that make me a princess?" I ask.

He nods eagerly.

I lean forward to cup his cheek. "Well, if you're a *prince,* that's okay then. In my humble human hovel, I've done nothing but lie on my bed, dreaming of the day that a demon prince would swoop in and rescue me from my dreary existence, stealing me away into his world. I even created a scrapbook dedicated to his horns—"

"You're being sarcastic, aren't you?" Sol's tail unwinds from my arm.

Strangely, I miss it.

I arch my brow. "What gave me away?"

He leaps to his feet, flashing his fangs in a way that I think is a grin...I hope. "It doesn't matter. My adopted father only wants an official Soul Bond. If we complete the ritual, everything else can be worked on, including the healing of my wounds from your cutting sarcasm. Follow me."

I scowl at his back, as he leads me further into the forest.

There will be no *working on* anything, no matter

how enthralled I am by the swaying of Sol's ruby tail, as it pokes out of a hole in his robe, or the tightness of his ass.

Sol thinks that he's bonded to Skye. I'll keep up this charade long enough to rescue my sister and get her safely home.

My chest tightens.

What if I have to keep it up forever to protect my sister from taking my place as Soul Bond?

Because I will.

Sol leads me into a larger glade. In its center is a pool, which is perfectly circular in a way that can't be natural. The water is sapphire blue. The ground around it is raised in ritualistic mounds that are scrawled with inverted pentagrams.

When Sol presses his hand to a tree, flames skitter from trunk to trunk but don't burn the wood, until we're encircled by fire.

It's breath taking.

The funnels of tiny whirlwinds spring up in the middle of the water.

"Fire, air, earth, and water," Sol points out. "The ritual demands all four."

I hug my arms around myself. "On the Stones, you're not about to do some dark magic shit?"

Sol's laugh is deep and rumbling. "I should tell my brother that: *dark magic shit*. All his studying to be a sorcerer would've been worth it." He steps closer, stroking my hair back from my face with aching tenderness. Why does he have to do that? "This ritual will announce to Father that I've returned and am confirming the Soul Bond. Don't worry, the connection is ours alone. Father will feel it, however, and prepare for my return to the demon court." His smile is hungry and dark. "In triumph for once."

He swaggers to the water, pulling his belt free and dropping it to the ground.

By the Hill, is he just going to strip off and jump in?

Seriously, *demons.*

"Woah," I shake my head. "No way. No naked bathing for you, Prince Sol."

Sol's already lifting his silk robe, however, and warmth curls through me at the sight of his lean, warrior toned legs. "Why? I have a glorious body. It's much admired. You're in for a treat."

I cross my arms. "I'm sure that I'll survive."

He cocks his head. "You say that a lot, sweetness. But *surviving* isn't the same as living. You know, where your bones, blood, and horns are seared, tingling, *awake* with pleasure or pain, but you're aware of every intense, stimulating moment. I wish to make you *live*." He studies me, baffled. "Humans."

I march closer. "*Demons.*"

I can see how fast his chest is rising and falling

and can feel his heat. Our gazes meet. I flush hot and cold.

He smirks. "Turn around then, if you don't wish to be blinded by my demonic beauty."

He whisks his robe off in one violent movement, before allowing it to pool around him like a snake shedding skin. Then instantly, he turns to dive into the pool.

My eyes widen, and I can't hold back the shocked squeak. I don't close my eyes fast enough not to see the strong, athletic lines of his body, and the gorgeous pale globes of his ass.

Now I definitely want to spank that delicious ass, after the water splashes across my face.

I shake myself like a dog and glare at Sol, as he emerges from the water, laughing.

He looks younger like this — adorable — and truly free for the first time. He pushes his hair out of his eyes and shakes his horns, spraying me again. Water droplets chase down his strong shoulders. His chest is submerged under the water, which is so brightly blue that I can't see beneath it.

And I'm not disappointed.

*Not.*

"Aren't you coming in?" He challenges.

"Sorry, but you'll have to wait to be blinded by *my* beauty." I crouch by the edge of the pool on my knees; twigs cut into my skin.

Sol's expression falls, but he swims closer to me.

"You need to be in the water for it to work. You're not frightened are you? The Soul Pool won't harm you. It'll only light with magic to confirm the bond. It'll look like flames, but they won't burn us." He gestures around the glade. It's strange how he's trying to reassure me. Unexpected. *Kind.* "Look at the trees. I'd never damage them, in fact, the forest's under the protection of Guardians. If I damaged it, they'd spank my horns." He shudders. How sensitive are his horns? They're so pretty I'd rather suck them than spank them. "How about you put your hand in? We can't have your clothes getting wet. Humans are weak. They're barely born before they die of some silly illness or another."

Okay, now I'm leaning more toward *spank*. On the other hand, why does he care? I mean, in a sociopathic way.

Worse, he's wrong. The water won't turn to flames. The magic won't work.

*Because he has the wrong twin.*

I'm not Sol's Soul Bond.

My heart's beating frantically in my chest. I'm trembling.

How the hell did this happen? How did this all spiral out of control so quickly?

Our disguises and masks are meant to keep us safe.

"Sol," I whisper, desperately. "I've been trying to tell you something."

*Too late.*

Sol clasps my hand and plunges it into the pool.

The water is surprisingly warm and thicker than I'm expecting, syrupy. It sucks at my fingers, tonguing them.

I hold my breath at the same time as Sol.

I realize the exact moment that his excited expression turns to confusion, as he stares around at the still pool that hasn't transformed to flames, and then to a darkening rage.

I've worn that expression many times myself.

I want to recoil from it, but he's still holding my hand in a vice-like grip.

Suddenly, he no longer looks snuggly, younger, or adorable.

He's a true demon prince now and he's pissed.

Sol's eyes flame, and fire blazes higher between his horns. I gasp, wrenching even more desperately to escape his hold

"You're not Skye." Sol's voice is cold with deadly fury, "Who the hell are you?"

# CHAPTER SIX

**Soul Pool, Eternal Forest**

Sol's dark gaze is intently on mine. His fingers tighten around my hand, still holding it under the water. I can't pull away. The heat from his horns is searing across my cheeks.

*Yet I'm flushed for another reason.*

My guts are churning with such conflicted emotions, it's like I'm about to go into battle without any armor, only a torn angel's costume, a crooked halo, and a demonic dagger.

All of a sudden, the temperature in the glade drops. I shiver, and goosebumps break out on my arms.

"What game are you playing?" Sol whispers, studying me like he can see through my eyes and into my Soul.

Then his lips curl back, revealing his brilliant white fangs, before he yanks.

I let out a startled yelp as I tumble into the water with an undignified splash and flailing arms.

*Shit, shit, shit...*

I don't close my mouth in time, swallowing several panicked gulps of water, which taste saccharine and too thick like treacle. I choke and splutter.

*I can't breathe.*

My lungs ache, and my nostrils burn.

The water is warm. It sucks at my arms, pulling me down.

I'm going to drown.

*By the Hill...no...*

I can see Sol above me: a haze through the blueness.

A horned shadow.

*Please, please, please...*

Then fingers twist in my hair, dragging me up.

Saving me.

My scalp screams with pain, but I'm breaking the sticky surface. How did Sol dive in here like it was no different to water? How strong is he?

This pool is deadly. Toxic. *A beautiful trap.*

Just like Sol because the only reason he's able to save me is because he put me in danger first.

Sol drags me up, holding me tight to his chest with one arm, so that I don't slip down again.

I tremble, coughing up the thick, sapphire water onto his chest, and he watches me with a cold expression that only makes me tremble worse.

I wrap my arms around his waist, digging my fingers into his skin. It takes me a long moment to remember that he's naked. The tips of my ears turn red, and I kick my legs through the thick water.

"Fucking demons," I mutter.

He arches his brow. "Is that your catchphrase or a secret fantasy of yours?"

I blush.

Sol's tail snakes side to side, helping him keep both of us balanced. Then Sol leans close to me.

Hot air gusts against my ear, as he whispers. "Now, who the hell are you? A pretty impostor? A shapeshifter? Doppelganger? A delusion that's somehow become real…"

When he slips his hand down to pinch my hip and then pat at my ass like he's trying to convince himself that I'm not real, I squirm. "Stop it, asshole. I'm not a figment of your imagination, although you probably are crazy. Can you feel this?"

I intend to pinch him because you soon learn with a twin that fair's fair: a pinch for a pinch. Yet I can't seem to make my hands let go of his strong back. It was too horrifying to sink down into the pool.

My face is so close to Sol's and the blackness of his large eyes. His eyeliner is smudged and running at the corners, but somehow, the messed-up look suits him. His butterfly eyelashes are thick and impossibly long, and his hair is wet and plastered to his head.

So, I do the only thing that I can.

I slowly move my lips towards his, never breaking his gaze.

Sol's eyes widen, but he nods.

Then I kiss him savagely, biting his lower lip. It's a quick, brutal attack like a stab from my dagger.

Quick, and then withdrawing.

He licks over his bitten lower lip and then smiles. "You're real. I encourage your choice of proof. Very stimulating. But that doesn't answer my question."

"Why do you think Skye's your Soul Bond anyway?" I demand. "You're the true trickster here. You schemed to get the post at the academy. You disguised yourself as a professor. And all to get closer to your victim."

When Sol's eyes gleam with hurt, I instantly regret my words.

"By my flames, she's not my *victim*. Don't talk about her like that. She's mine by treaty, and I intend...*intended*...to bond with her in love." He narrows his eyes. "I was marked with her name the

81

moment that I saw her. That was an...interesting lesson to survive without looking like I was having a heart attack at the same time as shouting a student's name in ecstasy."

I wrinkle my nose. "Marked?"

He waves his hand at a funnel of wind. Then I yelp, as the whirlwind blasts across the water at his command and surrounds us both, rising us out of the water.

I stare in shock at Sol's powerful chest, which glistens with water droplets. A single word is branded above his heart:

**SKYE**

My breath catches. The Prince of Fire truly is soul bonded to my sister. Even if I find her, how can I keep her safe?

Slowly, the whirlwind lowers us back into the water, and this time, I welcome the warmth, after the freezing wind.

My laughter is brittle. "You either got the wrong name or the wrong twin."

He freezes in shock. "Twins?"

He looks devastated, barely holding it together. *Broken.*

I hate demons. I shouldn't care. But I do.

Sol's destroyed, and I don't know how to fix this.

"You're marked with Skye's name, but she thought that *we* were the better match. She didn't ask you out for her, but for me. You know, we do have a lot in common. You don't want to cut your hair like Harry Styles, right?" *Why am I babbling?* "After all, we're the ones who had the date."

"You're *the sister*," Sol's voice is flat.

"Yeah, I'm the special birthday girl. My name's Blue." I attempt to smile. "Thanks for the dedication. No one but Skye's ever given me something as special as your song. But seriously, happy birthday to me, right?"

This is why your sister should never meddle in your love life.

"Blue," he says slowly like he's testing it out.

Why do I love hearing my name so much in his rich voice? Why do I want to hear him say it, while he's *begging* me for the stimulation that he's always talking about: *Blue, please, Blue, Blue...*

I bite my lip hard not to let my thoughts show.

He studies me seriously, however, and I don't miss the sadness lurking behind his eyes. "I claimed the wrong twin. You're idiots. I'm an idiot. And soon, I'll be a dead prince."

*WTF?*

I tighten my hold around him. "Are all demons so dramatic?"

Sol's gaze darts away from mine. "If not dead, then Father will take my horns."

I gasp, staring at his gorgeous, glimmering horns.

For as long as I can remember, I've feared and hated demon horns. They're from my nightmares: awake and sleeping.

Yet Sol's horns are part of him, both magical and beautiful. I don't fear them, and if taking them is punishment for something Skye and I have done, then I'm going to stop it.

Somehow.

"No way," I snarl. "Just *unclaim* me or whatever."

Sol snorts. "We're literally swimming together in the Soul Pool. My gorgeous naked body is pressed to yours. A demon loves once and forever. They only get one shot at a claiming. If they mess it up…"

I hiss out a shocked breath. "You're going to be alone forever because of this…?"

His gaze becomes steely. "I've already been alone for a long time."

"Don't tell me that a prince can be killed or tortured over a mistake?"

His jaw clenches. "*Adopted* prince."

"Then your *adopted* dad is a dick."

Sol's eyes sparkle with mirth, and he rests his cheek against mine. "Nobody has ever been brave enough to say that about the Emperor before. Promise that you never shall again. But on my tail, there's the *spark*. Why do I only feel it with you…Blue…and didn't with your sister?"

"Because this Soul Bond stuff is bullshit…?"

He kisses my forehead, before he draws back. "I'm taking you through the Stones to The Hill. Failing to claim my Soul Bond will cost me the chance to become Crown Prince, almost definitely my horns, and possibly my life. I won't let you suffer as well. You want to be free of me, right?"

*Do I?*

I stare into his midnight eyes, and I dig my fingers so deeply into his skin that I know it'll bruise; I want *my* mark on him. He winces.

"Nope, you can't get rid of me that easily. *I* summoned *you*, remember? I have my sister to rescue, and she could be at the court."

"Possibly. It's where we'll uncover the secrets and gossip. But would you risk dying for your sister?"

"In a heartbeat." I cock my head. "You said you had brothers. Wouldn't you die for them?"

He hesitates, and a curl falls over his eyes. "Wait until you meet them, before you ask me questions like that."

Crap, that doesn't sound good.

Sol's pink tongue darts out, wetting his lips. Why's he nervous? "The demon court is dangerous. If we go there to find out who took Skye, we need to make a deal."

*Never make a deal with a demon.* It's the first rule that Dad taught me.

Demons never break a deal, but if you're not careful, they'll end up owning you: mind, body, and Soul.

"What type of deal?" I demand.

"I'll help you find your sister," Sol says with a sly smile. "But here's the deal: the only way for us to be safe—"

"For us to survive…?" I say, dryly.

"You're wicked." Sol's eyes dance with delight. "And I was hoping that I'd need to corrupt you. Perhaps, *you'll* deliciously corrupt *me*. As you say, the only way for us to *survive*, is to fake our bond. You pretend to be…"

"Claimed by you."

His eyes darken. "You're already *claimed* by me." And there's the *possessiveness* again. "What you fake is that you're happy about it."

"So, fake dating. I can do that. What's a bond feel like?"

"Supposedly," he ducks his head, "as if your heart and blood are connected. It's not some fairy tale of perfect joy. It's a connection. Deeper than even love: the closest anyone can be to another. Like…"

"A twin," I murmur.

Sol's lips pinch. "Can you truly keep up this charade of lovers? To get away with this, we'll have to mask our real emotions. Fake date, as you call it. Plus, the others will believe it because no human would normally lie about a bond to a demon. Why would they?"

"What if they fell in love?" I ask, quietly.

"That'd be a shame, since demons are incapable of it, isn't that right?" Sol's lips ghost across mine. "Villains, all of us. Now, hold your breath."

"What?" I blink at him in confusion.

Sol's eyes glitter with mischief, as he takes a deep breath and drags me down, down, *and down*, deep into the pool.

I choke on the sweet water.

I'm surrounded by sugary blue.

And this time, I'm sure that I'm going to be drowned by a demon.

# CHAPTER SEVEN

**Elemental Palace Courtyard, Demon Underworld**

I rise up, breaking the skin of the pool like a rebirth.

Gasping, I cling to Sol, wrapping my arms around his neck. I no longer care how close I am to a naked demon or how my white top is now transparent. My heart is fluttering like a terrified hummingbird in my chest, struggling to break free, and I'm choking on water that's turned from sapphire to ruby.

I'm alive!

But how the hell was I dragged down into a pool in the Eternal Forest, only to emerge into...?

"Home not so sweet home," Sol announces,

proudly. "The demon underworld or more precisely, the Elemental Palace."

Shivering, I lift my chin.

Shit, this is real. It's truly happening. I'm here.

*Trapped in the demon underworld.*

It's night, and the sky is tinged a startling blood-red like fiery streaks in the black. Sol and I are on the edge of what looks like an ornamental pond with silver gilt around its sides. We're in the courtyard of a grand palace, which is lit with guttering torches bracketed to the walls in a way that painfully reminds me of the Heaven and Hell ball.

I bite my lip as I tip back my head to stare up at the obsidian palace that glitters with silver tipped spires and domes.

The four elements of the demon kingdom are carved above the archway that leads into the Elemental Palace. As I watch, they magically glimmer and move like they're alive. One moment, they're rolling flames, the next waves of water, then gusts of air, and finally, leaves blooming from the earth.

It's a never-ending, spellbinding cycle.

What would happen if the elements were combined? Is that their true power?

The Elemental Palace is Gothic and intimidating in a way that chills and excites me.

Yet it's a shock.

Aren't demons barbarians who can't do more than raid The Hill and then retreat to live in caves or trees?

How did they learn to sing rock songs, snark, and build grand civilizations?

"Not what you were expecting?" Sol says, knowingly.

I shake my wet hair out of my eyes. "Did you have to half-drown me?"

"Probably not, but it was the quickest way to get us to the demon court. Plus, fun."

"Asshole."

"Demon."

I push away from Sol in frustration, swimming to the edge of the pond, and he chuckles.

Why does the sound thrum through me so deliciously?

"Remember our deal," I hiss. "Faking love, while we hate."

*Hate, don't be hurt*, I remind myself.

Immediately, Sol stops chuckling, and his expression shutters. Then he fakes a yawn.

"So, you hate me," Sol says, flatly. "Because you're all sassy and stabby, and I'm a spoiled, sociopathic prince."

Does he want brownie points for self-awareness?

"Uh-huh."

Fire bursts to life between his horns, as he swims

lazily to my side; I fight to look away from his intense gaze.

"And yet," his eyes narrow, "you've already kissed me." My cheeks flush, and the memory shoots through me of savagely kissing his plush lips and *hell*, how much I wish I could lean in now and suck his lower lip, just to shut the haughty beauty up. He lets out a breathy laugh; the air gusts across my mouth in a desperately intimate way. "You're thinking about kissing me, *right now*...biting into the plumpness of my bottom lip." My eyes widen. *Am I that obvious?* He moves even closer, until the tips of our cold noses are Eskimo kissing. "Everybody in court despises me, but yet, they all kiss me."

"And you let them." A hot stab of possessive jealousy makes my words harsher than I intend, and I know that they hit home by the way Sol stiffens. "So, it says just as much about you."

Sol's eyes become half-hooded; he's coiled tight and dangerous. "And what's that then?"

Hell, I'm not answering that.

*Silence.*

Sol let's out a frustrated breath, before pulling back from me. "They won't be kissing me anymore. Not now that I've claimed you."

I can't tell if he's saying that as a good or bad thing.

By the way that he studies me, I'm not sure if he knows yet either.

Then he slams his hands onto the marble side of the pond, his powerful shoulders bunch, and he hauls himself out. Water glistens in tantalizing droplets on his translucent skin and streams down the strong planes of his back. I can't help the way that I watch it collecting in the hollow of his ass, before sliding even lower, past the base of his tail...

I flush, when Sol shoots me a cheeky look over his shoulder and catches *me* having a cheeky look at his ass. "You no longer deserve this treat, sweetness." When he shakes his ass, I can't even pretend that I'm not looking. "Or my demonic beauty."

I draw in a shocked breath, as dancing fire skitters down from his horns, across his skin, and finally covers him all the way to his ankles like a fire suit that's not burning him.

When he twirls around, I'm resolutely not disappointed that I can only see glimpses of his naked skin through the dancing flames.

His amused gaze meets mine, before he bends over and offers me his hand. "Would you like some help?"

"I'm not a damsel in need of saving." When I card my fingers through my hair, I realize that in the trip to the underworld, I've lost my halo.

Sol straightens, but his gaze becomes concerned.

"Really? It's just that if I were you, I wouldn't lounge around too long in that pond. Our thrashing around would've attracted the fish."

I snort. "I willingly summoned a demon. Do I look like I'm scared of fish?"

He tilts his head. "Demonic fish. And oh yes…"

I screech, when something nips sharply at my ankles…a lot of little somethings under the water.

My pulse thunders, and I scrabble wildly at the side of the pond, but my wet fingers keep slipping.

"…*they bite*." Sol's smile is sharp, but he crouches down to grab my arms and haul me out of the pond onto the marble floor of the courtyard. I thrash around like I'm a landed fish, trying to slow my ragged breathing. He crouches by my side, checking my ankles, which are bruised but not bleeding. He gives them each a gentle pat. "So do I, if you're wondering. But only if you beg very nicely. "

I'm wet. Cold. My ankles smart and ache.

*I'm* not the one who's going to be begging.

Snarling, I slide my hand to Light-bringer. The scabbard is as wet as the rest of me. I've spent years caring for this dagger with as much tenderness as Skye cared for her piano…or her hair.

*That. Is. It.*

I draw my blade and hold it to the fire that's sizzling over Sol's gut. The way that he only lifts his brow like he's bored is extremely unsatisfying.

The way that his breath is hot against my cheeks, as mine must be against his, is far more satisfying in a way that it shouldn't be.

"Sweetness, is it a custom of your family to point that thing at your *Soul Bond* because I'm adventurous, but we really need to negotiate first."

Shaking, I push my dagger back into its sheath, but Sol doesn't make a move to stand. We're too close; I can't breathe.

"Stop calling me *sweetness*," I demand. "That's the pet name you made up for my sister, right? I'm not sweet."

"I'd noticed. You're more stabby." Sol's eyes light up with delicious glee. "My sharp, sharp, *stabby*."

"Wait, I didn't mean to invent a new pet name..."

He brushes my wet hair back from my forehead, tucking a strand behind my ear, and I shiver. "Stabby, aren't you happy to be mine?"

Sol's gaze is soft, and I can't help the flutter in my stomach at how he rolls *stabby* on his tongue like he's balancing the line between using it as a pet name and an insult...or like he's fucking the word.

*How is that possible?*

And as much as my hands clench in rage, I want to make him call me that again just to hear the word on his tongue.

Is he acting like this because of our deal? I suppose that I should play along.

"You're mine too." I reach to stroke his horn.

To my surprise, he flinches back. I'm even more surprised by the hurt that sparks through me.

I wriggle away from him, pulling myself to my feet. "Careful, or your daddy will think—"

"Oh, do tell me what *I'll* think, darling," a cold voice that's threaded with an amused darkness calls from the shadows of the archway, "it's been a long time since a non-magical has had the arrogance to think they know anything of a Demon Emperor's mind."

*And there went my good first impression with the in-laws.*

I take a step back, dropping my hand to the hilt of my dagger.

Yet it's Sol who becomes ashen. "Father, we were just coming to see you…"

Anwealda, the Demon Emperor, strolls into the courtyard like a sleekly dangerous panther. His ebony eyes coldly survey me through the decorative silver and black mask, which covers the right side of his face. If I thought that the palace was Gothic, it's nothing compared to this gorgeous, regal, but night-marish demon.

He's even taller than Sol with huge spiraling horns and a mane of silver hair, which is threaded with glinting diamonds. A crown of magical fire flares like an unholy halo between his ruby horns. His broad shoulders bulge in his high collared black suit, which is marked with the four elemental symbols.

He screams deadly predator.

My throat is dry; it's hard to swallow.

I want to say something but can't find my voice.

Anwealda tuts. "And what kind of welcome is this for your Soul Bond?" His voice becomes hard. "*Kneel.*"

Instantly, Sol pulls himself elegantly to his knees, but his tail thrashes agitatedly behind him.

The move has been so fluid that it's obvious he's done it many times before. His back is straight, and his face is in the smooth mask that I'm beginning to hate.

"You know how messy bonds can be in the early stages," Sol says, not meeting his gaze. "I'll try harder."

"How delightful. You'll *try*." Anwealda pets Sol's horns but at the same time, drags his claws along them, digging in hard enough to make him wince.

*No fucking way.*

I knew Sol's adopted dad was a dick. *So what if he's an Emperor?*

"I *will* do better and make you proud, Father," Sol's voice is tight with pain.

"Of course you will. My sons aren't weak." Anwealda digs his claws in at the base of Sol's horns, and he bites back a yelp.

"Stop hurting him." I stride forward, wrapping my arms around Sol's neck and yanking him away from Anwealda's cruel touch, until he's leaning against me instead. Sol stiffens in surprise. "He's my Soul Bond now. *Mine*. And nobody touches his horns but me. It makes me feel possessive and sort of..." How had he explained the bond? I may as well lay the groundwork of our fake setup. "...like I want to vomit all over you because of our deep connection."

"Well, we can't have that," Anwealda replies, dryly. "And how about you throw in some *Your Imperial Majesties* because the only people who don't, are my sons or those who wish to die slow and painful deaths."

I tremble, holding tighter to Sol. I stroke him like he's a demon plushie.

Adrenaline spikes through me, and suddenly, my tongue feels too large in my mouth to even get any words out.

I thought that other demons would be like Sol. *What a mistake.*

The Emperor is a hundred times more dangerous.

"So...?" Anwealda taps his foot impatiently.

"Of course, Your Imperial Majesty," I whisper.

Anwealda's sharp teeth gleam, as he smiles. "Better. Perhaps, you are trainable. As long as you can learn to kneel."

I bristle but manage to force myself not to drop to

my knees.

Anwealda studies me like I'm a fly that he's considering swatting. "I said, *kneel.*"

"Nope."

"Sol," Anwealda warns, "control your human."

Seriously, *control* me?

Good luck with that.

Sol's jaw clenches. "I tried. It didn't work."

Anwealda smiles, as he grips Sol's chin. Then he slaps Sol hard across the cheek with a *crack* that echoes around the courtyard; he never stops smiling.

Sol's head snaps to the side, but he doesn't cry out. On the other hand, I do.

"Didn't I make my thoughts about *trying* clear?" Anwealda grips Sol's chin again. "Chastise her and make her kneel, or I will."

Sol's eyes flash with fire, before his gaze becomes defiant. "On the sacred elements, *never.*"

When Anwealda slaps Sol again for a second time, hard enough to leave a blossoming red mark and still with that maddening smile like he's a kind master correcting the behavior of a slave, I try to drop to my knees.

Yet I'm stopped by Sol.

"Don't," he barks, sharply. His tail wraps around my thigh. His chest is rising and falling hard, but he's not dropping his gaze from his dad's, even as Anwealda raises his hand to slap him for a third time.

"She's my bonded. She doesn't know the rules of the court yet; it isn't fair to punish her for that. I love her and I'll protect her. No one will lay a hand on my Soul Bond."

The silence is agonizing.

When Anwealda lowers his hand, he also drops his false smile. "Interesting. This bedraggled, rebellious specimen really is your Soul Bond. I did wonder if... but my obedient son would never talk back to me otherwise."

I don't miss the dark warning in his tone, but also...*WTF?*

Was that all a test to see if Sol would protect me? *Did Sol know?* Was he only acting?

*And did Sol really pass the test?*

Then for the first time, Anwealda's expression softens, and he draws a claw gently down Sol's reddened cheek. "I have missed you. Of course, I've been busy with intrigues and plots. You've been safer in the non-magical world. But we will celebrate your return with a delightful Bonding Revel tonight. Well, certainly a debauched one. This human needs to be presented to the court. First, both of you need to change into something more appropriate for a prince and his Soul Bond."

He grimaces like he can't even think of a way to describe how bad Sol and I currently look, which is harsh but totally fair.

"Thank you, Father," Sol replies with an earnestness that catches me off guard.

Anwealda merely nods before twirling around and gliding back to the archway. "Congratulations on being the first of your brothers to bring home his Soul Bond. I am rather impressed. Since I must name my heir to the empire and Crown Prince soon, it was a smart move. By the way, I summoned them back by portal, so they don't miss your big moment. Won't they be delighted? You've made me proud for once. Now, don't be late, no matter how tempting this darling one is to sample."

I don't miss the *for once*…or the *sample*.

Anwealda disappears back into the archway, leaving Sol and I alone in the courtyard.

I'm exhausted, cold, and damp. I've been attacked by demons, lost my sister, and been dragged to the demon underworld. The last thing I want is to start putting on my loved-up act at a special party in my honor.

But what choice do I have? And I'm beginning to realize, what choice does Sol have either?

When Sol's tail unwinds from my thigh, I move around in front of him, and this time, it's me holding out my hand to Sol.

He stares at it for a long moment, before he takes it, hauling himself to his feet. But then, he doesn't let go. His thumb sweeps across the back of my hand.

"You're a brave one." His smile reaches his eyes, and I wonder if it's the first truly genuine one that he's given me. "Not only do I respect it but it's seriously sexy. You know that, right? But you shouldn't have stood up to him like that." He hesitates. "Are my horns really yours?"

Wait, does that have some significance for demons? Like saying *your balls belong to me*?

I clear my throat. "I should, and they are." He looks far too happy at the thought. "You're scarily good at putting on an act. I almost believed you with your dad."

He gives me an inscrutable look but doesn't reply.

"Are all your family and friends that..." *Cruel, brutal, terrifying.* "...dangerous?" I can't resist reaching up to trace the rapidly purpling bruise on his cheekbone. "You know, since I'm about to meet them?"

Sol's fire suit blazes brighter in the dark night. "Until I came to your world, they were all I knew. By my horns, aren't all family dangerous? And I don't have friends at court. At least, ones that aren't also enemies." *Reassuring.* Sol's expression tightens. "In the name of the sacred elements, we can't make any mistakes. If we don't convince the entire demon court tonight that we're newly bonded and in love, then we're both dead."

# CHAPTER EIGHT

**Sol's Bedroom, Demon Underworld**

I 'm in Sol's bedroom, and there's only one bed.
*His.*

Of course there is...because his dad thinks that we're bonded.

I eye the offending bed warily, which is a large four-poster with crimson silk sheets and velvet blankets in the center of the room. Then I continue to rub my hair dry with what's admittedly the fluffiest towel I've ever felt, as I wander around the rest of the room.

Is it as weird for Sol to have me in what must once have been his childhood bedroom, as it is for me to be here?

Magical spheres of flickering orange light hover in the corners. Shelves groan under the weight of battered, ancient books and haphazard piles of glittering makeup and jewelery. They're like treasure hoards. On the far side is a large wooden wardrobe, which is carved with flames, and propped next to it is an acoustic guitar that's decorated with dragons.

My brow furrows. Why dragons?

A black, formal leather suit is laid out on the bed.

I sigh, taking a deep breath of the rich, bonfire scent that suffuses the room. It's powerful and weirdly reassuring. It makes me desperate to snuggle into the sheets and nest there, deep in the scent and safe from the court outside.

Instead, I run the towel over Light-bringer's scabbard, making sure to dry it fully so that it doesn't tarnish.

"Come on, why don't you get in?" Sol's voice calls teasingly, but it's sultry too. "I can clean you…or get you dirty."

I grit my teeth as I swing to the side and the remaining feature of the room: a demon in a round, marble bath.

A *naked* demon who's smirking in a way that makes me want to dunk him under the water or kiss him.

*Possibly both.*

Iridescent bubbles surround him, and he dips his

hand into the sparkling foam to soap his chest in lazy circles.

The **SKYE** brand above his heart spikes an irrational jealousy through me.

I hurl the towel onto the bed. "Pamper yourself like a spoiled, sociopathic prince before this psycho party if you have to, but I'm fine as I am."

I cross my arms.

My outfit is damp, wrinkled, and torn. My hair is a tangled mess. And I'm sure that I look a hot mess.

*Tough.*

They'll have to take me as I am.

Sol raises a skeptical brow. "The definition of *fine* has certainly expanded. Look, we've already bathed together. But this time, *I'll* pamper *you*. I'll wash you, stabby. Do you like shoulder massages?"

I shoot him a dark look, before lifting my foot. "You do realize that I could literally kill you with this spiky heel?"

His pupils dilate. "And you do realize that you're turning me on right now?"

I can't help a smirk of my own, as I saunter closer. "A pair of killer heels are a girl's best friend."

Sol laughs. "No matter what we face tonight, I'm glad to have you by my side."

His sentiment is unexpected, and it hits me hard.

My cheeks flush, and a warm feeling spreads in

my chest. Flustered, I look away, which is why I miss the moment that he rises out of the water with zero modesty, which is a demonic trait that I'm beginning to appreciate.

I can't be blamed for glancing up from underneath my eyelashes, as he strides to the bed. He's as perfect as a porcelain statue. Soap bubbles still cling to his skin in a delicious way, hiding some of his more interesting parts.

Although, is that a flash of silver?

Has he got a piercing...*down there*?

I hum "Happy Birthday" to myself, pretending that I'm not trying to sneak a look at what's clearly an impressive dick, before Sol turns away, and I admit that his ass looks deliciously tempting glistening and soapy.

The tip of his forked tail looks even fluffier than normal.

He takes far longer than necessary standing there wet and dripping, so I'm sure that he both knows and does it for my benefit.

*Tease.*

Then he waves his hand and fire skitters over his skin, drying himself. That's a useful feature. He doesn't even need to blow dry his hair but he somehow still manages to look like he's only just rolled out of bed.

Sol reaches for his leather pants that are black but scaled like dragonhide. He works them up his lean legs, without even pulling on any underwear.

My eyes widen. Why am I not surprised that demons always seem to go commando?

When he turns to me, he's looking far more serious than I'm expecting. "Okay, two rules. I'm not popular in the demon court. Prince means nothing, when you're not born to it. They'll try to get to me, through you. So, we have to play this perfectly. And don't mention that you're a twin." My stomach roils, but I nod. His elegant fingers tie the intricate laces at the front of his pants. "First rule: when bonds are this new, the bonded can't be more than twenty meters apart, or they're wracked by agony. It's a basic mechanism to strengthen the couple's connection. So, that means we'll be forced to stay close together at all times."

I groan. "What a wonderful honeymoon."

"Your sarcasm wounds me as always. Rule Number Two." He finishes tying his pants with an elaborate bow. It makes me wonder if he's had practice at tying things in a kinkier context. I force myself to concentrate. "We only have seven days and we've already had one of those."

*Seven days?*

I blink. "Seven days until what?"

"Until you and your sister will forever be unable to return to The Hill."

*WTF?*

I stalk to Sol, and his dark gaze meets mine. "Do you remember our conversation about my heel?"

"By my horns, it's a fantasy that I hope we can use as a roleplay sometime, but those aren't my rules. Humans can only cross into our world for seven nights, before they lose their memories of the non-magical world. If they're returned to their human lives after that then…" He grimaces. "It's been tried centuries ago, believe me. You won't know about it, however, because it's cruel: they lose their sanity, and The Hill refuse to take them back. So, seven days, if you wish to leave."

*Shit.*

I give a curt nod but I'm shaking.

Unexpectedly, Sol crushes me in an embrace, cupping the back of my head; his warmth is calming. "I'm sorry," he murmurs. "In the name of the sacred elements, I didn't want my bonding to be like this. Wait…" He draws back to look at me, panicked. "Hell, did I tear you apart from a boyfriend?"

I shake my head.

"Girlfriend?"

"Don't worry. The only person who I've truly been torn apart from is Skye, and you didn't take her, right?"

"Right."

Except, who did?

Can I truly trust that Sol had nothing to do with Skye being stolen, no matter how tenderly he's now holding me in his arms? I've already seen how good he is at acting.

If he's not popular at court but yet has needed to survive there, it's not a surprise that he's become excellent at wearing a mask.

"What about you?" I trace my finger along the **SKYE** brand, and he flinches. "Before this appeared on you like — *bam* — and you had no choice but to be bonded with this human, were you dating some pretty horned demon?"

Sol's grin is wicked. "Many demons have had the pleasure of kissing my pretty horns but none of them have claimed them as theirs. And they've tried."

Suddenly possessive of Sol's horns, I reach up and caress my fingers around the base of them. To my surprise, he purrs and melts against me; his eyes are half-hooded, and he's panting.

It's like I've stroked his dick. When I peer down; there's a bulge in the confines of his tight pants that looks painful.

Hurriedly, I withdraw my exploring fingers. "Sorry."

"What for? I thought my horns were yours?"

I pull away from him. "I just want my sister back and to free The Hill from you demons."

Sol's eyes narrow, as he grabs his leather shirt, which is scarlet like shimmering flames and hangs open over his pale chest. "We *demons* have as little choice in this as you *humans*. At least, those who are needed for the ancient treaty to hold. Are you shocked? Don't you understand that I've been sacrificed as much as you: the prince the same as the…"

"Pauper?" I suggest.

He's breathing hard, and his cheeks are tinted pink. "This treaty is needed to keep the peace between our worlds. This is my duty, and my brothers' too. Soul Bonds are the deepest love there is. Humans and demons are a perfect balance for each other. To be chosen as sacrifices is an—"

"Honor?" I suggest. He looks more amused than affronted. "Sorry, it just sounds like you've rehearsed that speech a lot."

He shrugs. "I've heard it a lot."

"From your dad?"

"Among others."

"And you promise that you'll try and get information on who took my sister tonight…?"

He looks weary but he nods. "I'll try."

As he fiddles with his silver cufflinks that are emblazoned with the flame emblem, I run my hand along the soft bed.

I shoot a quick glance at Sol. "There's only one bed."

"Smart as well as stabby."

"I'm not sleeping in bed with you."

"Of course not." He whirls around, before snatching a pillow off the bed and throwing it down onto the floor next to it.

Then he drags off a velvet blanket and adds that to the pile.

*Is he serious?*

Sol arches his brow at me like he expects me to thank him.

*Shit, he's serious.*

"You want me to sleep on the floor?" I growl. "I'm not a fucking pet."

Sol's pupils dilate, and his expression becomes dreamy. "You'd make a gorgeous pet. But that nest," he points at the pillow and blanket on the floor, "is for me."

I bite my lip. "Thank you."

Something about the thought of Sol curled in the nest on the floor feels strangely right.

Do demons nest?

Sol's cool gaze meets mine, before he starts to button up his shirt gracefully.

I drift closer to Sol, finding myself casually adjusting his collar and helping him to slip into his leather jacket, which is stiff and formal with thick ridges along the arms that remind me of a dragon. It makes him look even taller and more powerful, hugging his broad chest. Over his heart is the flame element like a military insignia.

Sol studies me. "I'll have formalwear sent up, which will magically adjust to fit you. Impressions are everything in this court. We can't have you turning up looking like a drowned angel."

"It sounds fucking appropriate to me," I mutter.

"I'm a prince, and Father will want you to look like the perfect princess on my arm in a beautiful dress, when we dance before the court."

I choke on my tongue. "D-dance? B-before the c-court? You know, demonic fish I can handle, but no way in hell am I wearing a dress and dancing. I get now why you were meant to be bonded to Skye. She would've made you the perfect sweet princess. But I would be more handy in a fight than a dance."

To my shock, Sol looks more excited than pissed off. "Good. I'm terrible at dancing too. Want to fight?"

Okay, not what I was expecting. But why the hell not?

My grin is sharp. "Bring it on, demon boy."

When Sol's grin becomes even sharper than mine, and his eyes flash, I only have one moment to regret my daring him into this, before he pounces.

*Hell*...

Sol tackles me, and we tumble onto the bed. I knee him in the gut, before he can pin my wrists, wriggling out from under him. I'm high on the adrenaline, buzzing. I'm loving every moment of this.

I dive over the other side of the bed, and Sol leaps straight after me. He's laughing the same as me, and I know that he's let me go. But I don't care.

When I reach for Light-bringer, he shoves me back against the wardrobe. I unsheathe my dagger, but his eyes are dancing, as he steps forward and grabs my wrist, knocking the blade out of it and spinning across the room. Then he presses me back against the wardrobe, pushing his thigh between mine. He's breathing as heavily as I am.

I haven't felt this alive…*ever*.

"Fighting is definitely superior to dancing," he whispers.

"Definitely," I agree.

He rests his forehead against mine, as I catch my breath.

His lips are tantalizingly close to mine.

"Do I have to wear a dress?" I sigh.

"Well, you could go naked but that would cause a bit of a stir."

I chuckle.

Then I glance at Sol's suit.

Who said I had to be the conventional Soul Bond? I've never been a conventional…anything.

I push Sol back, and he glances at me confused, as I wrench open his wardrobe and start to rifle through his beautiful array of shimmering suits.

"Ah-ha!" I pull out a suit, which is like the matching one to Sol's, except the shirt is black and the rest of the suit is a flaming crimson leather. It's gorgeous. "Can you adjust this to fit me? I'll be wearing your colors and element then."

Sol's expression softens, but his breathing quickens. "Smart, savvy human. You'll be the most beautiful person at the revel. You truly want to be dressed in my colors…?"

Weirdly, I do.

If the demon court is as dangerous as he says, then looking like I belong to Sol is the safest thing that I can do. Plus, it adds to the whole Soul Bond illusion. I can't examine the way that it also makes warmth unfurl inside me.

I settle for nodding.

Ruby magic unwinds from inside Sol, weaving around the suit and shrinking it to my size.

Delighted that I won't be forced into a thrice demon damned dress, I toss the crimson suit onto the bed and then sit on the side to pull off my boots.

My eyes widen, when Sol kneels down and gently pulls off one boot for me, and I didn't even have to demand it like his dad did.

A prince is willingly kneeling to me.

*A demon prince.*

Sol's eyes dance like he knows exactly what I'm thinking.

He takes off my second boot, before caressing over the arch of my foot, and I bite my lip to stop myself from moaning. Then he kisses the inside of each of my ankles.

I push myself to my feet, unbuckling my scabbard and placing Light-bringer on the bed, before wriggling out of my pants and top. It's way too late for modesty between us.

Sol stares at me like he desires my curves with an adoration that no man has before. Than his expression shutters, and I wonder if I imagined it. He stands, dressing me piece by piece in the leather suit that matches his own with a serious intensity like we're two warriors preparing for battle.

He stares at me in awe: dressed head-to-toe in a formal crimson and black leather suit. "Beautiful."

My skin prickles. Hot and cold washes through me.

He reaches up and glides his thumb across my lips, only to stumble back when the door slams open.

"Sol, my precious prince, why didn't you immediately come and find me to tell me that you were home? It wasn't right to let me find out through palace gossip. You're never too old for a horn spanking," a stern voice says from the doorway.

I glance up and am shocked to see that it's a human woman in her sixties who's scolding the demon prince.

She's elegant with ebony skin and graying hair that's braided like a snake on the top of her head with spiky combs. She's matronly and dressed in a long black dress that looks like a uniform with all four elements sewn on the sleeves.

Despite the threat of a horn spanking, Sol's face lights up. He strides across the room and throws his arms around the woman, who chuckles and hugs him back.

Wait, aren't non-magicals treated like slaves here?

I'd once believed that demons devoured humans. I know part of my Soul is being held captive by the Stones.

Yet I no longer believe the myths that they told me in The Hill. Since the stories are thousands of years old, and no one ever came back sane from the underworld to correct them, then it's no wonder that us humans have developed messed-up ideas about the demons.

What else have I got wrong?

Finally, the woman pats Sol on the back, and he grudgingly pulls back. Her smile is gentle, but she frowns, as she traces the bruise on his cheek.

She casts me a sharp glance. "Has something happened?"

Wait, she thinks that *I* slapped him?

"No more than the usual," Sol hurriedly assures her, before he holds out his hand to me. "And my Soul Bond would never lay a hand on me."

The woman *harrumphs*. "Considering that she's dressed as a warrior and looks more dangerous than you, I'm not sure I believe that, my precious prince."

Okay, now I know who's done the spoiling of my Demon of Fire. But since there doesn't seem to be a mum in the picture, I guess I'm glad about that.

*Time to start acting.*

I plaster on a smile, before strolling to Sol's side and awkwardly hooking my arm around his waist. "Please don't be cross with my dear Sol. It's such an honor to be sacrificed to him that I've selfishly demanded his attention and kept him to myself."

I try out a giggle for size, but I'm not sure I pull it off. Sol looks appalled.

Gallantly, however, he attempts to help me along with our act. He pulls me closer to his side and kisses me on my cheek.

"This is Bl..." He stops himself in panic, before smoothly continuing, "...bloody amazing to have my Soul Bond finally here with me. Mrs. Ward, this is Skye."

I hate being called my sister's name, even if this is pretend.

Luckily, Ward misinterprets my flinch, patting my arm comfortingly. "Don't worry, sweetheart. It'll get easier, and Sol's a good demon. The best in the court. The orphans here have missed him dreadfully. They need him." Sol glows, ducking his head. It's strange to see this woman, who obviously knows him well, praising him. Is she brainwashed or right? "Here's a secret: bond or not, things are always complicated or awkward at the start. Just get to know each other and don't expect things to be perfect. Love isn't. Wouldn't things be boring if they were?"

Is that the voice of experience talking because it sure sounds like it?

I tilt my head. "Are you bonded then?"

Sol says, softly, "You don't have to talk about this."

"It's all right, I'm not made of glass." Ward raises one elegant eyebrow and crosses her arms. "My beloved demon was killed in an attack by the gods. He died defending me. It was many years ago now, but I'll never lose the hollowness inside at his loss."

*Gods?*

Since when were gods the bad guys?

Sol clears his throat nervously. "I was going to tell you about that. You know, I just didn't want to overload you, right? Gods and demons are at war or most of them are. The Emperor has been working on a way for the demons to rise against the god's oppression of us."

I can't suppress my snort in time, and Ward's expression becomes steely.

"Don't disrespect the Emperor or his princes," she commands. "My lover died defending us from those gods. I'm honored to work in the Emperor's service as his housekeeper in charge of his other servants. I've always been even more honored to care for and raise the princes." So, this was Sol and his brothers' nanny then...? "The safest principle is not to speak about something you don't understand. You don't have horns, but you certainly have an ass that can be spanked."

I cringe back, only just resisting the temptation to shield my ass with my hands.

Sol smirks. "Don't worry, I'm certain that she'll end up over my lap."

My cheeks flame.

*And he'll be the one over my lap for that comment.*

I force myself to simper demurely. "I'm sorry."

Ward smooths her hands down her uniform. "Now, I must get back to the kitchen because I have preparations left for your Bonding Revel. It's going to be a grand affair. But first, my precious prince, is this... strangeness...in your bonded because you've banged her head?"

*Rude.*

Sol arches his brow. "I like her strangeness."

"Answer me right now young demon." Her hand is looking itchy. "How many times have I told you and your brothers that humans are breakable?"

Sol looks offended. "I was careful."

I remember Sol half-drowning, manhandling, and tackling me. Okay, the tackling part, which ended with our bodies pressed together, I didn't mind.

When Sol notices both Ward and me giving him long looks, he huffs. "*I was.* She's the one who gets all stabby."

Now, Ward's glare swings to me like I've skewered her precious prince in front of her; Sol looks smug.

"Listen here, I understand all about passion," Ward lectures, "but you're bonded now. That means you need to look out for each other. Sol's always needed someone like that in his life. I've prayed for the day, when he'd be blessed with it, especially in this court." She reaches forward and pats Sol's chest. "He deserves to be loved. Happy. And have wild, kinky sex."

I bite my tongue in shock.

*Ouch.*

Still, wild and kinky sex, since I saw how tempting Sol looked covered in bubbles, is definitely preferable than being presented to the entire court with danger, intrigue, and even worse, dancing.

Sol pretends to solicitously pull me closer and pet my hair, but his grin is bright. "Well, I guess we'll have to get to the wild, kinky sex then."

"Not until after the Bonding Revel you don't." Ward's face creases with concern. "I'm afraid that it's been organized by the Demon of Misrule and his gang. It's likely that they have some…games… planned." Sol pales, and his jaw clenches. So, not friends, and not fun games either. Adrenaline spikes through me, and my pulse speeds up. "By the way, your brothers are all here. Try and play nice. The Emperor will be cross if you don't."

I can't look away from the bruise on Sol's cheek.

I refuse to let him get another one. I remember his warning, however, that we could both be dead, if we don't pull off our act tonight. And I need to use it as an opportunity to find out about the raid and my sister's abduction. Somebody knows that the real Skye was stolen.

*And that means that somebody knows Sol and my secret.*

If they expose us, before we rescue my sister, then we'll also be slaughtered.

Is someone playing a game with all of us?

When Sol's gaze meets mine, I know that he's thinking the same thing.

"Just remember that this is the demon court," Sol

says. "Those who seem like friends are enemies and those who seem like enemies—

"Are friends?"

"Not quite." Sol's dark eyes flash with fire. "They're all enemies."

# CHAPTER NINE

**Emperor's Ballroom, Demon Underworld**

Awkwardly dancing at a ball in honor of my fake bond, while knowing that every single demon around me isn't even trying to hide their assessing looks, is a horrifying experience.

The only thing that lessens the horror, is the solid feel of Sol's arms wrapped around my waist, while I cling around his neck. We've long given up trying to properly ballroom dance.

Because Sol didn't lie.

He's just as bad at dancing as I am.

*Probably worse.*

He stands on my left foot, at the exact moment that I bump his nose with my forehead.

Then we both chuckle and hug each other closer.

The Emperor's Ballroom is like a cavern. Its high domed roof is gilded with glittering silver, which is studded with precious gems like we're inside a jewel. Silk banners that bear the four elements flutter from the walls. The moon shines through the circular windows and makes my breath catch, as it lights the revel with a wild and ethereal air. The room is decadent and opulent. I wrinkle my nose at the intoxicating scent of incense.

It's like falling into a dream that's hovering on the edge of becoming a nightmare.

Several musicians are playing violins and other string and wind instruments that I don't recognize, in fact, I don't think they exist in The Hill. The music is elegant but haunting.

There are tables, which are laid with food and goblets of blood-red wine, against the far wall. At the front is a raised dais with the Emperor on a throne that's chilling as well as spellbindingly beautiful. It's black and silver like the Emperor's mask but built up with spiked horns. It's as much a Gothic nightmare as Anwealda, who sprawls on it with his leg over the armrest.

Anwealda rests his chin on his hand, casually watching the revel. A gorgeous blue-haired demon with feathered wings stands sternly behind him in military stance like his personal guard, and on the steps up to the dais, are three intimidating but finely dressed demons, who I guess are the other princes.

*Sol's brothers.*

I'm trying to avoid catching their eye, and interestingly, so is Sol.

For now, we're lost in the whirlwind of dancers. It's making my skin prickle to be the only human in the midst of so many demons.

Where are the other Soul Bonds? Aren't they invited to revels?

Is this because I'm here as the sole attraction?

It feels like being a pet, who's been brought to the party as the novelty.

When Sol spins me, I sneak a look at the back of the Emperor's ballroom, which is covered in piles of velvet blankets and satin cushions.

*Demons definitely nest.*

Except, right now these demons, some of whom have blue, red, or even silver horns, as well as tails, are kissing as they strip each other, licking across each other's tits or savagely fucking.

Except, they're not all demons.

My eyes widen at the sight of the other creatures, most of whom are on their knees, both male and female, before the demons. They're ones who I thought were only myths before tonight: satyrs, kistune, and fae.

These creatures are untamed and stunning.

Were they also stolen to the underworld?

"Why's our Bonding Revel turned into an orgy?" I hiss.

"This is the underworld," Sol replies like that's explanation enough. "Wait, does that mean you want to join in? That male kistune looks cute — the one with the fluffy ears — and has been winking at you all night. If you really want to, we can go and join him. You can cuddle his tails..."

"Hell to the no!" I look up in time to see that Sol's eyes are dancing with amusement. "You were teasing. You didn't mean that, right?"

Sol's lips quirk. "I didn't mean it."

"Good." I narrow my eyes. "But *that* demon *has* been winking at you all night."

Sol spins us around again to look at the female demon with cruel eyes, who's dressed in a sweeping green dress like moss.

Sol's lips pinch. "She's just someone who once thought that she could own me. Jealous?"

"Of course not," I reply too quickly. "But I'm keeping up our front."

"It's understandable that you *would* be jealous," Sol continues, waving away my response. "But don't worry, you own my horns, remember?" *That thought is more comforting than it should be.* "How about we send out a message? We need to make this realistic."

He leans forward but hesitates when his lips are so close to mine that I can already taste them.

I nod.

*Hell, yeah…*

One thing that this demon knows how to do is kiss.

Then Sol's lips are on mine, but my gaze is fixed intently on the demon in the moss dress. She snarls, turning away with a flounce.

I relax into the kiss, swiping my tongue along Sol's lower lip and then opening my mouth, before our tongues dance with each other far more smoothly than we've managed so far on the dance floor.

I follow Sol with my lips, when he draws back.

"Did that achieve what you wanted?" He asks, coolly.

Is that the only reason he kissed me? Does he think it's the only reason that *I* kissed *him*?

I don't trust myself to talk, so I nod.

"We're making quite a stir in our matching suits," he points out.

I love the feel of the leather suit, and it was sexy as hell to swagger into this ball on Sol's arm, wearing his clothes. "As it should be."

He groans. "On my tail, would it really destroy our civilization to let me rock out at one of these revels?"

"Why can't you? You've got your own guitar."

"Because the Demon of Misrule, whose job it is to plan parties, has terrible taste in music."

"Yeah, it's as crappy as my sister's. I'd kill right now to see you do your rock god impression right in front of the Emperor." I grin. "You were on fire, when you played that song for me. I'm not kidding. It was... I've never been so caught up in someone's song before. It was like you were singing just for me: my heart."

His heated gaze meets mine. "I was."

Unexpectedly, the shadows in the far corner of the walls shift like they're dancing too; crimson eyes peer out at me. "Have they invited monsters to our party?"

"Shadow Demons. Scared, stabby? To be fair, you should be. They're destructive and brutal. They guard Father, sort of. I've never understood the deal they have, since not long ago they were his enemy and threatened the entire empire. Shadow Demons aren't even chaotic. They're pure anarchy and death."

I gasp, as he sharply twirls me. Then I tense, and my pulse quickens, as his lips are suddenly on my ear.

"What?"

"Don't react," he whispers.

Then he's kissing the shell of my ear, nibbling.

How the fuck am I meant not to react?

I shiver, and my skin prickles.

"Everybody will simply think that I'm ravishing

my beautiful new Soul Bond." His cool words are like cold water thrown on the fire between my legs. "But this is where you start to learn about my court. It's the only way to keep you safe, and by my horns, our only chance to find your sister."

He bites harder on my ear, and I moan.

When I look up, I realize that he's turned me so that I'm facing the dais. The Emperor is watching us, and his gaze is frighteningly knowing.

"Do you see the demon on the top step with the long military style coat and glower that makes him look like he's ready to leap off and rip open anybody's throat with his fangs who looks at him wrong?"

I swallow. "Yeah, Mr. Dominant Alpha."

I don't add Mr. *Gorgeous* Dominant Alpha like all the princes because I don't actually want to see if Sol also rips out throats with his fangs.

"That's Prince Breeze, the Demon of Air, and my eldest brother." Sol grimaces. "When we were in the orphanage, he once broke the horn of the keeper who was beating me. In turn, his tail was broken. As punishment, it wasn't allowed to heal right and it's still crooked."

I wince. "So, he's on your side, right?"

"Keep up. Since the Emperor adopted us, we've been trained separately in different kingdoms and in radically different ways. Breeze is a true warrior, who sees me as the lucky one. He wrongly thinks that I've been unfairly favored and pampered at court. Watch out for him because when he wants something or someone, he gets it."

I shudder. If I think that Sol's eyes are cold, then his brother's are like black ice.

Breeze is a ruthless, psycho warrior. Got it.

It's cruel, however, how the brothers have been kept apart and trained to be rivals. I can't imagine that being done to Skye and me.

"Now," Sol's lips are petal soft against my ear, "you see the cute demon next to Breeze? The one who has shimmering runes on his arms and a cheeky grin?"

"*Ehm*, he's waving at me actually."

"Well, wave back then."

Awkwardly, I do.

Shit, Sol's family is freaky.

"Is that a friendly wave or an *I'm plotting to kill you* wave?"

Sol chuckles, and his breath is hot against my skin. "That's Prince Roman, the Demon of Earth. The second eldest. You'd like him. Possibly. Well, if he wasn't such a cocky playboy. If you think I'm a trickster, I'm nothing next to him. And he's a sorcerer."

Cocky sorcerer, check.

"And the beautiful jock in the red and gold coat who's somehow managing to look lonely even in the middle of a revel...?"

Sol draws back. "You think Prince Caspian is beautiful?"

I study Sol's concerned face. Before we left his bedroom, he'd redrawn the black kohl beneath his eyes, which are large and thick lashed, and added a ruby glitter to his lips.

Sol's the most beautiful demon in this ballroom.

He offered to lend me makeup and jewels to add to my outfit, but I simply shook my head. Now, I'm loving being the least made up person in the middle of these sparkling demons.

They wear the glitter and glamor to hide themselves. I'm wearing Sol's clothes, but my face is bare. I may be having to lie right now, but I can keep some of myself: some truth.

Anwealda covers his face in a mask all the time. Why is that?

*What's he hiding?*

"I think Prince Caspian isn't you," I finally reply.

Sol gives me a searching look. "He's our youngest brother and he's...damaged. He's rarely allowed out of the Kingdom of Water."

"Why?"

"Because he's a monster."

My gaze shoots sharply to Caspian, whose head is ducked. He looks more in need of protection than being a danger. But what do I know?

*These are fucking demons.*

"And could any of them have taken my sister?" I demand.

Sol's gaze becomes flinty. "Just because we're rivals doesn't mean that I don't love my brothers. If any of them did steal your sister, just know that I'll stop you taking your revenge."

Fury surges through me. "You promised. We had a deal."

"To find her. And I will help you. But not to hurt my brothers."

All of a sudden, the music breaks off. A ripple of anxious chatter spreads through the ballroom.

What's happening now?

The dancing stops, and Sol pulls back from me, carefully schooling his expression. He holds tightly to my hand, however, keeping me close to his side.

The Emperor swings himself round in his seat and prowls to his feet. Instantly, everyone falls to their knees. Sol drags me down with him, and I wince, as my knees crack on the floor.

My heart's beating hard in my chest, and I don't look away from Anwealda, whose lips tug into a pleased smile, as he notices how Sol dragged me to my knees. He probably thinks that his son decided to take his scolding to heart and has been busy training and *controlling* me.

Well, as long as he doesn't learn the truth.

When Anwealda saunters to the front of the dais, I

don't miss how his sons all watch him like a predator approaching.

"This Bonding Revel is to welcome our newest Soul Bond, Skye, to our court," Anwealda announces. "She's now a princess. Treat her with respect and have a delightfully debauched time as always, darlings."

The demons cheer.

My cheeks redden.

*Princess?*

I should be loving this. Isn't it every girl's dream?

It isn't mine, however, and never has been. And I definitely never imagined that my Prince Charming would have horns.

Instead, I'm cringing and thrumming with anxiety, as everybody in the room studies me like I'm a fascinating new toy.

I never thought that I'd have preferred being the ignored cleaner in some rich kid's house. Did Lana or Maxton ever feel like this? The shiny toy on display?

As the Mayor's son or the Duchess, paraded around parties in pretty outfits like their parents' accessories since they were young, I bet they did.

Wow, I wish that I hadn't given them so much shit now.

*This sucks.*

Anwealda strolls back to his throne and hurls himself back in it.

As if all the tension has been released in the room,

the demons stand up and throw themselves into dancing or savage fucking.

Sol stands up and offers his hand to me, pulling me up.

"Princess?" I ask.

He smirks. "I did tell you that I was a prince."

*Princess Blue.*

I could get used to that.

Except, as soon as I find Skye, I'm leaving here and returning to a world, where I struggle over paying my electricity bills and definitely don't get called *princess*, unless it's a pet name by some douche.

Why does my heart clench at that thought?

"Come on," Sol leads the way through the dancers toward the table that's covered with cakes, muffins, and delicious cookies, "you must be hungry. I hear it takes it out of a human to be devoured by the Stones."

When my traitorous stomach growls, Sol passes me a chocolate cake that's smothered in cream and silver frosting that matches the ceiling.

The cake smells rich, velvety, and faintly vanilla. I can't resist taking a huge bite out of it. Immediately, I'm hit by such an intense burst of chocolate and cream sweetness, that I groan and stuff the rest into my mouth.

I lick the cream off my fingers, and my eyelashes flutter.

*Now I know why people sell their Souls.*

When I look up, Sol's watching me with a hungry expression like he wishes he could devour me. "Please tell me you always eat like that. Have you just orgasmed because, by my tail, I almost have."

I laugh. "Fuck you."

"Maybe later."

I flush. "You know, I was half expecting there to be a roasted human laid out here with an apple in their mouth. You know, since I was always taught that you dicks devour humans."

I take an unsteady step back, as Sol's face darkens to fury. His ruby tail whips side to side.

"You believed such lies and prejudice?" He snarls.

My expression hardens. "What do you expect? You stole my parents."

"I stole *nothing*." Sol wrenches me closer by my elbow. "The gods started those rumors about us *monstrous demons*. They're the ones who sparked the war between humans and demons in the first place. They fear the Soul Bonds because of the strength finding our fated mates gives to us. In a bond, the Soul isn't devoured: that's a mistranslation of our ancient texts. Instead, it's drawn inside the demon and creates something new: two Souls, together. It's precious, like Soul Bonds and every human who comes to our underworld."

*He means it.*

"Is Ward precious?"

"Don't speak about her. She raised me more than anyone did." Sol's eyes gleam dangerously. "Don't you remember what she told you? Humans aren't mistreated. And they *are* treasured. They're a gift."

"You mean a sacrifice."

"What's the difference?"

"Right, like you're not keeping them here as slaves."

"Aren't we all slaves?" He says, quietly. His tongue darts out to wet his lips. "I've been trying to end the raids on The Hill."

"Try harder."

Sol's eyes narrow. "Then help me become Crown Prince and take this Empire, and I promise to end them. Is that enough incentive to convince you to play nice?"

"What if the humans put an end to them all by themselves?" I counter. "Maxton believes that we can."

"Really? And who's Maxton? That *friend* of yours who touched you at the academy, stabby?" He asks with clipped control.

His magic is swirling around him in agitated waves.

Does he think that Maxton is one of my lovers, rather than an unacknowledged brother who I've spent most of my life fighting?

"My friend who hugged me," I correct.

135

"Emphasis on the *friend*. And why do you get to keep calling me *stabby*, when I don't have a pet name for you?"

"It's not my fault that you're not inventive enough."

*Wow, he's just made a serious mistake.*

My lips curl into a mischievous grin. "I'm plenty inventive enough, *kitten*."

Instantly, he bristles, and his claws extend. "What did you call me?"

"See, you're all bristly when you're angry like a cat. You hiss, spit, and even purr. Plus, you have fangs and claws. But still," I reach out and push a strand of his hair behind his ear, "silky to stroke."

"Can't I at least be a cat then?" He complains.

"Sorry, you're *kitten* because when I was a kid, I had two pets: a snake called Maxton," I smirk, when Sol scowls, "and a kitten called...*kitten*. I was less inventive back then with names. Kitten was meant to be my sister's. But adorable as he was, he'd nip or scratch you if he didn't get enough attention. My sister never loved him because of it. She was always scared by savage creatures. But me? I just learned how to handle him, and I never forgot that he was the type of kitten who'd never be tame. He was wild, and I let him be. A psycho cat."

"Sociopathic," Sol mutters.

"My sociopathic kitten."

"A lover's quarrel, is it?" A smooth Welsh voice asks with a false sympathy that makes *me* bristle.

Instantly, Sol lets go of my elbow and straightens. Even though his expression becomes a mask, he can't hide the tension in his shoulders or the way that his jaw clenches.

I stare at the new demon whose scarlet skin sparkles as brightly as his clothes, which look like they're made of crushed rubies. He appears to be only slightly older than Sol. His eyes are tawny and soft, but even though I don't know him yet, I can tell it's false.

He's hard and brutal underneath.

His gaze is darting between us like we're prey, and he's eager for new drama.

A second demon saunters up, who's taller than the first one, slipping his arm possessively around his waist.

Sol becomes even more tense, which I didn't think was possible.

The second demon's beautiful pastel green hair is braided to his waist, and his huge horns match it. He's palely beautiful but lithe. He's slenderer than the other demons. His black suit is lined with emeralds.

Why are they both dressed more richly than the princes?

"Won't you introduce us?" The first demon prompts.

Are these Sol's friends? But then, Sol told me in the bedroom that friends were enemies.

Are they?

"Nay, the Orphan Princes never did have any manners," the second demon's voice is Irish and mocking. His slitted eyes remind me of a snake's. "Away with you, what do you expect, when they raise wee poor brats above their station, expecting them to know how to interact with aristocrats? They should remain in their cages, where they belong. It would be less confusing for the wee dears."

The first demon's eyes dance with amusement.

*Assholes.*

Sol's hands clench. "This is Lord Oakthorn, Demon of Misrule."

The demon with pastel green hair sweeps me a lazy bow. "Call me Oran."

*Can I simply call him dickhead?*

"And I'm the Demon of Memories, Iago." The first demon catches my hand in his velvety scarlet one. I grimace. "I have a particular set of talents, see. I can borrow memories from one and grant them to another or drop you so far into your worst or best memories that you never surface."

I shudder, hastily pulling away my hand. "Is that a threat?"

Oran tightens his arm around Iago's waist, and he winces. "Nay, only a boast, unless you want it to be.

138

But why don't you ask your Orphan Prince. We've had a fine time playing with him at the revels and hunts that I organize or in Iago's experiments with memory."

*More like tormenting.*

So, the underworld has demonic bullies too.

"You've bowed to me but shouldn't you be bowing to your actual prince?" I arch my brow. "I mean, don't you have to call him *Highness* or else he can take your horns or something?"

All three demons wince. *Too far?*

"It's *Your Royal Highness*," Sol says, coldly.

Iago stares at him in shock, and Oran laughs like it's a joke.

Sol stands taller and continues to glare at them. "My princess is right. Call me Your Royal Highness." His voice becomes steelier. "I mean it."

"But here's the thing of it," Oran's green eyes open wide with pretend guilelessness, "when you're both dressed in such smart suits but also so pretty, how am I to know who's the prince and who the princess?"

This time, it's Iago who snickers.

Sol's voice is so deadly that I shiver, "*Now.*"

Oran rolls his eyes. "All right, I admit that I like the cute matching suits, Your Royal Highness."

"I don't." Iago shrugs. "Far too plain, Your Royal Highness."

139

"I'll just have to cry myself to sleep tonight," Sol replies. "Now tell me, there was another raid on The Hill earlier in the evening. You two always know the court's secrets. So, who led it?"

I try not to let my excitement show. But part of me hadn't trusted that Sol truly would help me find my sister.

Can I trust him now?

Iago tilts his head as he pets Oran's horns. "Thirsting for gossip already? What are you scheming?"

"You want to know if you have another rival, isn't that right, Your Royal Highness?" Oran smirks, and his too clever eyes seem to be making calculations. "Now, why would you be concerned about that then? Frightened that Da will love you...even less? Don't worry, there are enough demons here who are ready to *love* you in the special way that you're good for."

Sol ducks his head, and his hair tumbles over his eyes.

*Hell, no.*

No one talks to my fake bond like that. In fact, I won't stand by while anyone's talked to in that way.

"You forgot to call him Your Royal Highness, asshole," I snarl, diving at Oran and shoving him.

Surprised, Oran stares down at me. Perhaps, he's never had a human dare attack him before. Well, he'll have to get used to it.

"What a feisty creature." Iago's smile doesn't meet his eyes, as he nudges Oran. They exchange a glance that sends a chill down my spine. "I don't think you'll be so fast to defend your new Soul Bond, see, once you know what he's really like. How about I help? I only want to be fair to our new princess. Let me treat you to a gift of memories and show you our Orphan Prince's dirty little secrets."

"Hell fire, don't you dare," Sol growls.

But it's too late.

Iago snatches for my wrist, and it only takes the lightest brush of his skin against mine for me to be infected by memories like a toxin.

Then I'm falling down, down, *and down...*

I'm poisoned by a memory from a revel in this ballroom: one of Sol's very worst memories.

# CHAPTER TEN

**Emperor's Ballroom, Demon Underworld**

My mind is hazy, as I fall down into Sol's memory, but I flush with uncomfortable warmth like poison is creeping through my veins and making me fevered.

I draw in a desperate breath, but my lungs won't expand.

Sweat slides down my neck, and my leather shirt sticks to me.

I shudder with dread like I don't want to see — witness — what Iago has forced onto me. It's not my memory. He has no fucking right to steal it from Sol to sully him.

It's a violation.

What the hell is he going to show me?

The haze settles, and I'm in the same ball room, but it's decorated differently with bowers and summer flowers. There's a wildness in the air like blood could spill as easily as wine. There's a press of bodies in the middle of the velvet nest: demons and satyrs sprawled over each other in a tangle of near naked limbs.

And in the center is Sol.

I take a step forward like I can wrench him away from the demons who are kissing up his neck and the kitsune who's stroking his tail, but this is only a memory.

*This has already happened.*

Sol is younger here. Maybe eighteen. Demons have orgies. It's what they do. But the problem is Sol looks drunk, confused...vulnerable.

His gaze isn't focused, and the same woman in a moss dress who winked at him earlier is seated on his lap, resolutely keeping him pressed down amongst the others.

My hands clench at my sides compulsively.

Oran and Iago sit either side of Sol; they keep exchanging delighted glances with each other, and their eyes are too clear and bright to be drunk themselves.

"Here's the thing of it, Orphan Prince, it's tradition to play this game at a prince's first official revel,"

Oran announces with a smirk that tells me that's a fucking lie.

Oran nods at Iago, and Iago passes Sol a brimming silver goblet of red-wine. It's bubbling, and I can smell a stench like sulfur.

Okay, that's drugged or poisoned. But Sol forces himself to drink anyway.

Instantly, he doubles over in agony, and the other demons cheer.

Frantically, I look around for anybody to intervene. Where's his older brothers? His father?

Why's no one looking out for the prince?

"I won't drink anymore," Sol slurs, attempting to push away the goblet.

Iago shakes his head. "It's a sad day that the Emperor's son shows himself to be weak. He already has a pauper as a son and now a coward. He will be disappointed."

Sol's gaze sharpens just for a moment and becomes determined, as he raises the stinking goblet to his lips, struggling not to gag.

"Good boy," Oran coos. "Make your da proud. And if you don't finish it by the time we finish stripping you," Oran begins to unbutton Sol's shirt, revealing his pale chest, "well…"

He whispers something in Sol's ear, which makes him turn ashen and instantly, force himself to drink more of the poison.

The gang around him laugh, as he chokes, and the female demon kisses his horns.

"Let me out," I scream.

I can't see anymore. *I won't.*

I hadn't understood the danger of this court or the truth of Sol's position. He was forced to torture himself because if he didn't, he wouldn't have looked strong enough to remain a prince.

*Was it the same with finding his Soul Bond?*

Sol really is as much a sacrifice as I am. We're in this together.

If Oran and Iago thought that it'd shame Sol by showing this to me...make him look weak...then they're wrong. Instead, it makes me want to gut every bully who's ever laid a finger on Sol.

And I'll start with Oran and Iago.

Except, are they exactly the type of demons who'd have taken Skye?

"Let me out now, or I'll kick your asses," I snarl.

My mind becomes hazy again, and I can feel myself being dragged upwards.

The last thing I see is Sol gasping in pain, and Oran and Iago kissing each of his horns.

I burst out of the memory in a red haze of fury. I wrench my wrist out of Iago's hold and then raise my hand to slap him.

Sol slides his arm around my waist, however, pulling me back, even though I struggle.

"My dear father is watching," Sol whispers urgently into my ear.

I look over at the dais.

Anwealda is perched on the edge of his seat, studying our drama with fascination in his cold eyes.

I still in Sol's arms.

It's probably breaking royal etiquette to kick a Lord in the balls on the night that you're presented to court, right?

Princesses have no freedom. But then, I'm learning that princes don't have much either.

Sol said that we were all slaves. On the other hand, aren't some more slaves than others?

I spin in Sol's arms, and cup his cheeks, gazing up into his eyes.

"What did they show you?" He asks, as steadily as he can.

It's tearing him up inside not to know what I've seen or how I'm judging him now.

I don't judge others. What gives me the right?

"Something that made me want to get stabby on their asses. Nothing that makes me think worse of you," I reply. His shoulders slump with relief. "Now, since they're watching like your dad is, how about we put on a show and let them know that they haven't wrecked things for us?"

"You mean, pretend that they haven't damaged the bond?"

146

Oh, yeah. I'd sort of forgotten the whole *fake* part of this.

*Still...*

"Exactly." I stroke Sol's bruised cheek with my thumb, and his expression softens.

Then I kiss him, gently but insistently.

His magic curls around me. The sensation is electric.

When he pulls back, his lips twitch just for a moment.

Then he announces, loudly enough to make sure that his tormentors can hear, "Hell, I wish that we didn't have to be here right now or that the first *fuck* with a Soul Bond didn't need to be private." A jolt shoots through me at the way that he rolls *fuck* along his tongue like he's already pounding into me. His voice becomes a seductive purr. "Then I'd rip off all your clothes, bend you over this table, and rail you so hard that it'd rock. By my flames, I crave you so badly right now."

I gape at him.

So, I should've guessed that a demon prince excelled at dirty talk.

Shit, I crave *him* so badly right now.

I slide my fingers up his inner thigh, and he bites his lip. When I glance at his crotch, I can see how hard he is.

It's incredible to feel desired like this.

Time for a little revenge on the bullies.

"I love it when you take control." I slink my hips against Sol's. "You're so tall, strong, and powerful."

So, my dirty talk isn't up to Sol's level but it's not meant to be. It's sticking two fingers up to Oran and Iago. And by the glazed look in Sol's eyes, it's getting the job done with him as well.

"It's a fine thing to find a Soul Bond who can see past your wee flaws," Oran sniffs. I glance over my shoulder, as he casually readjusts his braid. "Why don't you show us your pretty brand?"

Instantly, Sol stiffens. "That's private."

Iago stalks closer, sliding his hand companionably onto Sol's shoulder. "You'd think that we hadn't seen every inch of your fine skin. What's the problem, Your Royal Highness?"

I wish now that I hadn't made a fuss about them using the title, when they say it in such a mocking way.

More quickly than a human can move, Iago slips his claw down the front of Sol's shirt, slitting it open and revealing the **SKYE** brand.

Sol hisses, stepping back and away from me. He tries to hold his suit together to hide it. The crowds around us have stopped talking.

I cringe back from their scrutiny.

Breeze, Sol's eldest brother, leaps from the top step like finally he's going to do something (how many years too late?), but Sol shakes his head at him.

"Touch me again," Sol says, his voice low and dangerous, "and I'll slice off your hands and pin them to the palace walls."

"Promises, promises." Iago smirks.

"And touch my princess," Sol's eyes blaze red, "and I will gore your throat with my horns, until you wish you were dead. Are we clear?"

Iago swallows and nods.

Oran snatches Iago by the neck and steers him back into the crowd.

When I try to touch Sol's arm, he shrugs me off and prowls away to his brother.

Does he want me to follow?

I'm torn between sticking close to his side because, hey, demon ball, and giving him some space.

I sigh, spotting a dark alcove, which is shaped like a gaping dragon's mouth behind the table. I squeeze past the table, trying not to knock into any of the food and spoil Sol's borrowed suit.

My temples are throbbing with the music, sparkling light of the bejewelled demons, and the overload of the memory that was forced into my head. I need a moment of quiet and dark. Except, then my heel hits something metallic with a *clank*, which is followed by a whimper.

I turn around and crouch in the shadows.

It's a small, golden cage.

And there's a beautiful naked man trapped inside the cage. He's so cramped that he can only sit with his knees drawn up to his chin.

In the dark, we stare at each other in shock.

I don't know whose heart is beating more rapidly. My breathing is ragged, but the man's chest is rising and falling so quickly, he looks close to tipping into panic attack.

He doesn't have horns or a tail.

Is he a human?

He's a beauty of naked muscles and sweet, blond curls. He studies me with large, amber eyes.

Who could be cruel enough to cage him like this?

Were all those things Sol told me about how humans weren't mistreated and held as precious a lie?

My guts churn.

When I rest my hand on the bars, the man's soft fingers tentatively reach to brush against mine like he hasn't had a gentle touch in a long time.

"Were you stolen from The Hill?" I ask.

I don't recognize him, but I don't know everybody. Some people try to hide their children because they think it'll make them less likely to be chosen as sacrifices.

It doesn't work.

The man's expression becomes haughty for a

moment, before his shoulders slump. "I'm a god, little girl. How far I've fallen that you can't tell."

*A god?*

I snatch my hand back quickly, and the god sadly clutches onto the bars, instead.

Should I feel sorry for him?

The demons are at war with the gods, right? Sol said that they were bad. But this one doesn't look bad. And how can it ever be right to keep someone in a cage?

"Why can't I tell you're a god?" I demand.

The god's expression darkens. "The cage steals my powers. Divinity. I was made to be worshiped." Then he wets his lips and shoots me a nervous look. "Are you here to hurt me? Is this more *training*?"

"Fuck no." Horrified, I reach through the bars to pet his curls. Hell, they're soft. "Who are you?"

"Nobody now. At least, I'm the Emperor's Pet." He pushes into my hand, and I stroke him, until he relaxes.

Yet someone's already hurt him. There are bruises and welts along his shoulders and back.

Is this what love is for demons? Am I going to be Sol's *pet*?

"Why were you put in this cage?" My eyes narrow. "What did you do?"

Pet ducks his head, and for a moment, I think he'll cry. "I fell in love."

Shit, what on earth do I do? Can I leave him like this? I'm not the kind of person who can just walk away from somebody in pain.

On the other hand, I don't know what's going on between gods and demons. I'm only here for my sister. I shouldn't be meddling in wars and political prisoners.

"Will you help me? Open the cage. That's all. Free me," Pet's whisper is as soft as honey. "Just let me out."

I gasp, as I'm grabbed by the back of the neck and dragged up, at the same time as Oran leaps over the table behind me and lands, before kicking the cage, hard enough to make it rattle.

Pet whines.

I struggle, but Iago is holding me too tightly.

"Leave Pet alone," I snarl.

Oran raises his eyebrow. "Mind yourself, human. First you stand up for the Orphan Prince and now for the fallen god. It's not good to ally yourself to lost causes."

He kicks the cage again, and Pet clasps his knees tighter.

"Has no one taught you not to be a bullying asshole?" I demand.

Oran's face clouds for a moment, before he replies, "The weak are prey. Knowledge is power: the power to know everyone's weak spot. And what I love most...? Discovering that perfect button to press to bring someone to their knees in front of me. Aye, it's a fine thing to play every courtier and make them dance. Especially, when they're princes or princesses." He snatches the god's curls through the bars, and he gasps in pain. "Or gods."

Iago shakes his head in mock disappointment. "What a shame, see, that we'll have to tell the Emperor that you've been a bad pet. I'm sure he'll make a public spectacle of you again. It's always entertaining."

Pet pales. "I'm sorry. Please, don't."

"It was my fault," I insist. "I spoke to him."

Oran claps his hands together. "Brilliant. Then you can take the punishment."

Wait, did he just play both of us?

Iago slams his hand over my mouth, before dragging me through a hidden door behind the alcove and down a narrow corridor into a room that's wood paneled with a mirrored roof. I can see my own struggling self being dragged inside and the door being slammed shut, reflected back at me, then as I'm thrown onto the satin ivory couch.

I stare up at my own frightened expression.

My pulse is thrashing in my ears, and I'm trembling violently.

I should have realized that Sol's been gentle with me so far. These demons are terrifyingly powerful.

I'm an idiot.

I should've looped the leather around the suit and brought Light-bringer with me, screw Sol telling me that it's tradition that no one bears weapons to a revel.

Demon traditions suck.

Plus, they already have their weapons on them: horns, claws, and fangs.

What's wrong with leveling the playing field?

Now I have a snake-like demon pinning me down, while another leans against the wall, watching with amused, tawny eyes.

How long before Sol realizes that I'm gone?

If we were true Soul Bonds he already would have. And yeah, I *am* bitter.

"I love this part." Oran flashes his fangs in a cruel smile. "It's a test for all newly bonded, when you're separated." He leans closer, and I try to draw back, kicking my legs, as he presses his body against mine. "So, scream for me."

My eyes widen.

Am I over twenty meters away from Sol?

What I truly want to do is knee Oran in the balls, but he's watching me with a sadistic intensity, waiting to feast on my agony. I secretly suspect, it's *Sol's* agony that he wants.

I force myself not to roll my eyes.

*Okay, let's do this.*

I grimace, before letting out a groan that I hope is

convincing. My eyes flutter closed, as I arch my back and scrabble at the couch.

Then I do scream, as high-pitched as I can.

When I open my eyes and peek at Oran, he's wincing.

*Serves you right, fucker.*

I take a deep breath, before screaming, "Sol, help! Murder! Fire! Bomb!" Iago straightens, looking around himself wildly. What else gets people to your aid as quickly as possible? *"Kitten, save me."*

Iago backs away as far as he can, bumping into the wall. "I told you this wasn't a good idea. She's crazy, see. Make her stop."

Oran slams his hand over my mouth, and I bite it.

*Hard.*

Oran howls, pulling away his hand and shaking it. "The bitch bit me. Humans don't fight back."

"This one fucking does." I grin fiercely.

Oran raises his hand to hit me, and I brace for it.

All of a sudden, however, a roar shakes the room from outside in the corridor.

Iago flattens himself against the wall, blanching. "Hell…"

The door bursts inwards, melting under the blast of fire.

A creature swoops into the room on ruby wings. Magic flutters around them, decadent and ethereal. They're spellbinding.

*It's Sol.*

Yet his eyes are wild and flaming red, sparks flare out of his mouth, which is razor-sharp with fangs, and his nails have extended to blood-red claws. Fire flares from his horns like a crown.

He's monstrous.

Terrifying.

*Savage.*

He's everything that I should be scared of…should hate.

Yet he's also everything that I want and need to see right now.

He's awe-inspiring.

Oran and Iago are screwed and they know it. I allow myself a wicked grin.

Sol glances at me, tilting his head like he's assessing whether I'm okay. He's vibrating with a searing, white-hot rage.

Then he bellows, and the deep sound rumbles through the room. Is he going to burn my attackers or gore them with his horns? His need to protect me is primal and ancient. It's driving him now, and I don't know if he'll be able to restrain himself.

I don't know if I want him to.

"Sol," I gasp.

Sol charges at Oran, grabbing his slender body by the waist and digging in his claws, until Oran howls.

Iago doesn't even attempt to help his friend. Oran swings his head around, trying to gore Sol with his horns, but Sol drags him away from me in one brutal move and hurls him across the room. Oran slams into the wall next to Iago with a *crack* that makes him scream.

He must've broken something.

Sol stalks toward them, and his wings beat behind him in a show of dominance.

"The shifter finally shows his fangs," Oran sneers. "*Aww*, how sweet. All for your Soul Bond. Is it true love? We were only doing a wee test."

"And I'll only be killing you like I promised for touching my Soul Bond." Sol's expression is cold.

"You don't want to do this, see," Iago warns, breathing hard. "Or do you want your private memories to be made public?"

"You know he can do it." Oran bends over, clutching his hurt ribs.

"That would be impressive if he's dead." Sol shoots out flames from his mouth, and my eyes widen in alarm.

If I'm honest, Sol is scorching-hot like this.

Oran and Iago holler and duck. The flames miss them, and they cower, covering their heads.

"Idiots as they are, I'd prefer my son and his friend not to be burned to a crisp right now," a gruff voice says from the doorway. "But since he's interfered with an official Bonding Revel, he deserves whatever punishment you think fit."

I sit up and stare at an older demon who's sober and statesmanlike. His hair is also pastel green like Oran's but it's short and lies between huge horns that are curved like a stag's.

Immediately, Oran snaps to his feet, dragging Iago with him. Even though he winces, he stands with his hands clasped smartly behind him.

He may be a dickhead but he's a dickhead who's afraid of his father.

Already, I'm getting better at reading these court dynamics.

Sol takes a shuddering breath, before stepping away from the other demons. His fangs and claws slowly retract, and his wings fold away.

He still looks just as deadly.

"Duke Oakthorn," Sol turns with studied politeness to the demon in the doorway, "I trust that you always know the correct severity with which to punish your son and his friend, who's under your guardianship."

"Away with you, don't be like that…" Oran whispers urgently, as if he's resentful that Sol isn't actually standing up for him against his dad.

Wait, is this Duke more terrifying than Sol, who's been threatening to burn Oran alive?

Apparently, *hell yeah.*

Oakthorn gives a vicious grin. "You can be assured of that."

Oakthorn marches toward Oran.

I'm surprised that Oran pushes Iago behind him as if to shield him. I'm even more shocked by the way that Oakthorn snatches them both by their horns and twists. They howl as they're dragged out of the room by their horns.

Sol gives a triumphant smile, before striding to my side and dropping to his knees in front of me. "Are you okay?"

I assess him. "Would you have truly burned them?"

"Do you truly want me to answer that?"

*Good point.*

Can I admit how much his protecting me has turned me on? Saying that he claimed me was just words but this was real actions.

He proved it.

I fiddle with the hem of my shirt. "Do demons have consciences?"

He blinks. "I don't think so. But I want to make you happy." He runs his fingers lightly down my thigh, and my breath hitches. "Very happy. And I didn't kill them, did I?"

"Give the demon a medal."

I clasp his hand, moving his fingers higher to the top of my pants. He pushes at my shirt, pulling it out, before he can play with my skin beneath. I feel like I'm fevered at his touch.

"Sarcasm." He glances at me from underneath his long lashes. "It makes me all tingly. Can I have a medal as well or...can I have this?"

He leans forward, and now it's his lips, kissing the revealed strip of skin above my pants. He's feathering kisses to my stomach, clutching my waist.

Do I want this?

*I've wanted it from the moment that I met Sol.*

Only, now I can allow myself to have it. Aren't we meant to have a first night tonight as bonded? What's stopping us from taking it?

Sol is never allowed to have anyone but me again, wouldn't it be cruel to deny him this?

*And I don't want to, even if he's only playing pretend still.*

Desire washes through me, and I'm flushed.

"Hell, yeah." I rest my hands on Sol's silky hair, but it isn't enough.

I twist my hands in his tumble of curls, tightening until I wrench back his head. He moans, and his pupils dilate.

"Unlace me and you can have a reward," I breathe.

Am I really doing this with a demon?

His elegant fingers reach for the laces at the front of my pants. Is this why they're made like this: convenience for kinkiness?

*Shit, I am doing this.*

"I've been desperate to taste you." Sol's eyes are dark and searching. "To take you here, where anyone could walk in and see us. By my horns, to show them what equality looks like because the human isn't the toy." He licks a stripe along my clit, and I hiss out a breath at the electric pleasure. "You have a demon prince willingly on his knees."

"Good demon," I murmur, tightening my hold in his hair.

I can feel the way that his lips smirk against my pussy.

"Bad demon," he corrects. "Do you still hate me?"

He circles his tongue around my clit, before sucking. Then he slips two fingers down and into my pussy, crooking them. I keen in pleasure, and my back arches. My heart's beating rapidly, and I claw at the couch.

I adore the way that a blush is creeping up his cheeks, and his eyes are flashing between black and red with excitement.

"Do you want me to hate you?" I gasp.

Yet in my head, it sounds more like *I love you*, than I've ever said to a guy. Than I've ever *let* myself say.

Sol's magic sparks out of him, and I gasp, as it prickles across my most intimate place.

"I *love* that you hate me," he whispers, pressing a

kiss to my clit on each word. "Why don't you hate me some more?"

Then his tail whips around and replaces his fingers in my pussy. My eyes widen in shock at the sensation of its soft, forked tip, as it presses inside me.

It's sparking with magic; it's the most intense pleasure that I've ever experienced.

"Sol," I scream, clenching my hand in his hair even tighter, as the twin sensations of his tail and wicked tongue overwhelm me.

Then ecstasy crashes through me like dying, and my mind is shocked to hazy white.

Is this the true meaning of being devoured by demons? If it is, then do I truly want to leave the underworld?

# CHAPTER ELEVEN

**Sol's Bedroom, Demon Underworld**

W hen I awake, I'm in Sol's bedroom, and a pale red-tinged morning light is streaming through the window.

I groan, rubbing my temples that are throbbing.

How did I get here?

The last thing I remember is having the orgasm of my thrice demon damned life and then...nothing.

If that means Sol carried me out in his arms or over his shoulder like I'm a real demon bride, while looking all smug and boasting of his conquest, then I never want to face any of those demons again. At least, not without Light-bringer in my hand.

Otherwise, I'll die of cringing embarrassment. I'm sure that's possible.

Still, Sol truly was an amazing lover and unselfish, which isn't something I expected from a prince. But then, Sol's surprised me at every turn.

He's not like I thought he'd be at all. None of these demons are.

I glance down at myself in relief, running my hand along the ruby silk pajamas. At least I'm not naked.

Except, does that mean Sol stripped and changed me into these last night, while my brain was fried?

Fuck. My. Life.

I trace my fingers further along the soft bedding and blink in amazement. The bed has been pulled apart and then reformed into a strange but highly snuggly circle around me. The blankets are pulled as close as possible and the satin pillows and cushions are almost like the walls of a…

Hell, demons *do* nest.

And talking of demons, where's my Demon of Fire?

I peer over the bed, but Sol's not sleeping on the floor in a nest of his own.

Instantly panicked, I sit up, not caring that my hair is at wild angles or my stomach is rumbling for breakfast.

*Where's Sol?*

Then I notice that there's something heavy around

my neck like a coiled necklace. Except, this necklace is warm, leathery, and moving.

I still and listen hard.

*It's snoring.*

I hiss out a breath and reach up, only to touch scales and the light flutter of wings. Then whatever is curled around my neck begins to purr at my touch.

*If demons put living collars on their humans, Sol is in for an ass kicking.*

I peer down but all I can see is the ruby tip of a snout and a tail curled around my neck.

"Hey, wake up," I hiss. "No snoozing around my neck without permission. I only give snuggles to those who I've been introduced to and not freaky but cute purring collars."

Instantly, the creature wakes up with a startled jerk. His black eyes open to stare up at me in panic. He chirps as if in apology and unwinds from my neck, flying to sit on the other side of the nest.

*He's a dragon.*

I gasp in delight.

The creature is tiny and beautiful. He's shimmering ruby, and magic flutters around him like smoke. His neck is long and sinuous, and his wings sparkle.

The look that he's shooting me is adorable, until he flashes his fangs.

I just had those small teeth way too close to my jugular…

*He's a demonic dragon.* I should have known.

"I take it back. As long as you promise not to bite me, you can snuggle me any time." I hold out my hand to the dragon, but he hops backward.

Then in a ruby spray of glitter, the dragon transforms into Sol.

I let out a yelp of shock, as Sol lounges in the nest, running his fingers through his hair. He's wearing the same pajamas as me, so at least we match.

Sol's smile is sheepish. "I can't promise not to bite, but thanks for the offer."

I stare at him. "You're a dragon."

*Of course!* Sol's guitar is decorated with dragons, and his clothes are like dragonhide. Plus, the way he half transformed last night into a monstrous creature that was growly, protective, and possessive.

"I'm a Shifter Demon," Sol corrects, "and my shifter is a dragon. I didn't intend to transform in the night. Instinct took over. Dragons are possessive of their treasure…"

"I'm not treasure."

He shrugs, and his silky top slips off one snowy shoulder. "You're sort of like treasure." He gestures at the nest. "Shifter Demons need to nest with their Soul Bonds. You must be enough like treasure to trick my biology into this…"

He picks up a pillow and reinforces the side of the nest.

"Can other demons shift as well?" I ask.

Hell, there's so much I don't know. Demons are as different and varied as humans are to each other. I wish Maxton and the others could discover the truth about this civilization, and I wish that other demons could truly get to know the human world.

Sol's expression becomes closed off. "Elemental demons are shifters. Some gods are. I understand if you don't want to… If you prefer to keep things solely business between us now."

*WTF?*

I edge on my ass closer to Sol, grabbing his hand.

He's been deliberately hiding this from me. But why?

"I told you before that I'm not judgey. I don't give a fuck what others think about Shifter Demons. It's incredible that you're a dragon. Why do they care?"

"Because it makes me a monster," he whispers.

He's studying me closely. He said that about his brother as well.

I get it now.

And I won't let him think that I'm the same as any of the assholes who've made his life hell simply for being born who he is.

"You're beautiful like that: a dragon," I say. His shocked gaze flies to mine, and his cheeks tint pink.

And he is, both this morning and when he half transformed last night. "Hey, how about if I walk around with you proudly around my neck? A princess wearing her prince as her collar."

He shivers. "And they say demons are exhibitionists."

So, I've hit a definite kink. Something to go back to then.

"But…" I bite my lip. "Only if you find Skye. I'm holding up my side of the deal here, and last night was a waste of time."

Sol snatches his hand away from me, narrowing his eyes. "I forgot that this was still no more than pretend to you. Nothing but a deal."

I wrap a blanket around myself, missing his touch. "I thought demons were all about deals."

"Of course, that and stealing and devouring," he sneers. "It's a wonder that I have time to hoard any treasure."

I squint at him. "You're being sarcastic."

"You don't have the monopoly on it. And I do like treasure." He points at me. "The evidence is in my bed. It's a dragon thing."

"Who am I to kink shame?"

Sol's expression becomes dangerous and dark, before he says, "Then it's lucky that I have a lot of kinks."

*Figures.*

I struggle to free myself from the nest and stand. "Ones that we won't be sharing, fake lover."

Hurt flashes across Sol's face, before he dives over the nest and hauls me back, pinning me to the bed.

My heart's beating too fast, and adrenaline spikes.

"I don't think that your excitement or enthusiasm was *faked* last night." He's holding me down by my shoulders but otherwise not touching me; he studies me with a desperate, open expression.

*I'm falling for him.*

It's a terrifying feeling like falling into a void. What if there's nothing but never-ending darkness?

Can I let myself fall?

I grit my teeth. "Find my sister. You promised."

Sol fights to get himself under control, before he lets go of my shoulders and sits back on his heels. "I have spies scouring the four kingdoms. I'm personally interrogating the court and even my brothers. What more would you have me do?"

"Whatever you have to."

His tail winds out, and its fluffy end strokes down my arm like he doesn't even know he's doing it. "There was gossip about you last night, but on my wings, nothing about the raid. Someone high up and with a hell of a lot of power decided to keep people quiet about it. Why?"

"You mean who."

"Sometimes, I mean what I say." His lips quirk.

"Why'd they go to all that trouble to keep it quiet? Did they intend to steal your sister? Was it an attempt to steal my Soul Bond or an accident? Did they want to set me up in my current impossible and dangerous position? Will they try and blackmail me now or was it all only a raid gone wrong? The answer to that will tell us whether your sister is even…"

He snaps his mouth shut, and his gaze darts away from mine, shiftily.

My stomach heaves.

*Shit, he doesn't mean…?*

"*Is even alive.* Go on. Fucking say it, if that's what you mean." My eyes burn with tears.

Sol's gaze darts to mine, and his tail wipes away a tear that's trailed down my cheek. "If she's even alive," he repeats, and somehow, I admire him for that.

*I will not let myself sob.* "Last night was the first time that I've slept in a different house to my sister, right? I mean, ever. Even when I had boyfriends, they came home to mine. It's this twin thing. Although, I used to piss her off with the noise. This separation is killing me. Once, she had to go into hospital, and we both kicked up such a fuss that the nurses pulled a bed next to hers and allowed me to sleep beside her, holding her hand."

Sol holds out his hand to me now, and I entwine our fingers. It's not the same, but it helps.

*Hell, I miss Skye.*

"When I was in the orphanage," Sol says, "my brothers and I slept together on a mattress on the floor of a cage." I tighten my fingers around his, too shocked to say anything. I remember Pet then, who's still trapped in a golden cage. How the hell can I just leave him there? "We cuddled together in the nest like a pile of puppies, holding hands. We could even shift without being punished. In the name of the sacred elements, we all loved nighttime best because we were together." He gives a bitter smile. "We were never parted, until the *lucky* day when us orphans were lined up, and my brothers and I were *honored* to be picked out and chosen to become princes."

I squeeze his hand. "If I can help you like you are me, then I will. But do you get why it means so much to me to rescue Skye?"

He snorts. "I always have." Then he tilts his head. "What will you do, when you find the demon who took her? Do you want revenge?"

My eyes flash. "Wouldn't you?"

"I'd want to rip the horns from their head," Sol replies. "But I've claimed you now, my princess. Revenge will lead to more blood and…I want you to be mine. Are you?"

And isn't that the fucking question?

I push myself up, and Sol's startled, as I shove him onto his back. I crouch over him with my thighs either

side of him. I clutch his tail between my hands. Then I
lick a long stripe along it.

His eyes are blown wide.

"The point is, *kitten*, you're mine." I take another
lick.

Sol bristles, and his claws extend…just like a
kitten's.

I smirk, slowly unbuttoning his pajama top.

Sol's eyes blacken to midnight. "Prove it."

Oh, he just dared me.

*Risky move.*

"Go on then, kitten." I nuzzle at his pale throat,
and he bares it to allow me more room. "Tell me some
more about these *kinks*. And if you're uncomfortable
at any point, things are too much, or you need to slow
down, just tell me. If you want me to stop, say *red*."

He glances at me, as if he's assessing whether I
truly mean it. Then he waves his hand at the wall. The
lights flare for a moment and then Bryce Fox's
"Horns" bursts out in its badass rock, bluesy glory.

Except, there's a difference.

*It's Sol singing.*

His voice bleeds through my blood, bones, and
Soul along with his guitar. I want to drink his voice
and devour his music.

It's spellbinding, *seductive*.

Warmth rushes through me, and I clench my
thighs together.

172

I shudder, and Sol watches me with his large, dark eyes.

"You're so fucking talented," I breathe.

And he is.

It's like he's already caressing me, and he's not even touching me yet.

Sol's face softens, and his smile is shy.

I realize that praise is what it takes for him to trust me.

When Sol joins in and sings the next lines to me like now I'm his princess, every word one of adoration for me and me alone, I'm officially melted to a puddle of desire.

"It's a spell," he explains. "It records my music sessions and stores them for me in the walls."

"Wait, does that mean you've been recording everything that happens in this room?"

He regards me for a long moment, keeping me in suspense.

*I'm going to make the asshole pay for that.*

Then he shakes my head. "It only records what I want. Although, if you're into that kink, I'm up for recording a sexy video with you. My demonic beauty looks amazing on film."

He looks at me eagerly.

I kiss along his jawline, before fixing him with a stern look. "We were meant to be talking about *your* kinks."

He licks his lips, before muttering too quickly, "*hornsclawstail.*"

I hear him but still, it's always fun to tease.

"What was that, kitten?" I suck harder on his neck, until it bruises.

I want to mark him, *claim him.*

Sol shudders. "Horns. Claws. Tail. And why can't my pet name be *dragon*? Look at my fierce claws."

He rakes his claws down my back lightly, and I gasp at the delicious sensation.

"Naughty kitten." I give him a wicked grin, as I pull one of his hands around to the front and then lick his claw.

He gives a startled hiss of pleasure, and beneath my hips, his dick hardens.

If even his claws are this sensitive, what will it be like if I suck his horns? But he's got more teasing to go before I get there.

I snake my free hand down and rub over his clothed crotch, watching Sol's expression closely. He bucks into my hand, and I keep his hips held down firmly with my legs.

Hell, he's huge.

I slip my hand into his pants and free his dick. Then I almost forget what I'm doing, as I stare at his dick in shock.

Wow.

I'd say that his dick is godly sized but I guess I

should say *demon sized*. It's fucking impressive and it's ridged.

Silver peeks out of its head: a small, curving bar. It's a Prince Albert piercing.

It looks scorching-hot.

I can't help reaching out and exploring, stroking my hands over the velvety soft ridges of his dick that hardens to steel, as he pants. His eyes are glassy, and he throws back his head, clutching the sheets. I touch the piercing, tracing around it.

What would it feel like to be fucked with that? What would the ridges feel like sliding against my inner walls in just the right way?

I clench my thighs together, as warmth floods through me.

I'm nervous, but hell, excited too.

For now, I have a demon to tame.

I edge Sol for a couple more strokes and then take my hands quickly away, leaving his dick painfully hard and throbbing. Sol groans, glaring at me.

I grin, before licking over two more of his claws.

He throws his arm over his face and moans. But I want to see him and his reactions, so I bend down, moving his arm away. Then I kiss him lightly.

"Look, you have claws just like a kitten," I hold his hand up in front of his face that I've been licking and is now shaking.

"I'm not…" His voice wavers.

*Just a little more…*

"Only kittens get kisses here." I kiss his next blood-red claw. He looks wrecked, as his dick pulses. "Say it, and I'll keep kissing."

His dark gaze is firmly fixed on me, but he looks like he's fighting an internal battle.

Finally, he breaks. "I'm kitten."

Inside, I whoop and happy dance.

I raise my eyebrow. "Not good enough."

I hold his thumb close to my mouth but don't kiss it.

He squirms. "I'm *your* kitten."

"Good kitten." I suck his thumb into my mouth, careful not to cut myself on his claw.

Sol's back arches, and his eyes flutter closed.

Quickly, I let go of his thumb and rise up, snatching his tail in one hand to stroke and sucking the tip of one of his horns into my mouth.

Sol's eyes shoot wide open, and he howls, coming in a pearly arc on his stomach, untouched.

"Blue," he murmurs.

My name falls from his lips — private and intimate — and just for me.

It's our secret. It binds us more closely than a Soul Bond.

I keep sucking his horn through the aftershocks. Then I gently pull away, curling his tail around his chest, away from the sticky mess on his stomach.

His eyes are hazy, but he's smiling.

I stroke his hair, and cuddle closer to his side, pulling a blanket around him. "You were perfect. That was amazing. So good for me. My kitten."

I feather kisses along his jaw, and he purrs.

Hell, I never knew how much a demon purring could both turn me on and make me feel protective at the same time. This demon prince truly is mine.

*What am I going to do?*

Sol trails his fingers through my hair. "If a kitten prince gets kisses like that, then hell, I *am* a kitten."

When he winks, I laugh.

Then he whispers hot into my ear, "Just you wait until you find out what *my stabby* gets."

I shiver. I can't wait.

All of a sudden, there's a shift in the air. Sol stiffens just a fraction of a second before I do. But even I can feel it: a dark, ancient magic.

And it's not Sol's.

"Go!" Sol yells, scrambling to push me out of the nest.

But it's too late.

Shadows burst from the four corners of the bed, snatching Sol and me in a hold that feels like death. I scream and struggle. Sol's snarling but he's more tightly bound than I am.

"What the fuck is happening?" I yell.

"An assassination attempt." Sol's eyes flash red.

"This is primal magic, either a curse or a hex. And whatever this plot is, it's focused on me and my new Soul Bond. The bastards are trying to hurt me, when my guard is down after the Bonding Revel. I should've known."

Unexpectedly, freezing cold water materializes in the air above us. I have a single moment to glance at Sol, who's frozen in horror.

"I love you." His voice is anguished and despairing.

And I know then that he's only saying those words because he thinks we're about to die.

The water crashes down on us: agonizing, terrifying, and cold enough to take away my breath.

And it doesn't stop.

I can't breathe, and my body is battered by the onslaught.

Soon, the hex will steal both our lives.

Why couldn't I have told Sol that I loved him, before we die?

# CHAPTER TWELVE

**Sol's Bedroom, Demon Underworld**

I struggle. I can't move, call for help, or breathe.

Freezing water crashes down on my face.

*I'm going to die.*

On the sacred Stones, somebody help me...

Water's going up my nose and throat. I'm choking.

Hell, make it stop.

*Please, please, please.*

My lungs burn, and I'd give anything to be able to draw in oxygen. Why didn't I know how precious it was?

*Why didn't I tell Sol that I loved him?*

I want to sob but I can't do anything but choke.

My throat's swelling. My brain's on fire. I'm convulsing.

Next to me, I can feel the same happening to Sol.

It's fucking agony. When will I black out?

The shadows that feel like death wind tighter around me, holding me still. My ears are ringing, and lights flash in front of my eyes.

This is it. The water hex is going to kill me.

*I'm truly dying.*

All of a sudden, there's a burst of silver magic. Then the water stops, and the shadows withdraw from me, seeping into the walls.

I twist off the bed, falling onto my knees next to it. Frantically, I hurl, spitting up the water. Tears stream from my eyes, as I gasp for breath. I'm never — *never* — going to take oxygen for granted again.

From the other side of the bed, I hear Sol gagging and coughing up water as well.

My legs are too shaky to stand; they feel like *they've* been turned to water.

Who the fuck did this to us? I'm going to kick their demonic ass.

I shiver, curling into a sopping wet ball. Tremors wrack me.

Sol crawls around the bed unsteadily, looking as much like a drowned rat as me; his pajamas are plastered to his body, and his tail is wrapped defensively around his waist.

When he curls around me, I flinch.

I can still feel the water battering me, and the sensation that I'm about to die.

"I'm sorry," Sol whispers into my hair.

"I should truly be very cross with you," Anwealda's cold voice drawls, "disrupting my morning by forcing me to rescue you. Not one day back and already almost dead by an assassin's hand. I feel like I should award you a medal or possibly execute you. I haven't decided yet."

I stiffen at the same time as Sol.

Then still shaking from cold and shock, Sol pulls himself to his knees. I only peer though the wet tangle of my hair at Anwealda, who's leaning against the wall opposite the bed with his arms crossed.

"She needs the Healer," Sol demands, although his voice is raspy. His throat is as damaged as mine feels. "The curse or hex was dangerous. Deadly. But she's human, and I'm discovering how easily they break. The aftereffects could hurt her. At least Ward should check her over. I can summon her now."

Anwealda's eyes flash with rage. "Am I not the Emperor?"

Sol swallows. "Of course."

"It's just that for a moment there, it rather appeared like *you* already were."

Sol glances at me. "Look, I can get Ward in here to—"

"Aren't you going to thank me?" Anwealda raises an imperious eyebrow.

"Thank you, Father," Sol grits out. "Now, may my Soul Bond receive medical attention? She's soaked through."

Anwealda waves his claw. Magic sparks from his crown between his horns. It lights up the bedroom, before skittering across the bed and drying it out like the attack never took place, before cocooning Sol and me.

I cry out. The magic's scraping over my skin with a heat that's too intense. I clutch onto Sol's arm, and he hushes me with a purr that's as gentle as a lullaby. Then it's over, and I sink against Sol's side.

We're both dry, but it felt like a second attack.

Sol's expression is guarded. "Thanks again, Father. But humans can't be dried off like a pretty bauble, no damage done."

"You astound me," Anwealda says, dryly. When he stalks toward Sol, my breath hitches with fear. He looks so much taller from the floor. "Any attack on my son, is an attack on me. It weakens my authority as Emperor. Now, what have you done that made someone think that they could make me look *weak*?"

A sudden image of Oran and Iago attacking me at the ball, then Sol protecting me, shoots into my mind. Followed by the way the bullying aristocrats were humiliated in front of Oakthorn.

Yet was that enough for them to risk an assassination in the palace itself? And where did Sol's dick of a dad get off victim blaming Sol?

Sol's expression shutters. "As you said, I've only been back a day. What could I possibly have done?"

Anwealda tilts his head, and the diamonds in his hair *clink*. "You're my son: *plenty*." He traces his claw down Sol's cheek. "Do you know why I chose you and your brothers in the orphanage out of all those other demons? Why I chose you alone to take home and elevate to lives of unimaginable power and privilege out of poverty and pain?"

Sol's lips pinch, and he shakes his head.

"Your magic was astounding. I've never seen four brothers, all different elementals. I could make you rulers: one for each kingdom. This land is nourished by your powers. But have you ever wondered why I picked *you* to stay by my side in the court, while I made your brothers great warriors or sorcerers?"

*Shit, don't do this...*

Sol is still gasping for breath and recovering from the attack, and Anwealda is about to kick him in the balls.

"Great trip down memory lane," I interrupt in an attempt to stop whatever poison Anwealda is about to say, "but shouldn't we be catching an assassin?"

"You won't be doing anything, little girl,"

Anwealda snarls. "Except *dying* if you forget to address me correctly again."

Sol hurriedly winds his magic around me, pushing me behind him. "I'll take it that your story to me, when I was a child, that I was your favorite, is a lie then. I'm crushed."

"When did you become cynical?" Anwelda snatches Sol by the horn and drags him up, hurling him against the wall. "Or filled with such rebellion?"

Before Sol can push away, Anwealda presses him against the wall with a clawed hand around his throat.

No. Fucking. Way.

I leap up, even though my legs are wobbly and my chest is aching, and throw myself at Anwealda. Unfortunately, it only takes a casual flick of his free hand, which sparks magic at me, and I'm flying back, bouncing onto the bed.

"Don't hurt her." Sol sounds wrecked. "Skye, I'm fine. Stay there. Don't move."

*And it wrecks me that he's had to call me Skye.*

Anwealda ignores me like I'm of less importance than a bug. I clutch my hands impotently in the blankets of what not long ago had been my nest with Sol.

"I chose you to stay at Court because you were the most beautiful out of your brothers. Sinfully so." Anwealda tightens his hand around Sol's throat. "*You* were to be the *pretty bauble* to show the blue-bloods like Duke Oakthorn that my adopted pets were docile, not a threat to the established families, but strong enough to survive." Sol winces. "How disappointing that you can't even do that." He scrutinizes Sol. "You're not hiding anything from me, are you?"

I hold my breath.

"Nothing," Sol whispers.

*Silence.*

We're screwed.

Anwealda eases his hand away from Sol's throat, and Sol doubles over, coughing. Anwealda pats his back.

"I *will* find the assassins who attacked you, and you *will* keep your guard up." Anwealda wrenches Sol up my his shoulders, staring intently into his eyes. A shadowed melancholy crosses Anwealda's face like there's something broken inside him: deep grief. His vulnerability is unsettling, and the moment is so intimate that I feel like I'm trespassing. "I've already lost my blood son to the Shadow Traitors, and I can't lose another son. I just *can't*. The murderers were executed, but someone was pulling their strings and that traitor is still at court. I swore that I'd do whatever it took to make my adopted sons strong enough to survive."

Sol straightens his shoulders. "I am."

Anwealda's full lips curve into a cruel smile. "Are you? Wonderful. I don't know why I'm worried,

185

despite the fact that I only moments ago had to save you from death."

Sol reddens and ducks his head.

"That wasn't his fault, Your Imperial Majesty," I insist.

Anwealda ignores me. "You've been in the non-magical world too long. Let me make this delightfully clear to you: while you were gone, after millennium of trying, I've turned the tide in our fortunes and triggered the Rise of the Demons."

Sol breaks into a wide smile. "We finally have a chance of winning the war against the gods!"

I glance between them. Is that a good thing? They cage beautiful gods. And what will happen if demons *rise*? Does that mean out of the underworld or to conquer all worlds?

I shudder. I don't think that I want this Emperor gaining any more power over gods or humans.

Will he attack The Hill? Enslave all gods and humans?

Anwealda merely inclines his head. "So, you understand why my adopted sons mustn't allow themselves to become the weak link in my chain." Sol pales, pulling back against the wall, as far as he can from Anwealda. His dad follows him, baring his fangs and encircling Sol's horn viciously with his fist. Sol gasps in pain. "Remember that, before I'm forced to break you."

Horrified, I scramble off the bed, searching on the floor for Light-bringer. It's been kicked to the side by the wardrobe, and I crouch, unsheathing it. Then I let out a snarl as I launch myself with the blade upraised at Anwealda.

I'm bubbling with white-hot rage.

All the times that demons have stolen humans from The Hill. All the nights that Skye and I have clung to each other, crying for our parents. All the hate that I have in my veins for the demon, who's kidnapped my twin.

*And all the times that Anwealda has hurt Sol.*

When I press the blade to Anwealda's neck, however, he only smiles. "Let me tell you, human, something about how our culture works. A demon's horns are their weapon, pride, and manhood. If you wish to hurt a demon, hurt their horns. If you wish to break them, break their horns. And if you wish to *destroy* them, then *take* their horns." He tightens his fist around Sol's horn, digging in his nails, and Sol's knees buckle. "Now, if you two bring me any more problems, I'll hurt his horns. If you make me appear weak again, I'll break one, maybe even two. And if you *ever* threaten your Emperor with a weapon again, I'll *take* his horns."

Sol's eyes are wide with panic, begging me to understand. "Put away your dagger. If he takes my horns...I'm nothing." Then his expression hardens. "I swear on the Stones, Father, you won't have to break me because I'm not weak."

Is taking a demon's horns like castrating them? *Worse?*

I feel sick.

Shaking, I throw Light-bringer onto the bed and step back.

Anwealda loosens his hold on Sol's horn. "You were right, you know. Trainable as she is, your princess is still human and should spend more time with other mortals here, until she understands our ways. Let her go to her…fascinating…kind. You have princely duties to attend with me. You'll have more than enough to keep you busy without a fierce Soul Bond getting you into trouble or do you have reason to refuse?"

*As if Sol has a choice.*

Sol glances over Anwealda's shoulder at me; his gaze is inscrutable. "Of course not, as long as we're kept within the safe distance for bonds."

My stomach sinks. How are we going to find Skye now?

How are either Skye or I going to escape this brutal and savage underworld in time?

I don't want to be apart from Sol. It's not safe, since someone is trying to kill us.

# CHAPTER THIRTEEN

**Sol's Bedroom, Demon Underworld**

T *wo days.*
Two days of being herded by Ward like human cattle away from Sol and into a room next to the Emperor's throne room and so within the safe radius for our bond, while Sol is guided with a firm hand on his back by Anwealda away from me.

Two days of listening intently to the drone of Sol's meetings through the wall, punctuated by roars and violent crashes.

Two days of missing Sol and pretending that I don't.

Two days of hating the dark shadows under Sol's

eyes, as he emerges from his princely duties with Anwealda, refusing to talk about them.

Two days of being crushingly aware that Sol has said *I love you*, but that I haven't said it back yet.

Two days of being lectured by humans drunk on the love of their Soul Bonds about the sensitivity of horns, the brutality of the gods, and the five kinkiest ways to use tails in sex.

*And the tail kink's just Ward.*

Ward could write the *Demon Kama Sutra* or perhaps the *50 Shades of Demon*.

Except, she still has no memory of her life before the underworld or The Hill. None of the humans do. If Skye and I don't escape soon, then we'll become just like them.

I shift, as the pale, early morning light filters over the bed. I stretch, yawning.

I love this hour, before Sol and I have to get up and separate. Then I squirm because should I be loving anything about my time in the underworld? Shouldn't I hate it all?

Does this mean that I'm becoming no different to the other poor assholes, who happily lounge around like sleek pets, drinking wine and boasting about the size of their demon's horns?

When I scowl, Sol tilts his head, studying me.

He's sitting cross-legged next to me in bed, with his guitar settled next to him. He's only wearing a pair of tight, ruby leather trousers, and his strong chest glistens in the morning light. Warmth unfurls through me at the sight of the v of his hips, and I reach out to stroke my fingers down his delicious trail that's only inches above the bulge of his crotch.

Sol's hips buck. "You do know that you're sending off mixed signals right now? What with the touching and the frowning…"

My lips tug into a smile, and I palm his crotch. "It's not you. I was just…thinking."

"Dangerous."

I squeeze his balls in warning.

He gasps, but his eyes dilate. "*Harder.*"

I chuckle. "Perhaps, later." I caress up the length of his clothed dick, which must be painfully hard now trapped in his tight pants (not that I'd ever suggest that demons should wear less tight ones), before I push myself up, leaning against the wooden headboard.

Sol pulls his guitar into his lap, probably to distract himself from his desperate need to come, and starts strumming a song, which is beautiful but haunting. I don't recognize it or the strange cadence, which is a lilting, waterfall of notes.

It's mesmerizing.

"On the Stones, I've never heard anything like this," I admit. "It's like you're weeping, but the tears are for my heart alone."

"They are." Sol's clever fingers dance over the

strings. "This is traditional demon music. My father — my blood father — was a musician." Sol's hair hangs into his eyes, and I get the feeling that he doesn't normally talk about his real dad. Has he ever told anyone this? "When I'm alone, I compose and play. It's why I spent my time doing it in your world. If I had a choice, it's what I'd do. But then, none of us are free, right? The Emperor has different plans for me, and sometimes, Fate calls you to step up and…"

"Become the hero?"

He gives me a long look. "Certainly not. Become a wicked leader."

"And what would your dad think about that?"

His fingers still. The silence is suffocating. *Overwhelming.*

Carefully, he places the guitar by the side of the bed. Then he leans over me, caging me in. His spicy scent wraps around me, and I grasp at his shoulders, pulling him closer.

"He'd say nothing." Sol curls back his lips; his fangs are close to my lips, but all I can think about is kissing away his hurt. "Because he's dead." I flinch. "No one allows me to forget that I'm the Orphan Prince who should be grateful for everything I have. It doesn't help to play pretend or *what ifs*. By my horns, we can't change the past."

I'm breathing too hard. If Sol's hands weren't on my shoulders, I'd be shaking apart.

"I'm not the same as you." Why do I say it like a plea? "I'm not a thrice demon damned orphan. My parents are still alive."

"Really? And are they still *your* parents." He rests his forehead against mine. "Do you miss them?"

"Do you miss yours?"

"Most days, I try to forget them." Sol's large eyes study mine. "You do realize that yours won't remember you."

Finally, a tear trickles down my cheek. I can't hold it back.

I swear on the Stones, I'd have given anything not to have shed it.

Instantly, Sol pulls me closer onto his strong lap, before cradling me and thumbing away the path of my tear. "I didn't mean... I'm sorry if I... Can I excuse upsetting you by playing my *sociopathic prince* card again?"

*Asshole.*

But also, *kind* asshole, whose tail is coiling around my wrist in comfort.

I stroke along the fluffy end of Sol's tail to accept his apology, and Sol sighs in delight. "As long as you remember that you only get one of those a day."

Sol's lips twitch, before he looks serious again. "I only meant that you need to think hard about whether you really want to find people who..." He breaks off. "It's your choice."

Then his tail unwinds from my wrist, and he gently pushes me off his lap.

Where's my snuggly demon lap going?

"There's only four days left for us to find your sister and give me the best chance of being elected Crown Prince." Sol leaps off the bed. "So, let's get on with it."

He snatches a black pair of leather pants and silk tunic with ridges along its arms out of his wardrobe and then tosses them at me. Magically, they adjust to my size. After the ball, it became a mutual agreement between us that I'd wear his clothes and that it turned us both on for me to do it.

I can't wait until I can walk around wearing *him* in dragon form.

I wriggle out of my pajamas and slip into the clothes that are already feeling like a second skin. "I figured that you wouldn't discuss this in front of your dad or where anyone else could hear, but that attack on you used water. It seemed like a pretty fucking clear message from one kingdom to another. Don't you think your brother, the Demon of Water could've—"

Sol freezes. "Caspian would never hurt me. *Never.* My brothers are rivals, and I guess that I don't truly know them. A lot changes over the centuries, and the cruelty they've suffered, which is so much worse than I have, could've changed them from the boys I know.

But we swore to protect each other, and I'd die for them." Sol's steely gaze meets mine. "So, they'd die for me."

Except, would they?

Yet I can't break his belief in his own family. I can see the importance of it burning in his gaze and the shaking of his hands.

He loves them, and they're all he's got.

*Apart from me.*

I nod, trying to smile. "So, what are your princely duties today?"

"Meet an ambassador from the Kingdom of Earth." Sol winks. "Secretly interrogate him about your sister. What about you?"

I groan, adjusting my tunic. "Ward's teaching me a class on the pleasures of fang fellatio." Sol's eyes light up. "Is it possible to die from embarrassment because I think I'll manage it. I don't know which of us has a more crappy day ahead."

Sol waggles his eyebrows. "We could wrestle for the title."

I bite my lip. "Seriously tempting."

Before I can dive across the bed and wrestle Sol to the ground because that's high on my list of fantasies, as well as the perfect excuse to fight and feel the flex of his muscles beneath me, Sol saunters around the bed with a leather belt clutched in his hand.

"Hold still." Sol fits the leather belt around my waist.

Except, it isn't only a leather belt. Looped to the side of it, is Light-bringer.

"You fucking legend." I grasp Sol and drag him into a slow, lazy kiss that's perfect.

When Sol draws back he looks dazed. "You need some way to have it with you, and I know you feel naked without your stabbiness."

"This is the most romantic thing anyone has ever done for me, kitten." I pull him into a second kiss that's deeper and more insistent.

*How the hell does he understand me so well?*

It makes my chest tighten, and butterflies flutter in my stomach in a way that I've never felt before.

No one but Skye has ever accepted me for who I am — loved me for it — before.

It's tearing me apart that I only have this short time with him. I should wish to hate him still and yet…

I never want to let him go.

*Bang — bang — bang.*

Sol and I startle at the loud drumbeat from outside in the corridor, which echoes around the palace, and our heads bump together.

I groan, and Sol winces.

My lips chase after Sol's, but he pulls back,

pressing a kiss to my sore head. His expression, however, is tight with fear and shock.

Outside, the jangle of bells and wild blast of trumpets have joined the savage beat of the drums.

Is it another revel or a demonic way to announce that the palace is under attack?

Sol clutches my hands between his; his whisper is frantic. "Oran has called a Devil's Hunt."

"And that's bad, right?"

"For us it is." Sol drags me off the bed, and we press against the wall away from the window. "He has the power as Demon of Misrule to plan these entertainments. But they're perilous because all rules are off during hunts. You're either predator or prey, and humans are always prey. It's meant to be a game but well," his eyes gleam, "a demon's games are always wicked."

"And you enjoy this?"

He shrugs. "It passes the time. What? We get bored." He clutches my hand tighter, as we edge toward the door. "But by my horns, my guess is that this is Oran's attempt to get back at me. During a Devil's Hunt, everything is topsy turvy, and the Demon of Misrule reigns: I'm no longer his prince, and he can hunt and hurt me."

"Passes the time, huh? Why can't you just play beer pong, strip poker, or dirty truth and dare like everybody else?" My eyes widen, and my pulse pounds to the rhythm of the frantic drumbeat. "Shit, the assassin could be out there too. What if this is set up to murder you...*both of us*?"

Sol arches his brow. "Then we need to escape the hunt, which breaks the rules but is better than dying."

He cracks open the door and peers outside.

The stone corridor is empty, but I can hear running footsteps and calls close by.

Are they coming for us?

Sol stiffens, and I shudder.

Sol nods at me, and I follow him out into the corridor. The obsidian floor is cold beneath my bare feet. I wish that I'd had time to slip on my boots. Sol isn't wearing shoes either. We creep silently to the end of the corridor.

The noise of the Devil's Hunt is coming closer.

Shadows dance along the walls. They're congregating. Becoming darker.

Are the Shadow Monsters hunting us too?

A scream is lodged in my throat.

I yank Sol on faster, and he directs me toward an iron, spiral staircase that leads downward.

The voices and howls follow us.

*Hunting us.*

We're the prey.

I bite my lip, as Sol and I burst out into the bright sunshine of a courtyard. The sky above is blushing pink with clouds like red streaks of blood.

*It's a dead-end.*

Sol growls in frustration, twisting around for another way out, but there isn't one. He bangs loudly on the only door, which is locked.

"This should be open. It's always kept open." He slams his shoulder against the wood, but it doesn't break. "It's been sealed by magic."

Behind us, the voices are becoming louder.

"What I don't understand is why those posh bastards treat you so badly in the first place." I skirt the courtyard, pushing at archways in case there's a hidden passageway or an alcove large enough to hide behind. "The Emperor chose you out of all those other kids to adopt. Shouldn't they respect that? It doesn't matter who you were before, now you're their fucking prince."

Sol's smile is brighter than the sunshine. "I'll just tell them that I'm the *fucking prince* next time. The look on their faces will be priceless." His gaze darts away. "My brothers and I may be rivals now, but in our own way, we're all rebels. We're the misfit Orphan Princes, who the other demons resent because of how we were raised up above our stations to play at rulers. And nobody hates us more than the high born who are forced now to bow down to us. They're spoiled brats who remember how they bullied us when we were kids. Yet increasingly, we hold the power."

Sol's horns flare with fire.

"Since we're hiding in a courtyard," I point out, "it doesn't feel like it."

Sol's dark gaze turns to the base of the stairway; the voices are so close now.

My stomach twists, and I drop my hand to the hilt of Light-bringer.

Should we fight? Allow ourselves to become prey? What will happen to us?

Sol's eyes glitter. "That's the point. My brothers and I are elemental Shifter Demons. We don't fit in. And the established, high born families want to greedily hold onto their power for all eternity. They won't be happy, until they've pulled us down again." I shiver, as his grin becomes sharp. "And we'll rebel, until they lose *everything*."

Suddenly, I catch a glimpse of pale green and bright red at the base of the staircase.

*Oran and Iago.*

They're here.

The drumming becomes more frantic. The trumpet blows in triumph.

The hairs stand up on the back of my neck, and I'm chilled.

Yet I tighten my grip on the hilt of Light-bringer. I won't be hunted, and I won't become prey.

Sol swaggers to the center of the courtyard. "Nice day for a fly."

"What…?"

Confused, my gaze swings to Sol, who in a spray of glitter, transforms into a huge ruby dragon.

I gape at him in shock.

He's awe-inspiring. Primal. Savage.

Sol opens his jaws and roars. The sound echoes around the courtyard like thunder.

Inside, the music abruptly stops.

I recognize Sol: he's a larger version of the tiny dragon, who snuggled around my neck and purred. He's shimmering ruby, which sparkles under the sun, with the same magic fluttering around him like a decadent outfit. His neck is long and sinuous. Scales rise into waves of ridges down his back, and his wings glitter. He studies me with midnight black eyes, which are framed by long lashes.

*How can he manage to be even more gorgeous in dragon form?*

How dare anyone shame him for this side of his nature? If it makes him a monster, then he's a beautiful one.

When Sol crouches down and offers me his wing, I'm grinning widely. My heart's beating rapidly in my chest, as I step onto his wing, and he lifts me gently onto his back. He's warm and smells of bonfires. I wrap my arms around his back, which is scaled and lustrous like a precious gem. Then his magic winds out, binding me safely in place.

When I glance over at the archway that leads to

the base of the stairway, Oran stands with his arms crossed, watching us. Behind him are a gang of demons. Oran's huge horns look like they're covered in painful stripes.

I pale.

Was he whipped by his father?

Is this his revenge?

Sol opens his jaws like he's about to breathe fire on Oran, who stumbles back in alarm, then spreads his wings wide, before flapping them and launching himself up into the air.

I holler, and my stomach falls. I guess that it's like being on a plane that's just taken off. But I've never been out of The Hill before, even on a train.

This is too much.

*I'm going to hurl...*

I rest my head on Sol's back to steady myself, screwing shut my eyes.

His magic tingles through me, soothingly.

*Up, up, and up.*

Then we're flying away from the palace more gently, and I struggle to open my eyes and glance down.

Okay, mistake.

The land below is a dizzying blur of greens: rich forests and undulating meadows.

I take a deep breath and try again.

Then it hits me.

This is truly the Kingdom of Fire in the demon underworld. I'm outside The Hill for the first time in my life. I'm flying on the back of a *fucking dragon,* who is also a demon prince and my fake Soul Bond.

A week ago, I could never have guessed that anything more exciting would have happened than getting tipped for my cleaning or having vodka and a cupcake on my twenty-first birthday with Skye.

Sol and I have escaped the Devil's Hunt. We're alone in the skies above his kingdom that he rules.

*This is freedom.*

Who knew that riding a dragon (and I'm definitely doing that in more ways than one), could be so much fun?

I laugh in joy, and Sol roars in response. Fire bursts from his jaws, lighting up the sky.

But then, he screeches in pain, swerving to the side. I shout, clutching his sharp ridges like those he wears on his clothes, as his magic holds me onto his back.

*What the hell?*

A savage howl bursts from the sky behind me, followed by another, and another, and...

Terrified, I twist around.

Neon blue eyes meet mine.

A giant black wolf — *a winged wolf* — is flying beside Sol's wing.

The winged wolf's eyes are neon blue, and blue

embers spark from his snarling mouth. His wings are leathery, coal black, and bat-like.

A whole pack of winged wolves are behind him, and they're circling Sol, watching me with hungry eyes. The wolf at Sol's wing howls, and the rest of the pack answer him.

Is he the Alpha?

On the Sacred Stones, we're still being hunted. And to these predators, we're truly the prey.

The Alpha throws back his head and howls again.

My adrenaline spikes, and my pulse is too loud in my ears.

Sol swipes at the wolves with his tail, but the Alpha dives forward and sinks his fangs into Sol's wing, savaging it. The Alpha has targeted Sol's weak spot, rather than the thick, armored hide of his body. My stomach lurches at the sound of tearing.

Why does everything in the underworld want to devour you?

Sol bellows in pain and tumbles from the sky.

I scream, as the ground rises up to meet me.

*The Stones save me, we're going to crash.*

# CHAPTER FOURTEEN

**Kingdom of Fire, Demon Underworld**

I struggle out of the black.

Groaning, my vision bleeds to gray. Agony shoots through the back of my head, and I feel groggy, sluggish.

Do I have a concussion? What's the bet that they don't have hospitals in the underworld?

My mouth is dry, and I rasp, "Sol?"

Instantly, Sol's arms are around me, helping me up. When did he turn back into a demon?

I struggle to sort through the confused memories in my mind.

*The beating drums of the hunt...winged wolves with neon blue eyes...tumbling down from the sky...*

My breathing speeds up.

*Fuck, we crashed.*

I stare up at Sol through my blurry vision, and he holds me to his chest. He's back in his demonic form, his cheek is swollen, and his lip is bleeding. He's holding his right arm too close to his bruised chest like it's badly injured. I can make out the teethmarks where the Alpha savaged his wing.

My eyes narrow in fury. Nobody hurts *my* demon.

I fight to right myself, looking around. Thank the Stones, I can't see the psycho wolves. Sol and I are on the edge of a thick forest, which is bounded by the rocky crags of a mountainside. There are no palaces with silver gilded domes and spires here. This is the type of wild countryside that I always imagined for the underworld.

That doesn't make me feel any better.

"Are you hurt?" Sol passes his hand over my ribs, and I wince. "I'll take that as *yes*. Humans are so breakable."

I lightly trace his arm, and he winces as well. "So are demons."

Sol huffs. "I'm used to it. I refuse to allow you to be. Here."

He dances his fingers across my ribs, and his

magic winds out. After a moment, the area numbs and the pain lessens.

"What did you do?" I demand.

Sol avoids my gaze. "I shared a little of my Soul with you."

"What?"

Sol turns away with affected casualness. He scans the sky on watch for the winged wolves.

"I should've known that Oran would set his pets on me." His tongue darts out to lick away the blood on his lips. "He's smart, and I am... sometimes...predictable."

I stare at him. "Those creatures are Oran's pets?"

"They're like our hell hounds: packs of shifters who are viciously trained, caged, and then let loose, *vicious.*" He pushes himself to his feet, and I notice how stiffly he's moving, while trying to hide it. "If they return, and we have to fight, don't kill them."

"That's a shit rallying speech." I clamber to my feet, brushing the dirt off my ripped clothes. "Aren't demon princes meant to call for *blood, slaughter,* and..."

"Disappointing, I know. But they're Oran's slaves." Sol's tail swishes side to side. "On my flames, *true* slaves. I never hurt them or hell hounds. Just like I don't hurt humans."

"Even if they're trying to kill you?"

Sol smirks as he swaggers toward me. "You've tried to kill me plenty, stabby."

"Not very hard, or you'd be dead."

He grins. "As much as you're turning me on right now, we need to take shelter, before they come back. I don't want to fight them in the skies." He struggles to raise his injured arm. "I heal fast, but my aerial acrobatics will be underwhelming right now."

I follow Sol, as he leads me along a narrow path into the forest. The trees are vast with a thick canopy and vines that block out the sky. Twigs *snap* and *crack* beneath our bare feet. I grit my teeth on each step.

Wait, is that a growl behind us?

Sol and I still.

*We're being hunted again.*

I glance behind me. There are shadows moving between the trees. The flash of fangs and blue eyes.

Sol takes a steadying breath, before he whispers, "Run!"

He grabs my hand, and together we sprint through the forest.

Haunting ululations echo through the trees. My heart is beating too hard in my chest, and I've taking panicked gasps. I can't draw in enough air.

My chest is speared with pain.

Does this wood belong to the winged wolves? Are we in their territory?

It feels like the forest is closing in, as the trees

grow closer and closer together, and no sunlight filters through the canopy at all.

My feet are slick with blood, sliced open on the forest floor.

At least Sol appears to know where he's going.

Finally, he drags me toward the largest tree that we've come across with wide, spreading branches. It's like an oak, but its trunk is skeletal white, and it grows in the middle of a small glade. He twirls to me, holding me by my shoulders.

"I know this forest," Sol says, urgently. "My brothers and I would play here. This was our Imagine Tree. Climb it. *Now*."

I shake my head. "Not without you."

Sol lowers his horns like he's ready to gore the wolves and he looks as dangerous as the entire pack of them. "Sorry, I have a prior engagement."

"You can't fight off a pack by yourself. You need me. Hell, you don't even have any weapons."

"I'm an elemental demon. My power is all around me. It *is* the underworld. Nature. I'm never without my weapons. It's why four brothers being elemental together...we'd be unstoppable." His expression softens, as he looks at me. "Please, climb."

I hesitate only as long as it takes for the Alpha to strut into the glade with his wings folded back, then I grab hold of the lowest branch and swing myself up. It's devastating not to look behind me at the sound of the wolves' snarls and Sol's roar. It's followed by the savage clash of their battle and Sol's muffled hiss of pain. Then I'm hauling myself up onto an especially broad branch that's wide enough for at least two people. I lie on my stomach, peering down through the leaves.

My breath hitches.

The Alpha has Sol backed against the base of the Imagine Tree, while the rest of the pack ring the glade. The Alpha's fangs lower towards Sol's neck. But then, Sol raises his hand over the Alpha's head, and a sparking light forms. It's magic like a miniature sun. I shield my eyes, as it grows bigger and bigger.

In the name of the sacred Stones, can my demon even control the *sun*...?

The Alpha and the winged wolves whimper and cringe back with their eyes closed.

Sol looks glorious as he stands in the center of the glade with the power of the sun between his hands. "Go back and tell your master that we're not prey."

Unexpectedly, the Alpha spins around with a snarl. His eyes are still closed, but he snaps out anyway in blind fury. His fangs sink into Sol's thigh and caught unawares, Sol stumbles and falls to his knees. His magic falters and dies.

The Alpha growls in triumph, shaking Sol by his savaged leg.

The rest of the winged wolves open their eyes and close in.

Shit, they're about to kill him.

I don't care what Sol said, I'm not staying out of the action.

*I'm not the fucking damsel.*

I slither down the tree trunk, jumping from branch to branch. As I go, I snatch Light-bringer out of its sheath.

Sol catches sight of me. "Stab the left wing. It's their weakness."

The Alpha looks up in surprise, but I leap from the final branch onto the Alpha's back.

The Alpha drops Sol's leg like a chew toy, and Sol slumps to the floor. Then the Alpha's ears press to his head, before he curls his lips back and snarls.

If Sol hadn't told me not to kill the Alpha, I'd have sunk my blade into his neck. This winged wolf tried to slaughter both of us. He probably still wants to. But if he's only acting under orders or some complex court dynamic that I still don't understand, can I blame him?

Is he really a monster?

So, I stab my blade in and then out of the Alpha's bat-like wing.

The effect is immediate.

The Alpha whines, bucking in agony and throwing me off. I crack against the trunk of a tree at the far side of the glade and sink to the floor. I shudder at the sharp pain, which is radiating through my ribs.

The other winged wolves howl in fury, as the Alpha collapses, flapping his injured wing. Then the winged wolves open their mouths, and a dangerous blue fire appears.

Hell, they mean to burn us in retribution.

Sol's expression becomes grim. He lowers his head, placing his palms flat on the ground. The land shakes and rumbles, before thin bursts of lava burst out of the forest floor like the bars of a cage, weaving around the winged wolves and their Alpha, who whimper in fear. I watch in wonder, as Sol controls the snake-like lava, suspending it just above the cowering winged wolves.

"I am the prince of this kingdom!" Sol bellows. "The Demon of Fire. I will not tell you this again. Go and don't return. Tell your master that if he tries to turn me into his prey one more time, then *he'll* be the one hunted by the entire court."

Slowly, the Alpha meets Sol's eye and nods.

Sol pulls back the scorching lava enough for the winged wolves to fly into the air with their tails tucked between their legs. The Alpha exchanges another long look with him, before dipping his head in acknowledgment and limping away into the forest.

Immediately, the lava falls back into the earth. I can still smell the smoldering twigs and the seared leaves. The glade is blackened and dead. It's been turned to ash.

Sol collapses forward. I struggle to my feet, clutching at my ribs. Then I stumble to Sol's side, crouching down and stroking his hair. I want to touch him but I can hardly tell what part of him isn't hurt. Although, his earliest bruises are faded to greens and yellow like he received them yesterday.

Clearly, demons do heal supernaturally fast.

When I settle for coiling his undamaged tail around my wrist and petting it, he lets out a breathy gasp like I'm stroking his dick, which I guess I am.

When he looks up and meets my eye, with cheeks that are tinged pink, I shoot him an innocent look, before petting his tail again.

"If it wasn't for all the..." I gesture down at my bruised ribs and his...bruised everything, "and the fact that the fight was terrifying, then that was *fucking amazing.*"

Adrenaline is still surging through me. The thrill of danger, violence, and triumph.

I glow with it.

I help Sol pull himself up onto his knees, and he shoots me a cocky grin.

"Nobody would've known that was your first battle," he replies. "*You* were amazing."

I flush, fiddling with my dagger's sheath. "Was your first battle like that?"

"Since it was against Odin and his bastard gods, I'd say it was more blinding terror, trying not to piss myself, and lots (and I mean lots) of disemboweling."

I wrinkle my nose. "I'll have the better story to tell…"

"Our grandkids?"

We both freeze.

*Did he really just say that?*

Sol is the first to look away with a laugh that's faker than our Soul Bond. "I'm joking, stabby."

Weakly, I laugh. "But winged wolves, really?"

"There are far more dangerous creatures than that in the underworld."

"Something to look forward to."

He grins, pushing himself to his feet with a groan, before holding out his hand to me. "Well, I wouldn't want to bore you."

I take his hand and let him pull me up. We both hiss in pain at the same time, and Sol looks concerned. He sweeps his arms down my left side, and I arch away from his touch.

"You're injured again." He frowns. "Let me heal you."

I take a step back, holding up my hand. "Not if it means taking a piece of your Soul. I went through the Stones, remember? I know how much that shit hurts, and you used a ton of magic to fight off those winged wolves. Why don't we simply fly back to the palace and get healed up there?"

"About that," Sol drawls like he's not worried, only I can tell that he *is*, "you're right. Using my elemental magic comes with a price. I'm connected to this land: I nourish it, and it feeds me. But if I draw from it, then I'm weakened after. I can't shift right now, and you're in no state to walk all the way back barefoot."

"You're not looking that great either," I point out.

He arches his brow. "I prefer to see it as looking like the roguishly whumped upon. Doesn't that make women hot?"

"I prefer you not getting your ass kicked."

"Surprisingly, so do I." Sol limps to the base of the Imagine Tree. "We can hole up in the branches, until I'm healed enough to fly us back tomorrow morning. You don't want to find out the other deadly creatures and spirits who live in this forest. They make the winged wolves look like cute puppies."

Sol pulls himself up into the branches with a pained grunt but he's so tall that he only takes a moment to reach the wide branch that I hid on earlier. I stagger to the tree as well, but this time, it's harder for me to climb. I grit my teeth, hauling myself up.

I steel myself against the sharp pain in my side.

*Breathe, fucking breathe.*

Then Sol's arms are around me, gently pulling me

the rest of the way, and I'm leaning in his arms against the trunk of the tree. His warm fingers trace my cheek, coaxing open my eyes. I stare up into his black gaze.

I tap my fingers on the hard white bark of the branch. "Why's this called the Imagine Tree?"

Sol smiles and turns me to face the trunk behind us. I'm shocked to see that four names have been carved next to each other in the bark:

**BREEZE**

**ROMAN**

**SOL**

**CASPIAN**

The four princes of the underworld's kingdoms. Elemental demon shifters.

*Brothers.*

Sol traces his thumb over each weathered name in turn; his gaze is fond. "We carved these here with our claws when we were still kids in the orphanage. I may shock you, but we were rebellious even then and ran away, despite the whippings that we received every time." I wince. "It was worth it for the adventure. This was our secret meeting place that no one knew about. We'd hide away here: our Imagine Tree. We could imagine that we were savage demons from primal times, living here in the forests, and that we only needed each other. How we didn't become some monster's dinner or worse, I don't know."

"But you were happy?"

Sol tilts his head, studying me. "No one from the orphanage ever bothered to ask us that, when we were caught and hauled back. Father has never asked me that since." He wets his lips. "In this tree, we could imagine anything and we were happy because we imagined that we were *home*."

My eyes smart with tears.

Hell, I know how that feels. Any orphan does, and only another orphan will truly get that you spend your life seeking that feeling.

Sol's expression shutters, as he twists away from the trunk, pulling me onto his lap. "It was stupid. We were caught. Every time. And we were punished. *Every time*. There's no such thing as *home*, and I've lost my brothers. What's the point in imagining happiness—"

I kiss him.

To stop his joy at the memories crumbling to sadness.

*To create a new home.*

I kiss him to make him *my home*.

Sol's eyes widen, and he lets out a startled sound, before he kisses me back. He's fire and passion. I lick across the cut on his lip, and he pushes his tongue into my mouth, entwining it with mine. His mouth is hot, and I can't get enough of the taste of him.

It's addictive.

I slide my hands down the hard planes of his chest,

circling around his pink nipple, before flicking across it.

His breath hitches.

Then I straddle him, and he bucks his hips against me. His dick is hard in his pants.

Unexpectedly, he breaks away from me with a sharp cry. His face is tight with pain, but he raises his hands to rest around my waist.

I force him to still, no matter how difficult it is, when pleasure is coiling through me. "Fuck, this is hurting you."

He winks. "Who says I don't enjoy a little bit of pain mixed in with my pleasure?"

*Hell, yeah.* And I'll return to exploring that later.

"And who says that I don't love the idea of you over my lap and squirming, as I pin your legs and spank that gorgeous ass of yours until its cherry red for being a brat prince, kitten?" I breathe, and Sol's eyes become glassy. "But this is not the good kind of hurt."

"Then since you already rode me in dragon form, how about you ride me now in demon form? That way, you do all the work, while I take a rest."

He smirks at me, shuffling around and lying back on the branch. He pillows his head on his arms, although I don't miss the wince as he raises his arms.

Clearly, he thinks the discomfort is worth the sexy, indolent look that he wants to pull off. Although I'm going to wipe off his smirk, and he'll be doing anything but resting.

I run my hand down his chest, and he shivers. "Good idea. Then you don't move because you're resting, right? I'll just *use* your dick."

I unlace his pants, and his dick springs out, already painfully hard. I don't know if it's the thrill of the battle, the closeness to me, or my dirty talk. But I've never seen anyone so ready to fuck.

I lean over him, and my hair brushes across his face; his breath stutters. "Why is it that even when you're being an asshole, I want to fuck you?"

"My natural charm...?" Sol tries to joke, but it turns into a moan, as I close my hand around his dick, exploring the ridges and toying with the Prince Albert in the tip.

Sol's hands clench, and he bites his lip.

*His dick's so large.*

I shimmy my pants down further, pleased at least that Sol goes commando and so do I.

I position myself over Sol, and he watches me avidly.

Just the way he looks at me makes me feel like the most beautiful woman in the underworld. In The Hill, I was invisible, but here, Sol sees me.

Warily, I hesitate over Sol's dick. "You're so fucking big. You won't fit."

"Trust me, you can take it. You're in charge here.

Fast or slow, how deep you want it. You take what you need."

I rub over the head of his dick in reward, and his breath quickens. "Tell me if it's okay too. I can't wait to feel your gorgeous dick inside me."

He nods.

My heart's beating fast, as I settle my hands on his chest gently, careful to keep my weight off him. Then I lower myself onto him slowly.

The tip of him enters me, stretching me.

"*Ahh*," I gasp. "Shit, that's intense."

I pause for a moment, before lowering myself again. The ridges are rubbing against places deep inside me that are coiling pleasure in sharp jolts that make me gasp for breath.

I never knew that it could feel this way.

It's overwhelming.

My thighs are burning, and I ignore the pain in my own ribs, to pound myself up and down faster.

"Fuck." Sol throws back his head. "Yes, hell, *yes*."

I lean down, kissing Sol in quick, pecked kisses like he's all that's holding me together, as I ride him. He's panting; sweat glistens on his abs, as he strains.

He's struggling not to move.

When his hips buck, I push them down, before pulling up and off his dick.

He looks at me, devastated. It's as if the world is ending. "Don't stop."

"I told you not to move. Aren't you resting?"

He nods, quickly.

"Then. Lie. Still." I rub my pussy tantalizingly against his dick that twitches, before deciding that he's been teased enough.

And so have I.

I lower back onto him, arching my back.

*Shit, that's good.*

He groans at the same time as me.

I ride Sol now with a frantic need that coils me higher and higher. Sol looks up at me like it's tearing him apart not to hold onto or touch me. He clutches his hands above his head, as if otherwise, he'll make a grab for me.

Then I yell out in shock, as his tail wraps around my waist like it's got a mind of its own and he's been pushed too far to control it. The end, however, traces downward, past the dimple in the hollow of my back.

*It's too much.*

The overwhelming sensation of Sol's dick pounding my insides in a way that nothing ever has before. Sol's dark gaze fixed on me like I'm his heart and Soul: his world. And then the soft brush of Sol's tail, snaking along the crease of my ass and sending electric jolts through me, as it starts to push inexorably inside.

I clench and come with a scream that echoes through the forest. "Sol…"

Beneath me, I pull Sol over as well, and he hollers, baring his fangs. He looks wild and savage. Fire skitters across his horns and down his skin. Exhausted by aftershocks, Sol and I are still connected, as his magic covers him and then me: we're joined in elemental fire that doesn't burn us.

*One being and not two.*

I stare at him in shock, as he stares at me in adoration.

He loves me.

And I love him.

How the hell did I let this happen?

# CHAPTER FIFTEEN

## Imagine Tree, Demon Underworld

I awake to cold rain on my face, as it drips with a *pitter patter* through the canopy, the hardness of the branch beneath my back, and a warm demon snuggling next to me.

*My demon.*

I study Sol's face in the pale morning light. He's relaxed like this, and so achingly beautiful. I wipe away a smudge of Kohl beneath his eye, and my gaze drops to his plush, kissable lips.

He never looks this peaceful and still. He's always active and energetic. Like he's got to be the one putting on a performance. I'm seeing a private side of him that I don't think many people do, and I seriously like it.

My heart feels like it's too full, and there's a goofy smile on my face.

I don't smile like this at guys, cupping their cheeks, as if they're precious, or shivering at the way my light hair is mingling on the branch with their dark.

I screamed with my Soul to allow me through the Stones and into the underworld to rescue my sister and get revenge.

Can I truly have fallen in love with this impossible, infuriating demon?

When Sol's eyes like the night sky flutter open, before widening with pleasure when he sees me, before he smiles sleepily, happiness spreads through my chest but it's bittersweet. His tail winds around my waist and pulls me closer to share his warmth.

"So, we weren't eaten in the night then." The pale, elegant fingers of Sol's right hand tangle with my bronzed fingers.

I'm transfixed at the sight.

"*Woah*, low expectations. And most of my one-night stands traditionally greet me with *morning* or *what would you like for breakfast?*"

"How boringly conventional." His eyes flash red with jealousy. "And it's lucky for you that I'm not a one-night stand."

His hand tightens around mine.

"Don't get me wrong, I am grateful that we survived the night," I add. "After all, we've already been attacked by psycho wolves, chased in a Devil's Hunt, and been almost drowned in an assassination attempt."

"On the other hand," Sol says, "you've had mind-blowing sex with a beautiful demon prince."

I lick across his lower lip, and his breath hitches. "Yeah, but then you've had mind-blowing sex with *me*."

"Then we're even."

"We're not even until I find Skye, and we've only got three days left to do that. Hell, she must be so lonely. What if…who knows what's happening to her? If she's in pain or… It's agony to be apart from her. Alone."

"You're not." Sol's intense gaze meets mine. "I promise, you'll never be alone again, if you don't want to be."

What does he mean?

There's no one here to pretend to. We're in the middle of a forest.

He can drop the act.

I give him a shrewd look. "And how long have *you* been alone? The Emperor separated you from your brothers and set you up to be isolated at court because he must've known that you'd be rejected by

225

those snobs. Hell, *I'm* rejected by the elite of The Hill and I haven't snatched any of their power from them. Then your dad sparked this crappy rivalry between your bothers over becoming the Crown Prince. How will anything be solved, even if you succeed in your ambition? Anwealda's made you think that your only worth is being his puppet like who you are now and all the stuff you do as prince in a kingdom means nothing. You told me that if you joined together with your brothers, then you'd be unstoppable. So, why do you kneel for that asshole? Why not rebel against him? Can't you just say *fuck him*?"

Sol avoids my gaze. "He's not my type."

I clench my jaw. "I'm being serious."

"And so am I. By my horns, your little rebel speech there was *treason*. If we were in the court, and we'd been overheard, then you could be executed. And so could I and probably my brothers too."

I pale. "You mean it."

"Just don't talk like that again. In the name of the sacred elements, we're not in The Hill with your human laws. Demonic rules and punishments are strict and harsher than you can imagine. My only protection comes from being the Emperor's son. I know you think he's a *dick*, and I criticize him more than I safely should, but you mustn't talk about rebellion." Sol's brow furrows. "And my father's also stood up for me and saved my life. I wish I could simply hate him but I can't. Losing his own son, it twisted something inside him. On my flames, he's my adopted father, and that means something."

I understand that.

Sol's already lost one dad, and I can't blame him for wanting approval from the second one.

"I'm sorry," I squeeze his hand. "I should've paid more attention in the demonic culture lessons, but the Soul Bonds' constant giggling over their favorite uses for tails was just too distracting."

Sol's expression lightens. "Tell me more."

"Not a chance. You'll simply have to show me those uses once we're back at the palace."

I study the bruises on his chest and face, which have faded to yellow. His lip is healed entirely. I can only see the pale scar on his arm, which shows the imprint of where the Alpha tore into his wing.

I have the sudden instinct to bite over it and replace the Alpha's mark with my own. "You look better. Do you think you can fly?"

"I told you: I heal fast. And your ribs…?"

I wince, feeling along my side. "I don't heal fast."

Sol helps me to sit up. I move stiffly, giving puffed grunts of pain.

*Attractive.*

I yelp, as Sol pulls my feet into his lap and prods at the cut soles. "What are you doing?"

227

"Helping you." He raises my foot to his mouth and licks.

So, demons *are* kinky.

Foot worship is Sol's thing then. No wonder he loves my spiky leather boots.

I squirm at the sensation of his warm tongue licking and then kissing the arch of my foot, tracing the cuts with loving care and devotion. By the way that I need to clench my thighs together, maybe this is a kink that I just haven't discovered yet as well.

There's definitely something to be said for a prince kissing your feet.

But then, there's a cool, numbing sensation, and I gaze at Sol in awe. He looks back, smugly. He's still holding my foot up by its heel, delicately in his hand, before he deliberately kisses the sole again, never breaking eye contact.

He's healing my foot with the power of his magic, which is tingling through his lips.

By The Hill, that's one of the most erotic things I've ever seen. Plus, one of the most romantic because how many people would heal another if it meant kissing their feet?

*Sol didn't even hesitate.*

Suddenly, the branch beneath ours shakes, and the leaves are pushed aside.

My heart races, and my adrenaline spikes.

*We're not alone in the Imagine Tree.*

Who the hell is climbing it or *what* the hell? Has the Alpha returned? Or other nightmarish, deadly creatures that stalk the forest?

"Someone's here," I hiss.

Yet before I can move, a demon pops his head up above the leaves and rests his elbows on our branch. He's huge and powerful.

Is he part of the Devil's Hunt?

He looks primal and savage like he belongs here in the forest. His gorgeous skin gleams like crushed sapphires, the same as his sweep of hair and curved horns. The muscles of his large shoulders are tight, as he hauls himself up onto the branch.

*He's also naked.*

I yank my foot out of Sol's hand and scoot backward, reaching for Light-bringer.

To my surprise, instead of snarling and leaping into attack mode, Sol sprawls back indolently like he's ordered a naked muscle-bound demon as a stripper.

"Sorry for interrupting your kinky fun." The sapphire demon grins. "Although, you do have an exhibitionist streak, and I'm a voyeur, so feel free to keep going."

"I'll pass this time." Sol returns his grin. "Only *you* could find me stuck in a tree in the middle of the forest."

The sapphire demon's eyes sparkle. "You never could win our games of Hide the Demon, mate." I startle at his casual use of *mate*. What happened to *Your Royal Highness*? He's more familiar than Oran and Iago, but Sol doesn't appear to mind. In fact, Sol's more relaxed than I've yet seen him with another demon. "Plus, I'm a spy and tracker with my lovers' magic helping me. When your lovers are gods, spirits, and reapers, it tends to give a bloke a boost."

I stare at him in shock.

How is a demon a lover of *gods*? Aren't they enemies?

Unfortunately, the sapphire demon catches me looking. "Are you enjoying the view?"

He wiggles his ass, and I redden.

Sol launches himself up, tackling the sapphire demon back onto the branch. For a moment, I think that he's finally been enraged into a fight, until I realize they're both laughing.

*Hell, it's a demonic bromance.*

Sol is still laughing and straddling the sapphire demon as he looks up at me. "Blue, this is Oni, my best friend." Oni's expression brightens at the *best friend*. "We grew up together in the orphanage."

My heart races. "You just called me *Blue*."

Oni's black eyes study me intently. "That's because he trusts me, love. My flame baby here and his brothers protected all of us orphans. They took beatings to save the rest of us, before the Emperor selected them. I'd have lost my horns if it wasn't for him. I owe the bloke everything, and I'd do anything for him."

"Apart from stop calling me *flame baby*," Sol corrects.

"You love it." Oni squirms out from under Sol, and Sol lets him. He catches me watching him warily. "Look, I'm an outcast. I walk between worlds, and I'm a Guardian of the Eternal Forest. I've learned there not to judge relationships or appearances because demons can even love gods. So, I only trust the burning truth of my own heart. My flame baby's been calling in every favor he knows to find your twin, including with me. And it's not because her name is scrawled across his chest, but because *you* want him to. The Emperor delights in punishing me for every minor rule I break, and I've never been good at following rules. But if Sol loves you so much that his blood sings for you, then I've risked returning to spy for him."

My throat is dry, and I find it hard to swallow.

*His blood sings for me?*

How much are all of these demons risking for my sake and Skye's? How much am I asking of them?

I reach across to take Oni's clawed hand in mine. "Thank you. I fucking mean it. I've only been in the Emperor's Court a short while, and it's terrifying. You're a brave guy for coming back here to help your friend."

Oni waggles his eyebrows. "Keep heaping on the praise. I want to remember what to tell my Soul Bond about why I deserve a reward because hers have me shuddering in ecstasy for long nights. How about a medal, so I can show her? I'm not sure where you'll pin it..."

He stares down sadly at his bare chest.

Sol sits up, suddenly tense. "So, report solider."

Oni looks affronted. "I'm no solider, mate. But I've found your missing human."

For a moment, I can't breathe.

Then I'm scrambling forward on the branch and clutching Sol by the shoulders. I twist him to face me, ignoring the way that he flashes his fangs at me.

"Where is she?" I demand. "Is Skye okay? Hurt? Is she...?"

"As far as I know," Oni replies, "she's alive."

My blood turns to ice, and my breathing becomes ragged.

As far as he knows? *WTF?*

Sol wraps his arm around my waist and hugs me to his side. I'm shaking, but my lips are pulled back in a snarl.

"What the hell does that mean?" I growl.

"Don't shoot the messenger, love." Oni's gaze swings between Sol and me. "I caught wind of a human who'd been brought over in a recent raid, when I was in the Kingdom of Air. But she's being kept hidden somewhere. The army's all sworn to secrecy."

Sol's shaking now too.

*Why?*

"But the only one with that type of power..." Sol's staring at Oni pleadingly.

"The prince. The Demon of Air."

Sol flinches but then he lets go of me and launches himself at Oni, knocking him onto his back. "It's a lie."

"Have I ever lied to you?" Oni wraps his arms around Sol, stroking his hair in comfort. "Breeze must've kidnapped Skye, hoping to hide away your Soul Bond. Perhaps, he meant to control you through her or thought someone else did. On the other hand, everyone knows that you're the Emperor's favorite to become Crown Prince, mate, and that you were under pressure to return with your Soul Bond. If you failed, then you'd have been punished, and as eldest..."

"The Prince of Air would become Crown Elect." I clench my fists.

I'm shaking now but with fury for the pain that his brother is causing Sol as much as me.

Breeze stole my sister to break her bond to Sol.

Possibly to control him.

*To take the power in the kingdoms.*

Sol's eyes are closed, and his eyelashes are matted wet. "He wouldn't do this. *He wouldn't.*"

"But he has." Oni puts his claw under Sol's chin. When Sol opens his eyes, they're gleaming with anguish. "Look, take a breath. We don't know his real reasons. He was always a smart one but also…"

"Ruthless," Sol whispers.

I lean over Sol, resting my hand on the hollow of his back. "We have to go and take Skye back. We don't even know what's happening to her, only that he's hiding her away."

Sol turns his head to look at me, and his lips are pinched. "If I do that, then I'm as good as declaring war. Breeze saw us at the Bonding Revel. He must've realized by now his mistake: that you're twins. But also that I'm lying and faking my bond. He could've exposed me, *destroyed* me." Sol's voice wavers. "But he hasn't. Why not?"

"I don't care," I snarl. "Skye's being kept prisoner, and I'm taking her back. Fuck your brother and all these politics. You gave your word that if I played along with your ruse, then you'd help me."

Oni draws in a sharp breath. "A demon can't break his word on a deal."

Sol scrambles away from us, and his back hits the trunk.

He wraps his arms around himself like a cornered animal. "I know…*please*…if this goes wrong, it'll be civil war with my own brother. Give me time to think of a plan. My brother's tail is crooked because he tried to protect me. It'd kill me if... But I won't — I'd never — break my promise, Blue."

"Even if it means that I take revenge on your own brother?" I whisper.

I don't even know if I can make myself do that, after everything Sol's told me. Yet how can I trust Sol now that I know it's his brother who took my sister, if he breaks his vow?

Sol tears at the trunk, and his claws scratch through the names, which he'd once carved on it with his brothers as kids.

When he nods, it's like I can feel his heart break. "My deal was to find your sister. And I warned you that if you try to hurt my brother, then I'll stop you."

# CHAPTER SIXTEEN

**Emperor's Ballroom, Demon Underworld**

I skulk at the back of the opulent ballroom by the dragon alcove like a human princess is an abandoned piece of luggage, while important affairs of state take place.

A *damp* princess because the flight back on Sol was through cold drizzle. Thank the Stones that the day is brightening now, and hot sunlight is shining through the circular windows and drying my skin and clothes. I push my tangled hair back from my face and grimace. My silk tunic is ripped down the ridges on the arm and torn on the side of my injured ribs, and I wish that I didn't know how tight and scratchy leather trousers are, when naturally dried from wet.

It must be worse for Sol in his, since they're all he's wearing and are even tighter than mine, pulled over his dick. *Not that I'm complaining at the way they hug his gorgeous ass.*

I try to discretely rearrange my crotch because having a camel toe in the presence of an Emperor, who's also the dad of the demon who I love, isn't a good look.

And I do love Sol.

I don't know what a Soul Bond should feel like but this…*love*…burns through me. It's like I've always known Sol, and it'll kill me to be separated from him. I want to hurl at even the thought of it.

*I did warn Anwealda about the vomit.*

Fuck it, I'm not good at romance.

But then, this is demon romance, right?

And Sol is *my* demon. I crave, claim, and *devour* him. I get it now. I want to protect him from every bastard in this court, as much as he possessively wants the same for me.

Except, right now he's elegantly kneeling on the hard floor in front of the raised dais at the other side of the ballroom. His back is straight, and his hands are smartly clasped behind him. He looks regal on his knees, which is impressive.

I shiver.

The moment that Sol landed in the courtyard and transformed back into his demonic form, the Shadow Demons surged from the walls, trailing black tendrils toward us like chains.

It'd felt like nothingness.

The void.

*Death.*

Sol grasped me by the waist. "Don't touch her. By my flames, if Father has summoned us, then we can walk without shackles or are we prisoners?"

The Shadow Demons hesitated only a moment, before parting from the doorway and allowing us to stride to the spiral staircase without binding us in their tar-like tendrils. My pulse thrashed in my ears, and I clung to Sol. But he walked with his chin tilted up defiantly, every inch the prince.

The Shadow Demons seeped over the walls, guarding us. There was no escape.

"Try to restrain your stabby impulses," Sol whispered, as we reached the doors to the ballroom. "What happens next is between Father and me. I broke the rules by taking you out of the palace. I did it knowingly and willingly. I'd do it again."

I snorted. "Can we hire a defense lawyer first because if that's your testimony, then you're screwed."

Sol's lips quirked. "Whatever made you think that I'm getting a trial?"

"Fucking demons."

Anwealda sprawls on his black and white horn throne, staring down at his son. The same gorgeous blue-haired demon with feathered wings stands guard behind him. If anything, he looks even more like a military commander than he did at the Bonding Revel.

Anwealda's eyes are hard, but he's silent.

The silence is cold and oppressive. It's as violent as a beating.

This is worse than if Anwealda was hollering and kicking Sol's ass. And it makes me want to scream just to break it.

I clench my hands.

Say something. *Fucking say something.*

Hell, I'm going to scream.

Anwealda's expression is furious; he's like a snake about to strike. He's the true predator, who rules over the entire court, weaving plots and making every other demon into his puppet.

Except, his son has gone rogue.

I can't help the grin.

When Anwealda shoots me a sharp look, I take a steadying breath, before choking on the intoxicating scent of incense that's flooding the room. Anwealda's lips twitch, before he fixes his gaze on Sol again.

"If you wanted to get my attention, Sol," Anwealda raps his long claws on the arm of his throne, "I can think of at least two hundred and three less painful ways you could have achieved it."

Sol shrugs. "I'll have to remember to go for positive attention next time. I'm always too quick to choose the negative route."

I smother my laugh in my palm.

To my surprise, Anwealda looks like he's trying hard not to smile as well. "Indeed you are, darling. If you wanted some private time with your Soul Bond, then I'd have arranged it. You didn't need to take her away from the palace to indulge in delicious debauchery." I redden, but to be fair, he's not entirely wrong. "Even if Oran is an insufferable brat, however, he's also the Demon of Misrule, and you broke the tradition of the Devil's Hunt. How can I uphold my position here, if I make one rule for everybody else and one rule for my son?"

Sol ducks his head. "You can't."

Wait, is Sol agreeing to punishment?

This is more court politics bullshit and manipulations, right? Or is it Sol being a good leader?

Finally, Anwealda's expression softens. "How delightfully agreeable you're being. Don't worry, I'm not turning you over to Oran for discipline, as he requested."

Sol's head snaps up in alarm.

I gasp, rushing forward, but Sol twists and waves me back.

Who knows what torments Oran would put Sol through? I may only be a human in a demonic underworld, but I'll fight tooth and tail to stop that happening.

Anwealda tuts. "So hotheaded. I said: *I'm not*. His father, the Duke, is also…"

Oakthorn marches into the ballroom and up to the dais. He stops next to Sol, towering over him. I admire the way that Sol doesn't flinch away but remains smartly kneeling up.

Oakthorn runs his hand through his pastel green hair like he's trying to control himself, before shaking his head side to side; I'm transfixed by his huge horns that are curved like a stag's.

Oakthorn looks close to goring Sol with his horns, when he turns and points down at him. "The prince has gone on too long the rebel. My son has informed me what has occurred, aye, and the instances of his previous misbehavior. He hides behind his adopted title but he has no control or self-discipline." He gives a vicious smile, as he looks at the feathered guard behind Anwealda. "This one's brother would know how to sort out a pampered prince. Give him directly to the military academy and stop spoiling him. Beat the weakness from him."

The guard looks appalled, shaking his head violently. "Your Imperial Majesty, it would break him."

Anwealda arches his eyebrow. "How strange. I imagined that *I* was Emperor, and yet you would all assume to tell me what to do."

The guard pales and instantly, takes a step backward, wrapping his wings around himself. He shoots Sol an apologetic glance.

Oakthorn clenches his jaw and falls silent.

I freeze. Goosebumps raise on my arms, and I glance frantically between them.

Could Sol's decision to protect us truly lead to him being sent away? Hurt? *Broken?*

Sol's expression is shuttered. He's staring at the floor, and he hasn't spoken once in his defense. But then, he told me that this wouldn't be a trial.

*Fuck that.*

"Why the hell are you punishing him?" I growl, flooded by a red mist. "Because of stupid *tradition*? Your Imperial Majesty, *you know* that in a hunt like that our lives were in danger, and you made your son promise not to put himself or me in that position. He was keeping his promise. What kind of dick are you that you'd make your son suffer simply to keep face? How fucking weak are you?"

The moment the words are out of my mouth the red mist of my rage lifts, and I'm left with one thought.

*I'm screwed.*

Perhaps, not learning to wear a mask in a court that never shows its true face, makes *me* weak.

Sol half-raises himself off his knees. "She doesn't know what she's saying..."

"Oh, but I think she does," Anwealda's voice is darkly amused but a lot more dangerous because of it. "You have exactly one second to get out of my sight, human, before I forget my own rule that no Soul Bond shall be killed. And then I'm going to decide if I'll now need to execute my son."

Sol lets out a strangled sound, and I scrabble backward into the shadows of the alcove. My heart is beating wildly, and my eyes are burning.

I've made things worse for Sol and for myself.

I won't let Sol die. *I won't.*

But what if I can't stop this? What if I have to watch...?

I can't hold back the sob and press the back of my hand to my mouth, desperately attempting to hold the gasping, grief inside.

My chest hurts, and I watch through blurred vision, as Anwealda snatches Sol by the shoulder, dragging him to the back of the dais, where they talk in hushed tones.

What if Anwealda's planning to kill Sol?

Will I be stuck here like Ward after the death of her demon? Will I have to spend my life, losing my memory of The Hill and the truth, then believing myself to be the widowed Soul Bond of an executed demon prince? Will I never be able to find my stolen twin?

As tears pour down my cheeks, I turn away on my knees and *clang* against something metallic. I look up in shock and find myself face to face with a small, golden cage and the beautiful man inside.

The same beautiful naked man with sweet, blond curls who I saw at the Bonding Revel.

*The fallen god and Emperor's Pet.*

Now that I've got to know the Emperor better, I feel even more sorry for the bastard.

Pet's sitting, crushed against the front of the cage with his knees drawn up to his chin.

He snakes his soft fingers through the bars to pet my cheek in comfort, and I startle. "Don't cry, little girl."

I wipe my tears away roughly on the back of my hand. "I'm not a little girl."

He scrutinizes me with large, amber eyes. "And I'm not a pet, but it's what everyone calls me. I'm caged like one. My divinity stolen."

He hunches his shoulders, and I can't look away from the livid welts that mark his shoulders.

"Who hurt you?" I blurt.

He bites his lip. "Everybody."

I shudder. What must it be like to be a prisoner of your enemy? A god amongst demons?

As if he can tell what I'm thinking, Pet leans closer to me, and I stroke his hair.

"Please, free me. I only want to go home," he says, softly.

*Home.*

Hell, I've long ached for home.

It was hard enough to leave Pet here last time, but how can I now? No prisoner should be treated like this.

I glance at Anwealda, whose back is turned still, as he stands with Sol. The guard is chatting with Oakthorn. At the back of the alcove is the entrance that Oran and Iago dragged me through.

Will anyone know, if I open the cage and allow Pet out? He could escape through the corridor and leave the underworld. And if I am discovered, then will I truly be in more trouble than I already am?

Can I claim to want to free The Hill from the treaties — to save the humans from being stolen — if I ignore the enslavement of gods? If I stand by and do nothing, then do I have any right to cry about unfairness, when I'm the next one to be caged and turned into a pet...because who the hell knows what Anwealda will do to me or Sol?

I slide my fingers through Pet's silky curls.

"Free me," Pet whispers, urgently. He peers up at me through his dark lashes. "*Hurry.*"

A cold ball of doubt forms in my stomach.

Uncomfortable, I demand, "How do I know you're not dangerous?"

Pet looks at me with puppy dog eyes. "Do I look dangerous?"

He looks beautiful and hurt. If Sol is a dark statue come to life, then this fallen god is a golden statue.

Yet the Soul Pool was pretty and toxic. Most things in the Eternal Forest and underworld are beautiful traps.

I pull my hand away from Pet's hair, and he whimpers. "The demons are beautiful and they're anything but harmless."

I watch, as the spark of hope dies in his eyes. *And I did that.*

Pet turns away his head from me, leaning his lashed shoulder against the cold bars with a wince.

"Then leave me," he mutters. "I'm only the Emperor's Pet now. I don't know why I thought that you'd help me...why anybody would ever love me again. Nobody has truly loved me, as I love them. I've already been taught that cruel lesson."

My heart aches.

Is Pet here because he fell in love with the wrong person? Did they betray him to the demons?

"Wait," I hiss. "I'll let you out."

I can't do it. I can't leave Pet here like this.

*Shit, this is stupid.* But still, I can't walk away from this.

Pet turns back in shock and joy. His hands rest on the bars.

I cast a hurried glance back at Anwealda to check that he's still distracted, before I fiddle with the door of the cage.

It's not even locked.

*If I can just push the latch...*

I scream in shock, as cold fingers snatch me by the back of my neck and claws bite into my skin. Then I'm pulled up dangling onto my tiptoes, until I'm staring into Anwealda's furious face.

*Shit, shit, shit...*

How fast can the bastard move?

I'm trembling, and my breathing is ragged.

"Did you not think that I'd have my Pet's cage protected by magic, and that I'd sense if anyone tampered with it, darling?" Anwealda's voice is as cold as ice.

Sol appears at Anwealda's shoulder. "She didn't know—

"You say that a lot," Anwealda drawls. "As if ignorance is a defense."

"Don't hurt my new worshiper," Pet commands.

He sounds nothing like the submissive, gentle Pet who he'd been a moment ago.

I stare at him in shock.

He was playing me.

*Of course he was.*

I'm a fucking idiot.

Still, at least Pet's standing up for me. Considering that Anwealda looks like he's about to tear out my throat with his fangs, then that's brave, right?

Anwealda snarls, as he tosses me into Sol's arms. Sol catches me, and I stare up into his face with relief. Except, I'm shocked how frostily Sol looks back at me like he's restraining his own rage.

What's wrong?

Is he truly pissed that I tried to help Pet? Does he think it's okay to cage gods?

Anwealda crouches by the cage. Pet cringes back, but there's no space, and he can't escape.

"You have no idea how cross I am with you, Pet." Anwealda reaches through the bars to grip Pet's chin. "Perhaps, I'll show you later, won't that be fun? I think you've forgotten that you're here to pay penance. Will you enjoy being my footstool again before the entire Court?"

Pet's expression darkens, before his gaze darts to me, and to my shock, he smiles.

*It isn't a nice smile.*

"Do what you like, demon." Pet looks smug. "I'll always find a way to create new worshipers. Unlike you, I'm lovable."

Anwealda's hands clench, before he turns to me with repressed fury. "Congratulations on being the first Soul Bond who's also a traitor on the side of the gods."

I twist to Sol, who's staring at me with that blank, detached look that I hate.

Wait, do they think that I'm conning them? *That I was sent here to free Pet?*

Does Sol think that everything we've said and done together was me *tricking* him?

*I want to hurl.*

I back a step away from Sol, trying to clear my head.

Behind me, I can see Oakthorn and the guard blocking the exit like they think I may try and run.

"Look, I'm sorry," I gasp. "I was an idiot. But by The Hill, this wasn't some big scheme or something. He just kept asking me to be set him free, and how can I see someone caged and hurt and not help them? I'm not a dick. How can you treat someone like that?"

I gesture wildly at Pet, who this time, doesn't even try for puppy dog eyes.

He no longer looks innocent.

Sol's shoulders relax, and he now appears more panicked than angry. He gives me a slight smile, before glancing at Anwealda.

"On my wings, she's soft hearted," Sol offers. "It's not like gods are normally kept out here, rather than the dungeon." Hold up, there's a fucking dungeon? *Of course, there is.* "The humans may find sights like this…uncomfortable."

"Fuck yeah, I find it uncomfortable. Let's call it a cultural difference." I gesture at Pet. "Let him out."

"Was that an order?" Anwealda asks dangerously low.

Sol shakes his head at me frantically.

I lick my lips. "More like a strongly worded suggestion, Your Imperial Majesty."

"And at long last she remembers what to call me in order not to die." Anwealda stalks toward me, and I battle not to back away. "I can either believe you a dangerous rebel who's also a traitor or a naïve simpleton. Which are you?"

"Naïve simpleton," Sol mouths at me.

"Is there a third option?" I ask.

When Pet chuckles, Anwealda shoots crackling fire from his horns at the cage, and Pet screams as he's electrified.

"Stop it!" I try to run forward, but Sol catches me and holds me back. "Please, he's hasn't done anything."

The magic cuts off.

Anwealda gives a bitter laugh. "*Naïve simpleton* it is then. Do you even know who this is?"

I glance at the fallen god, who's still shuddering in the cage, before I shake my head.

Sol's brow furrows. "Would you have opened

Pandora's box too, if it looked pretty? The moment that you freed that god, you'd have been dead."

I gasp.

Pet struggles to look up at me, wincing. "She wouldn't. I like her. I'd have taken her with me to rebuild my cult of worshipers."

Anwealda's eyes are like ice. "This charmer is Bacchus. His magic holds his worshipers under the thrall of ecstatic frenzy. They become a pleasure cult. And those who are unwilling..." His jaw clenches. "Bacchus is learning a lesson about being caged because he's spent Millennia caging mages, shifters, and other gods. He's violated and..." I'm shocked by Anwealda's anguish, as he looks down. "He hurt one of my lovers, my darling Lopter. Then he killed him."

I take a harsh breath, but Pet — Bacchus — merely looks bored.

"He didn't stay dead," Bacchus objects. "He has an annoying habit of reincarnating. And I loved him too."

"A toxic love." Anwealda's nostrils flare.

Bacchus smirks. "I never said it was healthy."

Sol grips my arm, pulling me closer to look intently into my eyes. "Bacchus meant to kill all shifters...like me."

"I enjoy taming them too." Bacchus' eyes gleam like he's imagining it. "I may have kept you *caged*, Shifter Demon."

Bacchus no longer appears sweet but poisonous.

"Not a word more, Pet," Anwealda warns, "or I'll leave you out in the courtyard for the week."

I shudder, before wrapping my arms more tightly around Sol.

Hell, I almost freed a psycho god who killed Anwealda's lover and wants to commit genocide on Sol's kind.

*Bacchus is deadly.*

I've stepped into the middle of a war that I don't understand, and I didn't trust Sol enough to talk to him about it, before I acted.

From now on, I fucking will.

"I'm sorry," I whisper against Sol's chest.

Sol nods in acceptance, but his expression is still tight. I turn in his arms to face Anwealda and take a deep breath.

"I really am sorry," I say. "But I can't stand seeing anyone hurt."

"How are you with seeing *yourself* hurt?" Anwealda adjusts his cuffs, before stalking toward me. "You're lucky that I believe humans to be such pretty idiots. Twelve lashes."

I blanch, and my stomach drops.

*No, no, no...*

Sol's arms tighten around me in alarm, and he drags me behind him.

Oakthorn marches toward us, unhooking a short leather whip from his belt.

This can't be happening.

"As Soul Bond, she's the other half of me, and so according to tradition," Sol's voice is cool, but I can feel the tremors wracking him, "I wish to take her punishment."

"No fucking way." I stare at the stiff set to Sol's shoulders, but he doesn't turn around, and I can't see his expression.

I don't want to be whipped.

Spanking for sexy fun is as far as I go, and I'm not a masochist. Even if I was, this isn't about pleasure, it's discipline, and it's going to agony.

Yet there's no way I'll let Sol be hurt on my behalf.

All of a sudden, however, the guard's feathered wings are around me, dragging me back.

I struggle. "Sol…"

"Keep out of it," the guard says into my ear. "You're only making it harder on the prince."

I fall still.

Anwealda studies his son thoughtfully. "How chivalrous. And by the Stones, you are responsible for failing to control your Soul Bond, as I commanded. I only warned you for your own good. Do you see where your weakness has now led?"

"I do, Father." Sol kneels down, presenting his horns.

Oakthorn tests the whip, snapping it through the air. I wince at the sharp sound, but Sol stays eerily still.

He can't really be going to hit Sol's horns with that thing...? That's like whipping Sol's dick. His horns are sensitive.

"Please, don't," I whisper.

Anwealda's gaze meets mine. "You're the cause of this horn whipping. A Soul Bond should bring joy and completion to their demon. I wonder why you're bringing him pain and confusion?"

Oakthorn lifts the whip, before bringing it down. It lands with a sharp crack right across the tips of both horns.

Sol lets out a hiss. By the way that he's clenching his hands on his lap and shaking, I can tell how much he's struggling to hold in his pain.

I'm glad of the way that the guard's holding me because otherwise, my knees would've buckled, and I'd have fallen into a crumpled heap on the floor.

I don't cry because if Sol isn't letting himself, then I won't. He wants to look strong, even if this is being done to him.

Then I will too.

As Oakthorn lays down the other lashes methodically onto the horns so that no strike crosses (and I should be glad of that mercy, but in my distress, I'm fucking not), Sol struggles more and more to remain still. He winces and pulls out of position but then forces himself back in. He half raises his head after a particularly brutal blow and then struggles back down again. And at the half way mark, he gives in and gasps, then shouts, and on the final stroke, he screams.

I can't take it.

I just...*can't.*

I need to hold Sol, soothe him. I never want to hear him scream again.

The guard finally loosens his hold, and I run towards Sol. Before I can reach him, however, Anwealda snatches me by the arm.

"I could've had to kill my own son today," Anwealda hisses, and I jolt at each word. His gaze flicks to Sol, who's shaking like he's holding in moans of pain at his feet. "Never make me do this to him again."

It sounds like Anwealda's close to tears. But he can't be, right? He's the one who ordered this. He may as well have been wielding the whip himself.

I wrench my arm away from Anwealda and fall to my knees beside Sol.

I hardly notice, as the other demons leave the ballroom. I only notice the way that Sol curls around me, when I drag his head to rest on my lap and stroke his hair, careful to avoid his beautiful horns that are striped with painful purple welts.

The way that he's bitten his lip bloody, holding in his pain.

The crescent marks in his palms, where his claws have cut in.

How he holds onto me like I'm what soothes his pain, rather than having been the cause of it.

Once, I hated all demons. I blamed Sol for the actions of every demon. Yet Sol has never hurt me. I asked him to get the Stones to devour me. I willingly struck our bargain. And he didn't steal Skye as his Soul Bond. He wanted to get to know her and fall in love, since her name appeared on his chest and because the Emperor ordered him to, as his duty.

Sol's tried as much as he can to be a rebel to his own traditions, and now, he hasn't hesitated to take my punishment.

I can't even pretend that I don't love him. And I don't want to.

"It's okay, they're gone," I murmur. "You don't have to hide it anymore."

Sol's face is pale and drawn, as he looks up at me. There are shadows beneath his eyes. But his cheeks are dry. He takes deep breaths, steadying himself from the agony. Then he holds tighter onto me.

Unsure, I bend to kiss his horn in apology, trying

to say everything I mean in the gesture, but he hisses in pain.

"I just watched the demon who I love almost die because of me and then be whipped," I say, fiercely. Sol's gaze snaps to mine on *love*. Once I start, I can't stop. My heart is beating too fast, and I'm trembling. "And the worst thing is, I thought for a moment that I'd never get to tell him that I love him."

Sol breaks into a brilliant smile "Well, I imagine that demon would rather like you to tell him now."

I smile in relief. "Hell, I love you."

Sol presses a gentle kiss to my knee. "Then every lash was worth it."

I jump at Bacchus' dark laugh.

Bacchus' eyes glow from the shadows of his cage. "And so it begins. Love is pain. It didn't free me; it caged me. Little lovebirds, what cage are you weaving for yourselves here in the underworld? Do you even still wish to escape?"

# CHAPTER SEVENTEEN

**Fire Dining Room, Demon Underworld**

I t's my sixth day in the shadows of the demon underworld, and tomorrow, will be my last chance to find my sister and escape it, or else I'll forget my human life forever.

It should be an easy choice, right? Stay and be unable to even remember The Hill, or go and lose a fake Soul Bond.

Except, curled on Sol's lap and caught in his strong arms, it isn't.

*Because it no longer feels fake.*

I snuggle closer to Sol's hard chest. I'm sitting on his lap in the Fire Dining Room, still lazy and warm with sleep. This is the first time that he's brought me here for breakfast, rushing me to dress in matching black and crimson ridged suits, rather than having Ward bring it to us in his room on trays.

What's he plotting?

One thing I've learned about Sol is that he can play the game at Court as well as any demon. And after the disaster that happened yesterday, I know that he needs to do something drastic. I just hope that it doesn't get us both killed.

Honestly, that appears to be *my* talent.

I wince at the remembered crack of the whip, and Sol's bitten back screams.

Sol loops his arm around my waist, before lightly kissing the crown of my head. Then he forks a piece of yolk off the huge plate of egg and bacon that's on a silver plate on the oak table, before holding it to my mouth.

Okay, being fed by a demon is pretty much the opposite of what I thought would happen in the underworld.

Shit, I thought that *I'd* be the one on the end of the fork.

*But it doesn't suck.*

I bite the egg off the fork with a moan. It's delicious. I catch Sol's eye, as I lick my lips, and his pupils dilate. I moan again, just to feel his dick harden in his tight pants beneath me.

The air is heavy with smoke and rich, meaty aromas. I take a deep breath, as I glance around the dining room. It's painted scarlet with huge fire pits along one side. On the opposite side are floor to ceiling windows that look out over an orchard; something silver glints on the branches of the trees.

*Are even the apples silver?*

Three long, wooden tables and benches run down the center of the room, and all different types of demons mingle together with satyrs, kistune, and fae. Some are naked and sprawl over the tables like they're waiting to be eaten, but only in the most pleasurable ways.

A kistune is having his tails stroked, while a male fae is pinned to a table as he's savagely kissed by the female demon in the moss dress.

I struggle to hold back a growl.

Next to her, is Oran and Iago. They lounge on the bench like they're kings holding court, surrounded by a gang of demons who are fawning over everything they say. A mountain of food is piled in front of them: muffins, gooey pastries, cheese, and fresh, baked rolls.

There's a roaring fireplace behind, which casts a fiery light over them. The fireplace is large enough for an entire boar to be roasted, as it turns slowly on a spit.

*I used to imagine that demons would be turning humans on a spit like that.*

I wish I could tell Maxton that I was wrong and coordinate his efforts with Sol to change the Demon Sacrifice treaties. But if I stay here, I'll forget Maxton, won't I?

My chest tightens at the thought.

Maxton has no one but Skye and me, apart from his asshole dad. I know he told me that he could handle the revolution. Can I trust that he's become a man now, as much as I'm no longer the scared kid, hollering *devour me* into the forest?

Sol nudges a piece of bacon at my lips, and I nibble it.

*Hell, that's good.*

"Are you trying to turn me into a pet?" I grumble.

Sol's lips quirk. "I thought we agreed neither of us was a pet, but that it'd be a fun roleplay?"

I flush. "I must have missed a memo."

When there's a burst of raucous laughter from Oran's table, Sol's expression darkens. "The Demon of Misrule is holding court again."

"The Court of Assholes," I mutter.

Iago catches Sol's eye and nudges Oran.

Oran turns to study Sol for a long moment, before rubbing his hand over his own horn in faux sympathy for Sol's pain.

His sycophantic gang break out in mocking laughter.

I glance at Sol's horns, which still bear the dark purple stripes of his beating.

I hate how sore they must be.

How much he's hurting and hiding it.

I grip Sol by the chin and make him face me. "Fuck them. They don't matter."

Sol's dark eyes twinkle. "Then who does?"

"You."

I kiss him, tenderly. I sigh, addicted to the taste of him. I can't get enough of it.

*I need more.*

I wrap my hand in his hair, tightening my hold to the point of pain, holding him close. He tightens his arm around my waist, and his kiss deepens.

Hell, I need this.

*Don't stop...*

Unexpectedly, there's a polite cough behind us. "Young demon, I'd tell you to get a room, but I know that you already have your old one. I'm glad that you've taken my advice and appear to be indulging in wild, kinky sex."

I startle, breaking away from Sol.

Sol merely grins, smugly. "I have indeed. But don't worry, I've been careful to remember she's breakable."

"*She's* right here." I cross my arms, as I dart a glance at Ward, who walks around to lean against the table.

She looks as elegant as ever. Her hair is braided today and then coiled on the top of her head with pearl combs. She's dressed in the same long black dress with all four elements sewn on the sleeves.

She appears to wear the same thing every day, and I've come to realize that she, more than anyone apart than Anwealda, runs the palace.

Ward ignores me, slipping a small, round tin out of her pocket and passing it to Sol in a practiced way, which tells me that she's done it many times before

She smiles at him sadly. "My precious prince, for your poor horns."

Sol ducks his head, hiding the tin as quickly as he can, as if he's ashamed of it, in his own pocket. "Thank you."

Ward squeezes his shoulder, then her sharp gaze lands on me, and I squirm.

"I warned you not to disrespect the princes and especially not my dear Sol," she says sternly, and I shiver. "I heard what happened. The entire palace has because gossip spreads like fire here. I'd be giving you an ass spanking over this bench, if I didn't think you weren't so insanely in love. Even for Soul Bonds, such sacrifice so early is rare."

I *eep*, trying to wriggle free, but Sol merely arches his brow at me, holding me firmly on his lap.

*Traitor.*

Ward's expression softens. "I've never seen my

precious prince open up the way he does to you. The way he looks at you, when you think he's not looking like you're the sun…"

"Ward, please." Sol reddens.

*Is it true?*

Ward fixes me with a steely glare. "But if you ever get his horns whipped again, sweetheart, none of that will matter to me. Do we have an understanding?"

I freeze, staring up at Ward.

"Did you just give *me* the shovel talk?" I demand.

She shrugs.

I gape at her. "Why doesn't *he* get one?"

Ward leans closer to me, and I stiffen. "Because just between us girls," she cups my cheek, "*you're* the dangerous one."

I like Ward.

I give a fierce grin. "Fuck, yeah."

Sol bites his lip to stop himself laughing.

Ward snorts, straightening. "Look after each other." Her gaze flicks to Oran, who's watching us with an intense gaze. "A Soul Bond, no matter if it's between a demon and a human, or a demon and any other creature, can strengthen them in ways that they can't understand, before they experience it. We're always stronger, if we let someone else share our burdens and life's journey."

I huff. "And why do you have to be bonded for that?"

Sol looks panicked. "So inquisitive this one. I'll just take her back to my room and—"

"Hush, young demon," Ward snaps. "I still remember when you had baby fangs and every sentence you asked as you followed me around holding my skirts began with *why*."

I struggle to hold back the *aww* because the image of an adorable kid Sol is so cute. Sol grits his teeth.

But then, realization strikes me, and my eyes widen.

I struggle off Sol's lap and face Ward. "How in the name of the sacred Stones do you remember that? How old are you?"

She frowns. "Don't you know that it's rude to ask a lady her age?"

Except, I'm not sure that she *is* a lady.

I still quail back under her stern gaze.

When Sol snickers, however, her gaze swings to him. Then it's *his* turn to quail.

"And haven't you explained *anything* about Soul Bonds to your beloved?" She places her hands on her hips.

"I've been rather busy with the whole not dying business," Sol drawls.

"Don't get fresh with me. There's nothing more important than your Soul Bond." When Ward turns to me, I admire the hell out of her. She's formidable. She came to this underworld, and even after her lover died, she stayed and raised princes. She totally *schools* demons and puts them in their place. "I'm centuries old. To be honest, I've lost count. Once you've bonded, your life is extended to the same length as a demon's. Your Soul is truly bonded, so that you can become compatible. In some supernaturals, it is one-sided, as with fallen angels, and you even die, if they do." I gasp, but she reaches out to pat my arm. "Don't worry, not with demons. This way, you can truly live your entire life here, together in the underworld. You'll never be parted. Alone. Unless…"

She looks away, and her eyes gleam with tears.

Sol stands hurriedly, pulling Ward into a hug. "You have me."

Ward sniffs. "I told you, I'm not made of glass."

"I wouldn't dream of thinking it."

Ward gives Sol a final pat on the back, before pulling away.

She smiles at us both. "My precious prince, I'm just so happy that you're not alone."

My guts roil. No pressure, right?

I feel like I'm being torn apart.

I watch, as Ward leaves the dining room.

"We're not really…" Sol murmurs.

We both know the missing word is *bonded*.

His arm is touching mine; warm and hard. His fingers brush against mine.

"I know."

"We only have today and tomorrow to find your sister…"

"I know," I say, harsher than I mean to.

Sol grabs me by my arms and twists me to look at him. He's so fucking handsome, it takes away my breath.

"We don't need that," he insists. "We can love… be in love…without…"

"We can because we're already rebels, right? But then, humans have an expiration date."

His hands tighten on my arms like he never means to let go. "But I forgot. In a day, you're leaving me anyway."

I open my mouth and then snap it shut.

What can I say?

My heart is desperate to reassure him that I'll stay with him forever.

I want to…I need to. But if I find my twin in time, don't I owe it to Skye to leave the underworld with her? If she wants to go home, I can't separate from her. We've never been apart.

How can I promise Sol forever, if it means that I never see Skye again?

Sol swallows. "By my horns, I know what I'm asking isn't fair. But can this be my sociopathic prince card for the day? If I find a way to get your sister safe, but also us bonded, will you take it? I love you, and I need your stabbiness by my side forever."

I'm caught between laughing and crying, as I rest my forehead against his.

He hisses out a sharp breath. "Hell, please, say something."

"Find a way," I whisper. "And I'll think about it."

All of a sudden, there's a clatter of sharp footsteps, and Oakthorn marches into the dining room, followed by the Emperor's personal guard. Oakthorn is grim faced, and there's a sudden tension in the air that makes my skin prickle.

Instantly, the other demons sit smartly in their seats or stop their lazy kissing.

Wary, I slip my hand to the hilt of Light-bringer and twist to stand in front of Sol, even though he's over a foot taller than me and could throw me over his shoulder like a ragdoll (and has done).

Oakthorn doesn't storm to Sol, however, rather to his son.

Oran uneasily shifts on the bench, resting his hand on Iago's shoulder in an action that's both protective and possessive.

"On your feet," Oakthorn barks.

Oran reddens, glancing around at the other demons who are watching his humiliation with relish. Weren't they his friends a moment ago?

Except, does that really make them his enemies?

Iago's tawny eyes are wide with genuine emotion for once: *fear*.

"What's going on?" I mutter.

Sol watches with a shuttered expression and doesn't reply.

Oran slowly stands, and when Iago hesitates, Oakthorn snatches him by the horn and wrenches him up and next to his son. Iago winces but doesn't resist.

The woman in the moss dress pushes away from the fae beneath her and strolls away like she doesn't even know Oran.

My eyes narrow.

I may think Oran's an asshole who deserves whatever he has coming to him, but so much for friendship. Perhaps, Oran will take note of the way his kingdom has crumbled so fast. The only one who's standing by him is Iago, and it's not like he has a choice.

Oakthorn throws Iago with a grimace of distaste to the guard, who catches him in his wings and then turns him, twisting his arms behind his back to hold him still.

Iago gasps in pain.

"Don't hurt him," Oran demands.

"How dare you give orders? You're for the dungeons," Oakthorn growls, "traitor."

The room falls silent, and I hold my breath.

Oran pales. "Traitor?" He whispers. "W-hat's...? On my h-horns, what the hell is going on? Why would you p-put me...? W-what?"

I'm shocked by how young and vulnerable he sounds.

The guard's gaze flicks to Sol, before he raises his brow. Sol's lips quirk. Then the guard gives a nod, as if in approval.

Sol's face smooths to a cool mask again.

But I didn't imagine that.

*What the hell has Sol done?*

Oran clasps Oakthorn's elbow like his dad will actually help him, and this is all a misunderstanding over a broken vase or a curfew. "Father, can't you straighten this out?"

Oakthorn shakes him off irritably. "A disgusting display. You plot treason with a fallen god and then you beg favors."

My eyes widen.

The room is filled with horrified gasps.

If Oran had any supporters left, I can tell by the disgusted and contemptuous looks being cast at him now that he doesn't any longer. It was a painful lesson, but I've learned just how deep the war between the demons and gods runs.

Being in league with Bacchus is the worst accusation that can be leveled at him. Even if it's not true, that public smear will destroy him.

It won't be forgotten.

Sol's a fucking genius. I know — somehow — he's behind this.

Sol crosses his arms like he's as shocked as everybody else.

Oran's pastel green eyes are wide with shock. "Nay, we didn't do this."

"We're innocent," Iago yells, struggling.

The guard only tightens his hold. "Settle down."

"Da," Oran begs, "you've got to believe me, I'd never—"

Oran is silenced by Oakthorn's backhand that cracks across his cheek loudly enough to resound through the room. It breaks his lower lip, and blood trickles onto his chin.

Into the silence, Oran licks at the blood, breathing hard.

Oakthorn straightens his shoulders. "You're no longer my son. By my horns, for years I've covered for you. I've rescued your idiot arse from your indiscretions, cruelties, and the consequences of your scheming. No more." I almost feel sorry for the asshole now. I mean, I would…if he'd hadn't attacked me and probably tried to kill me. "Do you hear me? Not. This. Time."

Oran's expression crumples. "Da, please…"

Oakthorn snatches Oran by the arm and drags him out of the dining room. The guard follows with Iago, who doesn't resist. He looks as distraught as Oran, but then I would too, if I knew that I was being taken to some demonic dungeon.

271

I shudder as I twist to Sol.

Sol shrugs. "Well, that was entertaining."

I poke his side. "They say they're innocent."

"We're demons. We're all wicked."

I push myself onto tiptoe, wrapping my arms around Sol's neck. He grins, hooking me beneath my ass and pulling my legs around his waist. Then he carries me to the far wall, away from the other demons, who are excitedly gossiping about the shock arrest.

"Bad kitten," I murmur into Sol's ear, masking our own gossip with pretend but enjoyable passion; he slams me against the wall and pushes his hips against mine, "you framed them."

Sol's breath gusts hot across my ear, as he ruts against me like we're about to truly test out his exhibitionist streak right here in the dining room (why are we wearing so many clothes?). "Did I? Then I'm smart. And it must be because no one gets away with hurting my stabby princess."

Warmth surges through me, and I rake my nails down his back. "Fuck, yeah." I nibble his ear, and he shivers. "So, I'm not the only one who wants revenge…?"

Sol's dark gaze meets mine. "Demons are simply more Machiavellian about it."

"I'm getting that. But how…?"

He pulls back and kisses me to stop my words.

"Not here." Then he licks across my lips, and I melt against him. "On my wings, I have an idea what to bargain with to get Father to allow me to visit Breeze with the least risk of sparking civil war. Then we can secretly search for Skye ourselves. It's dangerous. But then, everything here is deadly. Want to risk your life with me?"

I stare into his beautiful midnight eyes, as my legs are wrapped around his waist, and I pull him closer, devouring his lips again.

Panting, I draw back. "Hell, yeah. Let's make a deal with the devil. What could go wrong?"

# CHAPTER EIGHTEEN

**Elemental Palace Dungeon, Demon Underworld**

Anwealda slams Sol against the stone wall at the top of the dungeon steps, hard enough to crack the wall. I shake, edging to stand next to him. Anwealda snarls, wrapping his hand around Sol's neck. When his claws dig into Sol's skin, I notice the crimson glistening under his nails.

Is it blood?

Has he already been down in the dungeons, interrogating Oran and Iago?

I wince, battling not to kick the Emperor's ass and instead, play the good Soul Bond, as I promised Sol I would.

Although, Anwealda would definitely kick *my* ass, even if I try to pull him away from his son.

The landing at the top of the ancient stairway is narrow and dark. There are no lights, and Anwealda's crown of magical fire, which flares like an unholy halo between his ruby horns, is the only thing that illuminates the tiny space.

It's claustrophobic being trapped here with two huge, predatory demons in a face-off.

Especially, when one of them is as deadly as the Emperor.

Anwealda's eyes narrow. "You truly do like to play with fire, don't you?"

"It has been known," Sol rasps.

Anwealda's cold gaze darts to me. "After your discipline the other day, why would you seek me out now and request a favor? I thought that I made it clear that you're on thin ice. Shall we call it probation?"

"I'd never ask a favor of you, Father. You taught me better than that," Sol replies. "I'm talking about a deal."

*We decided on a deal with the devil, right?*

Anwealda's eyes light up, and he lets go of Sol, stepping back. "Explain. You have a minute and make it entertaining. The last hour in the dungeon has been a boring litany of *I didn't do it, please, mercy,* and….well, screaming."

When he flashes his sharp, white fangs, I shudder.

*Paternal motivation at its finest.*

"I request that you send me to visit my brother, the Demon of Air," Sol says, speaking quickly.

Immediately, Anwealda shakes his head. "You're needed here. By my side."

Sol gives a slow smile. "By my horns, of course I am. But what Duke Oakthorn said about me after the Devil's Hunt hit me hard. I need to be able to represent you, Father, in the best way. I shouldn't let you down but also, we both know that the academy would put me through hell."

Anwealda's touch is gentle, as he pats Sol's arm. "I'd never send *you* there. You're not your brother, darling. I want you obedient but not to break you."

Is that true?

He's threatened to *break* Sol's horns and execute him. Does Anwealda really care what happens to his adopted son?

Surprise flashes across Sol's expression, before he's able to mask it. "That's why I thought you could send me to the Prince of Air for tutoring, instead. He always knew the best way of drilling discipline into me as a child. I bet he has even better ideas now. I swear on the sacred elements, he kept my brothers and me in line; his merciless guidance would do me good."

Anwealda tilts his head, and the diamonds in his

hair *clink*, as he studies Sol. "How self-sacrificing of you."

I hold my breath. Has Sol overplayed his hand?

When Anwealda chuckles, both Sol and I startle.

Anwealda shoots Sol a sharp look. *"Lies."*

I pale.

*We're screwed.*

I edge my hand into Sol's, and he squeezes it.

"Father…" Sol tries.

"Oh, keep your petty secrets. Boys will be boys." Anwealda adjusts his cuff links. When the blood on the tips of his fingers smears on his cuffs, he hisses in frustration. "Simply tell me what I get out of the deal."

Sol straightens. "If you send me, along with my Soul Bond, to the Kingdom of Air for retraining, then I'll find out who was responsible for the assassination attempt that made us both look weak."

Immediately, Anwealda stops fussing with his cuff and looks with disconcerting intensity at Sol. "You've impressed me. I thought that you'd hide in your room, licking your wounded horns and pride for days. Instead, you're demon enough to bargain with your Emperor and you know how serious the consequences will be if you fail."

Sol clenches his jaw. "As you said, I like to play with fire."

Anwealda's smile is dangerous. "Spoken like my

son. And where do you intend to start your search for the assassin?"

Sol's return smile is equally as dangerous. "I know exactly where."

He drags me away from Anwealda and down the stone stairs. Our footsteps clatter in the dark quiet. Fire surges on Sol's horns to light the way.

As we descend, it becomes as black as hell. Plus, just as hot.

I expected the dungeons to be freezing cold, but instead, as we descend, deeper and deeper below the palace, it heats up like the lava that lies beneath the Kingdom of Fire is turning the dungeons into a furnace.

Sweat drips down the center of my back, plastering my hair to my head. I try to breathe through my nose. The air is thick, musty, and stinks of sulfur. My eyes sting with the heat.

I hate to think how oppressive it must be for prisoners who are stuck down here, even assholes who deserve it.

*Like Oran and Iago.*

Sol's shoulders are stiff, and his expression is tight like he hates it down here as much as I do. He pulls me down a narrow corridor with rows of cells with heavy iron doors, which are set in the stone.

"Have you been in these dungeons before?" I whisper.

Sol casts me a quick glance. "Not on this side of the doors."

My eyes widen, and I swallow. "You were a prisoner?"

"Why? Do you imagine that this gorgeous demon is always a good boy?" Sol tries to smirk, but it falls flat.

I snatch him by the shoulder, and his surprised gaze meets mine. "This gorgeous demon is *my* good kitten, and I swear on the Stolen, he's never being thrown into the dungeons again."

Sol's eyes flutter shut for a moment, before he swings away from me, laying his palm flat on the iron door next to him. "Then we must find out the truth of the assassination." Fire sparks out, heating up the iron. "They're sealed by magic."

At last, the door swings open.

Sol's expression hardens, as he stalks into the cell.

I take a deep breath.

I don't know what I'm going to see now — what I need to do — but this is the next step in our plan. And I meant it about doing anything to stop Sol becoming the prisoner again.

I can do this.

*For Sol and Skye.*

I follow Sol into the cell, which is small and as hot as hell. I choke on the suffocating heat, and the stench of sulfur that catches at the back of my throat.

By the Stones, that stinks.

I hold my sleeve over my nose.

Oran and Iago hang next to each other by chains that are shackled around their bruised wrists in the center of the stone chamber. Their toes only just touch the floor, which must put a hell of a lot of pressure on their shoulders. Their heads are ducked low, and their tangled hair hangs over their faces. They don't look relaxed and in control now.

They look a fucking mess.

Their rich clothes are torn and bloodied, and their feet are bare.

I'm trying hard not to look at their striped horns, which match Sol's, but I don't miss Sol's wince, before he's able to school his expression into a cold mask.

We both need to play our roles.

When Oran looks up and realizes who it is, I'm surprised that it's relief that washes over his face. He nudges Iago, who looks almost unconscious. Iago struggles to open his eyes.

"Thank the sacred elements you're here, Your Royal Highness," Oran rasps like he's worn his voice out screaming (and I seriously bet that he has). "Here's the thing of it, you need to tell the Emperor that we're innocent."

I frown. Why's he looking at me?

"Are you still trying that line? How boring." Sol

fake yawns. "And am I *Your Royal Highness* all of a sudden? If I'd known a stint in the dungeons was all it took to get you to call me that without sounding like you smelled something disgusting, then I'd have thrown you down here years ago myself."

Oran gapes at him. "The Emperor will kill us."

Sol shrugs. "Well, you are traitors."

Oran struggles wildly in his chains. "Nay, we're not."

"That bastard Pet set us up, see," Iago says, slurring each word like it hurts to talk, "he said that we were the ones who told you to release him because we were trying to get Sol executed. But we didn't. Please, believe me."

When Sol circles Oran and Iago, my skin prickles. He's dominant and in charge in a way that I haven't seen before.

It's hot as hell.

He clutches Iago by the scruff of the neck. "I do." Iago lets out of a sigh of relief. "Because all plots have a grain of truth in them."

Iago's eyes widen with understanding, before he lets out a furious yell and struggles in his chains. All it achieves is to wrench his bruised wrists.

Oran doesn't fight, however, to my surprise. Instead, he studies me. His eyes remind me of a snake's, attempting to mesmerize its kill.

"I'll rip off your horns and feed them to you," Iago

growls. "Forcing your Soul Bond to lie about us is a new low even for you, Orphan Prince."

Sol pinches Iago's neck, and he yips. "I did no such thing. Pet told the Emperor what he did because his new worshiper," he smirks at me, "was kind to him, and he *fucking hates* you."

"I underestimated you." Oran arches his brow.

"You always did. I hope you learn from this."

"We can't learn much if we're *dead*," Oran mutters.

"Father won't kill you." Sol lets go of Iago and circles around to face Oran. "I've had long enough to learn how he thinks. He's going to make an example of the bluebloods and bring them down a peg or two. He wants everyone to remember that they're not untouchable. Then he'll hold this over you, so you become his puppets at court, won't that be fun?"

Okay, my turn. "Yeah, it's not the Emperor that you have to worry about. It's me."

I unsheathe my dagger and prowl to stand next to Sol, before holding the blade under Oran's chin. Oran hisses and raises his head to stare into my eyes. His breathing picks up, even though he tries to hide it.

I bet he hates being frightened of a human for once.

Sol studies his nails. "I never can control my princess. She's fiery."

Oran becomes ashen. "Now, hold on…"

"Not a fucking chance." I press the blade harder against his neck, winding my hand into his long hair, which is now free of its braid, and yanking back his head.

He hisses, and Iago watches with panicked, tawny eyes.

Rage simmers through me, as Sol prowls to stand behind me at my shoulder.

I remember being pinned under Oran's weight on the night of the ball. The flash of his fangs in a cruel smile.

"I love this part." I throw Oran's words back at him that he used that night, and his eyes flash with rage and fear, as he remembers too. "So, *scream for me.*"

Fire from Sol's horns dances over Light-bringer's copper hilt. Oran's stuttered breath is loud in the oppressive dark.

"Wait," Iago cries. His gaze darts between Sol and me, before he spits out a mouthful of blood, which puddles on the floor between us. "Are you just here to gloat and torment us then?"

"What do you think?" Sol drawls.

"I think," Iago's brow furrows, "that you could've destroyed us centuries ago but you didn't. And by my horns, you've brought us low to make us your puppets."

"Then if you're my puppets," Sol waves his hand,

and his magic heats Iago's chains, until he gasps and squirms, "I can make you dance."

"Just tell us what you want, Your Royal Highness," Oran snarls.

*My cue.*

Sol cools his magic, and I ease back my blade.

"Who tried to assassinate my Soul Bond and me?" Sol demands.

To my shock, Oran laughs. "You're not such an idiot, you're thinking that I want you *dead*...? I mean, I do...I simply mean that if *I* had planned it, then you'd *be* dead."

I roll my eyes. "All demons need to learn about self-incrimination because seriously, if trials existed here, I'd suggest you got yourself a good barrister."

Oran smirks and for the first time, despite the fact that he's the one in chains, he looks like the one in control. "I've breathed plots and schemes since the moment that I was born. Unlike the Orphan Princes, I'm not stumbling around in a world that sees me as prey."

Sol snatches him by the horn, and he yelps. "Except, you're the one hanging from the ceiling."

"And you're the one trying to find out who wants to kill you."

"Well, who tried to make it look like they wanted to kill you," Iago muses.

"What do you mean?" I demand.

Oran's eyes narrow. "Will you swear on the sacred elements to put in a good word with the Emperor for us, if we tell you?"

We could say *go to hell* and force them to tell us. Sol is right: they're his puppets now.

*Yet Sol isn't his dad.*

And I hate the idea of anyone locked away down here.

I give a subtle nod at Sol, but he deliberately takes a long moment before he replies like he's thinking about it.

Oran looks like he's barely breathing.

Then Sol's wings burst out with a flare of blinding magic. They beat behind him in a show of dominance. The other two demons quail.

"I am your prince," Sol has never sounded so commanding and regal, "and if I petition on the behalf of prisoners to my father, then I'll be doing them a favor and not a deal. One that shall forever put them in my debt, do you understand?"

My heart speeds up.

Sol's a genius. Not only has he played the two aristocrats to get his revenge, but now, he can look like the merciful one and put them in debt at court.

Perhaps, he really does know how to play demonic politics much better than his dad thinks.

Oran and Iago exchange a defeated glance, before they both nod.

"I will be in your debt, Your Royal Highness," Iago whispers.

Sol raises his brow at Oran, who looks like he's having difficulty getting the words out past his gritted teeth.

"Fine, I'm in your bastard debt. Now, do you want to know about the assassination attempt that wasn't? Then come closer."

I snatch Sol's shoulder, shaking my head.

There's a trick here. Oran's looking far too smug. There's a vicious cruelty lurking in his eyes.

But Sol leans closer to Oran.

What the hell is he going to tell him? Who tried to kill us on the night of the Bonding Revel?

"There was no assassination attempt," Oran says, triumphantly. "It was a deliberately botched *fake* assassination attempt. If you weren't such a blinded idiot, you'd have worked it out by now. Who'd want to make you look weak? The Emperor fears losing a son more than anything. It'd rock his reign, destroying its stability. Even the thought of it has made him doubt you, hasn't it?"

Oran watches Sol's devastated expression, greedily.

I'm frozen.

My pulse is racing too fast, and my mouth is dry. Each word is more poisonous than the last, but I can sense their truth.

And that's worse.

Dread churns in my guts.

Oran's eyes light with malicious glee, and I just know that what he says next will be his way of hurting Sol: his revenge.

I have to stop it.

Yet what if this is the only way to fulfill the deal with the Emperor and reach the Kingdom of the Air to save Skye?

"Sol," I grab his elbow.

*But it's too late.*

"Who would want to tarnish the Prince of Fire's reputation just as he was bonded?" Oran's voice is cold and cruel. "Who had the means to control an attempt by magic or water. Why, either the Demon of Earth or Water, of course. Your *brothers* are the true traitors."

# CHAPTER NINETEEN

## The Silver Orchard, Demon Underworld

I sprawl in the afternoon blood-tinged sunlight in the grassy orchard — naked — watching an equally naked demon setting up what looks like a dangerous ritual between the trees.

The vast orchard lies behind the palace; the air is sweet and cloying. The sprawling trees grow close together and are heavy with fruit: silver apples. The light glints off them; I can sense the magic, worming inside.

Once, I'd have been worried that Sol was about to devour me.

Once, I'd have been embarrassed about the whole nakedness thing.

Once, I'd have hated him for being a fucking demon.

But now, I'm not only surviving. *I'm living.* And I trust Sol, even if he insisted that we sneak out here and strip out of our clothes, before he created an inverted pentagram out of mounds of mud and leaves.

Now, he's sprinkling water from a wooden bowl on each of the pentagram's points, while chanting something in a demonic tongue.

Weirdly, I'm not freaked out by that. It's not even the strangest thing that I've witnessed today.

I haven't asked Sol yet about what Oran told us in the dungeon.

If I was told that Skye had betrayed me, then I may go a little crazy like Sol as well. If it only goes as far as nakedness and chanting, then it doesn't hurt, right?

And hell, I get to check out his gorgeous ass again.

I sigh, and the brand on my wrist tingles. I rub at it absentmindedly. I lick my lips, as I eye a fallen apple that's on the ground close to me.

My stomach grumbles.

Sol's been too preoccupied with setting up whatever this ritual is for us to grab lunch.

It won't hurt to steal one apple from the Emperor's magical orchard.

Right?

I reach for the silver apple, but with a speed that takes away my breath, Sol darts forward, crouching beside me. He drops his bowl, spilling the water over me, and snatches my wrist, before I can touch the fruit.

"On the name of the sacred elements, have humans totally forgotten what happened to Eve?" He demands.

"Seriously?" I grimace at the sensation of a wet crotch (and not in the fun way). When Sol arches his brow, I pout. "But it's so temping."

"And you wonder why humans fall to sin." His grin is wicked. "Luckily for me."

He kisses me, before pulling back.

I cup Sol's cheek; this is going to be tough. "Look, I know you don't want to talk about it, but what Oran said—"

"You're right, I don't want to talk about it." Sol's tail swings agitatedly side to side. "I feel like I've been gutted. I need to work it out in my head, before I can... But I don't believe that my brothers did it. I can't."

"Okay, I'm here if you do want to talk, yeah?"

"Thank you." He looks down. "I've spent years with Iago violating my mind and sharing my worst memories and emotions with others for their amusement. The feeling that I can hold onto this...the privacy of that...it's precious."

I stroke his cheek with my thumb. "You're safe with me, and I'm safe with you."

All of a sudden, his expression becomes determined.

Have I said something wrong?

By The Hill, I'm trying. I don't normally do *relationship stuff*, beyond one wild night of pleasure. I don't know how to talk about all this crap like *feelings*, but then, Sol's as bad as me at that.

Am I screwing it up?

Sol shifts around, until he's on his knees on the orchard floor. I startle, as a bed of red roses that have petals of flame blossom around him and up the surrounding trees in a bower.

Just as they did in the Eternal Forest.

Sol's tail whips out and coils around my wrist like he never wants to let me go.

"The last time that I did this, it went wrong because I didn't know who I was really talking to, but by my horns, I do now." Sol's midnight gaze meets mine with an intensity that makes my breath hitch. "I, Prince Sol and Demon of Fire, claim you...Blue...as my Soul Bond."

Last time, I was disgusted by his claim. It blinded me with white-hot fury.

I mocked him and made a joke out of it.

But this time, I understand how much it means to Sol. His sincerity shines through his eyes, and the way that his tail is trembling.

I pick my next words very, *very* carefully. "I, Princess Blue, claim you, Prince Sol and Demon of Fire as my Soul Bond."

Sol gasps, and his face lights up like the sun with delight. His tail drags me into his arms, as the roses burn even brighter.

He kisses me like he'll die if he doesn't, and I kiss him back like *I'll* die, if he stops.

He spins me around, never breaking the kiss, lying me down in the center of the pentagram. The fire from the roses jumps and burns along the five points. Sol's hard body presses me to the ground, and I flush hot and cold, lost in desire.

Reluctantly, Sol draws back, licking across my lips, before he feathers kisses down my neck. I arch against him, shivering.

"On my flames, I love you. I want you to be mine, forever. I need you," Sol murmurs, his voice is threaded with an anguished desperation.

"I love you too." Concerned, I wrap my arms around his waist. "What's going on?"

He gets in a final hard suck on my neck, before peering up at me beneath dark lashes. "You know that you said you'd think about it, if I could find a way to get your sister safe, but also us bonded?"

My heart misses a beat, and I clench my fingers into his hips, hard enough to bruise. "You've already managed it with my sister, if we tell Anwealda that your brothers are likely the ones behind the assassination attempt. Then he'll let us go to the Kingdom of Air to find her."

"I know." Sol's jaw clenches. "But will you bond with me?"

"If I do that," I say, slowly, "I won't be able to leave the underworld."

*Or Sol...*

We both hear that.

But could I anyway? Even if I find Skye now, could I truly return to a human world, leaving behind the demon who I love? Could I abandon him to be alone for the rest of his long life...to face the wrath of the Emperor?

*Hell, no.*

Sol's expression is studiedly blank like he's being careful not to influence my answer. Yet I can tell by the twitching of his tail and the way that fire is flaring between his horns that it's killing him not to.

It must be hard not to be able to fully hide his emotions or perhaps, I'm just getting better at reading them.

I wrap my ankles around Sol's, pulling him even more flush against me; his hardening dick rubs against me, sending delicious sparks through my core.

"You're mine, and I'm yours. I could never leave you now."

Sol lets out a relieved huff that gusts against me, and his shoulders slump.

Then his lips quirk. "So, you don't hate me anymore, stabby?"

"Let me show you just how much I hate you." I rock my hips against him, and he moans. "Fucking…" Another roll of my hips, and he bites his lip hard. "…demons."

I slip my hand around to his ass, stroking the base of his tail. His eyes dilate, and he pants, as I stroke past his twitching tail to the crease beneath. My thumb circles the sensitive rim, and he ruts against my leg.

He forces himself to still with an insane amount of self-discipline. "Hold. That. Delicious. Thought."

Reluctantly, I draw my hand back to rest it on his ridiculously perky ass. "I thought that demons were exhibitionists?"

"We are." He grins. "But kinky as I am, I also want to bond with you."

My brow furrows, as I glance at the **SKYE** brand on his chest. "I thought that my sister kind of already did that?"

He pulls a face. "I never loved your sister, nor did I claim her. And this week, while you were off getting lessons on fang fellatio and sexy uses for tails, I was being trained on my role in the palace. But that also meant I was left alone with the ancient demon texts to study. Who said that I was a good prince and studied what I was meant to?"

Excitement surges through me.

What's he found out?

"You're a total bad boy, kitten. Got it. So, what did you discover?"

Sol cards his fingers through my hair. "I looked for cases of identical twins bonding. There hasn't been one for centuries. When I did discover one... Skye and you have identical Souls. You're two halves of the *same* Soul, split in the womb. I only have Skye's name on me because she must have been born first."

"She was, by three minutes." My heart beats faster, and I swallow. "What's that mean?"

"The Soul Pool works on simple magic. But I discovered something darker and primordial. It only works for elemental demons, which is why I've added all the elements around the pentagram: fire, earth, water, and soon, there'll be wind. This type of magic is risky and dangerous." He gestures around at the ritual he's set up. "It's from an ancient time, and by my horns, maybe it'll consume our Souls."

"Wow, reassuring."

"Sorry, was I meant to be?"

I slap his ass, and he shivers in delight. "Hold that thought as well. But this magic will reveal my true Soul Bond, while linking your life to mine."

"So, I'd live as long as Ward…"

*I'll pretty much be immortal.*

The reality settles around me as heavy as a cloak.

*This is really happening.*

Sol strokes a strand of hair away from my face. "If it works, we won't have to fake anything again. You'll be an equal princess by my side forever, and no one will be able to take that away from us. *No one.*"

"What we're talking about is weighing the risk of a dark ritual consuming our Souls, against the chance of eternal love?"

Sol smiles, brightly. "Exactly."

"Let's do this."

Sol clicks his fingers, and the flames surge brighter around the pentagram. A sharp breeze picks up, shaking the trees' branches, but it doesn't blow out the fire.

All the elements are combined.

Sol's eyes flash red for a moment, and I shiver, but this time, with desire.

"What do we need to do?" I whisper.

"Since this is sex magic," Sol drawls, "it's self-explanatory. Unless you wish me to draw you a diagram?"

I gape at him. "Are you sure this isn't simply an excuse to have kinky sex?"

"Since when do I need an excuse for that?" His lips brush against mine. "Sex magic is one of the most ancient, powerful magics there is. Roman's a sorcerer who's renowned for it. But this won't be sex. This will be making love."

Sol's expression softens, and his eyes crinkle.

My heart aches. "Hell, I need you."

"And you have me."

He lowers his hand to between my legs, finding my clit, which he circles. Then his dick nudges between my thighs, before he pushes in with an aching slowness that makes me feel — *demands* that I feel — every inch.

I give a breathy moan, and my eyes flutter closed.

"Don't look away," he whispers. "Keep your pretty blue eyes on me."

I struggle to follow his command, under the onslaught of sensations, opening my eyes.

"You're so beautiful." He kisses my nose and cheeks. "Perfect."

I gasp, as he starts to thrust, slowly.

Looking into his eyes and watching every flickering expression of pleasure, is the most intimate thing that I've ever done. It's like I can see his Soul laid bare, and I'm sure that he can see mine.

He captures my lips, and I sigh with desire.

I need more, just *more*.

"Deeper," I murmur against his mouth.

I grip his hips harder, as he doesn't speed up but

instead, adjusts his position and pushes in even deeper.

And I gasp because there...*just there* is the spot. The one that sends electric waves of pleasure through me. I moan, and Sol's eyes become glassy.

"Don't ever look away from me." He winds his hand in my hair, pulling hard. "Blue, *my Blue*."

And that's what it takes. My name on his lips.

I howl, tumbling over the edge into screaming ecstasy at the same time as Sol.

His back arches, the same as mine, as if we've become one.

A sharp wind blasts through the orchard, blowing out the fire.

And I feel it. *The moment that our Soul Bond snaps into place.*

It's a connection that surges through me like burning fire. The world becomes vibrant and new. I can't see inside Sol's mind but I can feel his emotions like lace across my skin, and I know as much as I'm sure that Skye's the other half of me, that Sol is mine.

*This* is what we were missing before...? Yet we still fell in love: with each other's fierceness, humor, bravery, and beauty, inside and out.

But our heart, lives, and Souls are connected now.

I'm as immortal as a demon, and my humanity runs in Sol's veins.

For the first time, I understand the point of

humans bonding with demons and both species drawing closer to each other. Yet that doesn't mean I won't find a way to break the cruel reaping of Demon Sacrifices, unless they're through love.

Sol's staring at me with an adoring look that I've never seen directed at me before. "My true Soul Bond. Tell me that you feel it too?"

"Yeah, it's overwhelming and beautiful. In the name of the Stones, just like you. But also, you're still sort of inside me and heavy."

I push at his shoulder, and he laughs.

"Both fair points." He tosses his rock star tumble of hair out of his eyes, and I reach up to rub a smudge of eyeliner away from his cheek.

I love his messed-up look.

Then he sits up, gently pulling away from me.

I draw in my breath, sharply. "Look at your chest."

Confused, he peers down at himself. "Now I'll never forget who I belong to."

The **SKYE** brand has magically transformed to the word **BLUE** beneath his heart.

The sight does funny things to my insides, and by Sol's smile, it must do the same to him. He traces over each letter with his claw like he can't quite believe it's real.

But then, he becomes ashen. "Time to get dressed. Enough fun nudity."

He throws my pile of clothes at me, before dragging on his top, hurriedly hiding the branding.

Hurt, I frown. "What's the rush?"

I wriggle into my leather trousers, as Sol kicks over the mounds of earth and obscures the evidence of our ritual having taken place.

"Well, nothing." He slides into his own matching trousers, and his elegant fingers do up the lacing. "Unless you count the fact that we've been pretending that you're Skye, and I'm Soul Bonded to you. Plus, that if our whole charade is discovered, a trip to the dungeons, followed by a painful, public execution is the most likely outcome. No one makes a fool of my father."

"Oh, *that*." I push my arms into my crimson shirt, and Sol kneels over me to do up the buttons. "And what would we have done if we hadn't been Soul Bonds, after all?"

Sol gives a long blink, before tossing my suit jacket at me. "We'd have simply enjoyed a session of mind-blowing sex, before we had to tell my father what we'd discovered."

I fidget, as I let Sol help me into my jacket. "What are you going to tell him then?"

Sol bites his lip. "The truth. By my horns, Father can see through anything else, and it's the only way…"

"I understand the passion of new Soul Bonds,"

Anwealda's frosty voice calls across the orchard, and both Sol and I stiffen, frantically looking around to check that we've hidden enough evidence, "but I'd rather not come across your sweaty bodies in the middle of my orchard. I see enough naked debauchery at the revels, and as much as I encourage it, even a demon needs a break from orgies once in a while."

Sol smartly pushes himself to his feet. "Sorry to disappoint you, Father, but it's hardly an orgy when there's only two of us."

I hold back a snort of laughter.

Anwealda glides from between the trees; his face behind the mask is in shadows. He's tossing a silver apple from hand to hand.

Sol holds his hand out to me, pulling me up next to him. His ruby magic winds out from his back, forming ethereal wings.

I'm holding my scabbard on the other side and hurriedly buckle it around my waist.

*This is it.*

Sol has already kept his promise to bond with me. And I've kept my deal up until this point to fake bond with him at Court.

Yet the first part of his bargain was to help me find my sister, and she's in the Kingdom of Air. The only way to get there is for Sol to betray his own brothers.

I know that a demon can't break a deal. I wish that I could let Sol out of this one, but I don't know what's happening to Skye with Breeze. Is she a prisoner? Is she hurt?

Love is about more than promises and passion.

It's also about sacrifice and fucking pain.

I edge closer to Sol, resting my hand on the hollow of his back. His tail wraps around my ankle. Air gusts against the back of my neck from the beat of his wings.

If he does this for me, then it shows more love than any number of declarations, primal fucks, or beds of flaming roses ever could.

Even if its devouring him inside to do it.

Anwealda chuckles. "Do you wish me to let your friends out of the dungeon so that you can make it a true orgy then? I remember they used to talk about having some delightful times with you."

Sol's expression tightens. "Why not? It's what those posh brats are good for, right? They've had a scolding and a spanking. I'm sure they'll never try anything like it again."

Anwealda takes a long, slow bite of his apple.

When he replies, his voice is deliberately light but much more dangerous for it, "Why the change of heart?"

"Because then they'll owe me a favor, and you an even greater one. I wish to make them dance."

Anwealda gives a sharp grin. "You vicious thing. You're learning." He circles us, and I stiffen. The fluffy end of Sol's tail strokes my ankle. "If you're lying around in my orchard, I assume you've already discovered the identity of the assassin."

I don't miss the underlying threat in those words.

Sol tilts up his chin. "I don't have any evidence but I don't think it was a real attempt, more likely a smear on me: a way to weaken me in your eyes."

*One that worked.*

Anwealda cocks his head. "Keep talking."

Sol clenches his hands. "There are only two people who would want that, when you're deliberating who's to become Crown Prince on the night of my Bonding Revel. Two who have the talent and the motivation. At least, someone has made it look that way." I can tell by the light tremor running through him, how hard this is for Sol. He steels himself. "Either or both of my brothers, Roman and Caspian."

Anwelda stiffens for a moment in surprise, before forcing himself to nonchalance and taking another bite of his apple.

*Silence.*

Fucking say something...

Sol is staring at Anwealda, desperate for him to reply.

Is Anwealda going to arrest or hurt Sol's brothers? Is Sol going to end up needing to save the other princes?

I grit my teeth at the sound of Anwealda's deliberately slow munching on the crisp apple.

*For fuck sake...*

At long last, Anwealda swallows. "The wicked imps. How clever of them."

I gape at Anwealda in shock. "What?"

Anwealda throws his applecore down on the grass. "Close your mouth, darling, or are you catching flies?" I shut my mouth with a snap. "Your brothers are impressing me no end with this rivalry. In fact, all of your ambition to become Crown Prince shows me a streak of ruthlessness that's impressive."

Sol blinks. "So, do I have permission to travel to the Kingdom of Air for Breeze's tutoring?"

Anwealda swaggers closer, pulling a folded silver parchment that glimmers with a dark magic, which prickles across my skin even from this distance. "Go on then. But remember, you asked for it. Take this letter with you and don't open it on pain of another horn whipping." Sol winces. "It's my instructions to him about you both."

Wait, that doesn't sound good.

Breeze is a psycho warrior prince who's also probably stolen my twin. Now, we're traveling to his kingdom to be under his control, and the Emperor is giving him special instructions about us...?

I lean closer into Sol's side, as he takes the letter

from Anwealda. Sol encircles me protectively in his wings.

Anwealda's cold gaze darts between us. "You know, darling, I doubted your bond at first. One could almost think you hated each other, although I'm the first to admit that most of my relationships begin at the end of the blade and end in between the sheets. But now, your bond is so bright that it's glowing." His lips curl up, revealing his sharp fangs, and the crown between his horns flares. "The Kingdom of Air is harsh and deadly. It's a land of warriors. I've pampered you at Court. But now your brother is all grown up, he's more...beastly...than you." His gaze flicks to me. "Are you ready for the Demon of Air?"

I sheathe Light-bringer, sharply.

Then I grin; I'm a princess, Soul Bond, and a sister seeking revenge for her twin. "Is the fucking Demon of Air ready for me?"

**The End...For Now**

**Continue the adventures in the demon underworld in MY DEMON OF AIR (REBEL DEMONS BOOK TWO)**
https://rosemaryajohns.com

Thanks for reading **MY DEMON OF FIRE**! If you enjoyed reading this book, **please consider leaving a**

**review on Amazon.** Your support is really important to us authors. Plus, I love hearing from my readers!

Thanks, you're awesome!

Rosemary A Johns

X

**Become a Rebel here today by joining Rosemary's Rebels Group on Facebook!**

# WHAT TO READ NEXT: MY DEMON OF AIR!

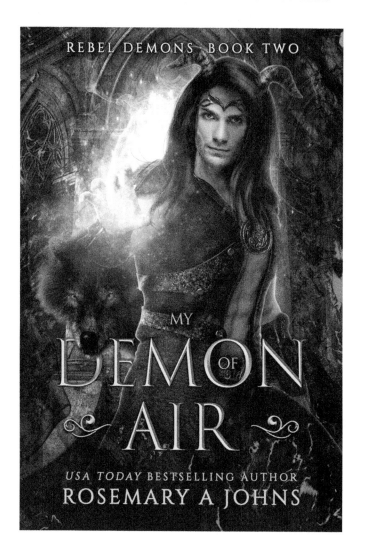

REBEL DEMONS · BOOK TWO

MY
DEMON
OF
AIR

USA TODAY BESTSELLING AUTHOR
ROSEMARY A JOHNS

**When a warrior demon prince locks me in his dungeon, I never expect him to claim me…**

I'm a broke music student, only loved by my twin. After a raid on my human town, however, I wake up, staring into the cold, black eyes of the Demon of Air. He's the mysterious, lethally gorgeous leader of the demon army, who's also a hell hound shifter.

But if he's my enemy, why does he keep saving me?

He's the beast who wants to make me his princess but keep me hidden and disguised. *His sweet secret.* But why?

I'm trapped in the middle of a war, and no matter how much attraction simmers between us, I have one chance to escape. In this perilous battle, will only one of us be left standing?

*If you like sexy, powerful heroes, thrilling adventure, and steamy romance, then you'll love this series.* **Devour this devilishly tempting twist on *Beauty and the Beast*!**

# OTHER BOOKS BY ROSEMARY TO READ!

## REBEL GODS

**Want to read more demons, Oni, Bacchus, and bad gods?**

The destruction of the godly Realms begins with a demon's kiss.

I lean through the silver bars of the cage and accept the kiss of the demon who's my best friend and first lover.

*Loki doesn't count.*

Plus, I allow myself to forget in the desperation of the moment that this is my *ex*-lover.

*It's complicated.*

His lips are soft, but they spark with a dark magic

that shudders through me. Its aroma winds through me: a warm cinnamon that makes me desire to taste it.

*Sweet Hecate, my soul aches.*

I'm empty. The place inside me, which was hollowed out of my own chaos magic, tries to reach out in response. But there's nothing there...*never anything there.*

I sacrificed it to save the god who I worship, Bacchus. Now I can only taste magic second-hand in my sorcerer lover's...*ex*-lover's...power.

Merlin's prick, why is it so hard to remember that?

*My demon's magic is delicious.*

Oni's gorgeous skin gleams like crushed sapphires, the same as his sweep of hair and curved horns. I wish that I could reach through the bars and stroke them to reassure him because he loves that.

Horns have many...*creative*...uses.

The muscles of his large shoulders are tight with the stress that he's trying to hide from me. He's naked (*does he have an allergy to clothes?*), and he's been forced to his knees. He's far too tall for the cage.

*He hates to be trapped.*

Reluctantly, I pull back from the kiss.

Just for a moment, I flash back to the night over a thousand years ago, when I lost my magic, to a white wolf in a silver cage just like this, before it stands freed next to a black stallion with flaring green magic...

I shake my head, grimacing as I snap the thin band around my wrist, as Ecstasy has taught me to do if I spiral about *that* night.

Bacchus gave all us Bacchants immortality. I've now lived for over a thousand years. Yet sometimes, it feels like no time has passed at all.

*Bubbling cauldrons, that scares me.*

The Bacchants have gained power and influence around the entire world, while I've been trapped *for my own safety* because I don't have magic in the Eternal Forest (just like once I was kept in the House of Ecstasy). Of course, as a teenager, there was the time that I attracted the Shadow Demons crawling around the walls by accidentally blotting out the sun (an eclipse, Ecstasy called it), or *accidentally* transported the entire West Wing into an alternate universe.

I rather enjoyed that universe: *they* didn't scream at me for the *accidental* mistakes of my magic but planned to crown me Queen of Chaos. Plus, Loki was imprisoned in a jail in Asgard for badmouthing the other gods. I believe they told me something about him being *tied to a rock, while a snake dripped venom on him for all eternity.*

*Win-win.*

Ecstasy brought me back, however, for *my own safety*. She was fiercely protective of me, just like I was fiercely protective of her. Yet I think it was more that the Bacchants feared that *I* wasn't safe.

*I'm not.*

What's wrong with an inquiring mind or the way that wild magic spills out…?

Yet after giving my cult immortality and placing me like a delicate toy that's already broken in the Tree of Life at the center of the Eternal Forest, Bacchus disappeared.

In a thousand years, why's he only visited me once? Does Bacchus love me or has he forgotten me?

Bacchus' golden curls and amber eyes still haunt *my* dreams. I crave my god, who possessed me and then was reborn through me…*for whom I gave up my magic.*

Ecstasy has spent the long years hunting and hurting Loki. Yet I no longer hope that Loki will be caught. I definitely don't wish to break him.

Loki cared about responsibilities, and I have mine like the one who's trying to give me the *demon puppy eyes*, even though he's got himself into trouble again.

Oni attracts trouble in the same way that my sister attracts cocks.

My lips twitch, but I ruthlessly smother my grin.

The cage is bound in ropes and swings from the high yew tree. I glance up at the thick branches. Oni's lucky that I came across him on my patrol before the Shadow Demons, who are massing in greater numbers every day.

Shadow Demons don't have loyalty to other

demons. They're beings of destruction and death. Just like they tore apart my parents, they'd have killed Oni.

My stomach roils.

The Eternal Forest is on the edges of Oxford, in England. Yet it's also a meeting place of the godly realms, where the veils meet the Other Worlds, the underworlds, and portals to places that are beyond even my imagination. It's dangerous and the spirits, demons, and gods are equally deadly.

*They're as vicious and wild as I am.*

This has been my playground for a millennium, and I'll protect it with my last breath.

The gloomy grove is a ring of dying yew trees. Vines hang between them like shrouds. The thick canopy of branches blocks out the late afternoon sun. My boots sink into the bed of curling, fiery leaves that crackle like paper. I wrinkle my nose at the scent of damp moss.

The Eternal Forest doesn't change with the natural seasons but adapts to those who dwell inside it. Plants from across the Realms grow next to each other, preying on the weak.

*I'm not weak.*

Yet there's beauty in the ancient forest. Luckily for me, I find that the deadliest are usually the most beautiful. Oni, for example, is a psycho but he's also a *beautiful* psycho.

I love him, until my Soul bleeds. I just can't give him as much of me as he needs.

Once, our love was the only thing that held me together. Oni stopped me from breaking apart, when I was first brought to the forest. Demons are immortal. He became my best friend, tearing through the shadows at night with me, swimming in the river that gushes through the heart of the forest, and climbing trees to battle spirits, rather than treating me like I was weaker than any another witch.

Like he could make me strong through his love and as if I was just another demon at his side in the dangerous black of the night. We were two creatures of the forest, and we fucked with the same savagery.

We simply can't be together now like we once were. *And it tears me apart as well.*

Oni's black eyes study me intently, as he wraps his clawed hands around the bars. "Come on, love, help a bloke out."

The cage swings in the breeze.

I raise my eyebrow. "You stole a kiss. What more do you want?"

He shoots me a lady-killing smile. "*Stole?* I offered, and you accepted. That's called a deal in the underworld."

"You're a rogue."

He grins. "I never pretended that I wasn't. Don't

we know each other well enough for a little familiarity?"

"Over familiarity."

*What am I saying?* I'll kiss him a thousand times if it calms his ragged breathing.

*Who's hunting him?*

I eye his glorious nakedness (and his dick hardens but then, he's always been an exhibitionist; demons mostly are). "It's freezing in the forest right now. The breeze is like needles under my skin. Where's your striped pelt or at least a thong…?"

"*Thong…?*" He tilts his head, and his horn hits the bar with a *clang* that makes me wince; his horns are sensitive. He does a good job of concealing his own wince, but I know him too well. "Of course, you're wearing such a lot yourself."

I mock gasp.

What's wrong with these leather pants and top, which are laced down the side? They're comfortable.

Forest creatures don't wear much. Perhaps, Oni has a point on the nakedness, apart from the twigs, rocks, and beetles sticking in uncomfortable places.

I lean closer. "Sass is a dangerous when you're inside a trap, asking for help."

"Sorry." Oni's eyes sparkle in the way that I love. "Even my spinster aunt would approve of your outfit."

I narrow my eyes. "You don't have a spinster aunt."

"Good thing too or demon or not, she'd have a heart attack over what you're wearing," he mutters.

I slam my hand against the bars. "And this imaginary aunt loves naked asses?"

Oni wiggles *his* naked ass. "Aren't you enjoying the view?"

He sounds sincerely disappointed.

I roll my eyes. "What did you do this time?"

Oni's expression becomes serious.

"Nothing," he says, affronted.

*Liar, liar, demon ass without pants on fire...*

"Then what's the Demon Emperor punishing you for?" I demand.

My heart clenches, and I scuff my foot through the leaves. I've never been able to save Oni from the other demons, and he's never asked me to.

I can't leave the forest to kick some Emperor ass. Who knows what dark plots go on in the kingdoms of the demon underworld? Yet I'd give anything to be able to hex their Emperor with a Ginger Root Hot Horn Hex.

For a demon that's worse than shoving the ginger root somewhere far more intimate.

Oni puffs up his chest. "By my claws, there were twelve gods, and they attacked me from behind, or I'd have crushed them with a single blow from my hammer..."

"It *was* the Emperor, wasn't it?"

Oni deflates, pushing a strand of blue hair behind his ear. "Work with me here. Allow a demon some pride."

"You could easily crush twelve gods in one go with your hammer," I reassure him.

He brightens. "Really?"

"Of course not."

He rattles the bars of the cage. "Just a *minor* disagreement over *minor* infractions of the rules. How about you let me out, before I'm eaten by something in a *major* way?"

*My rebel demon...*

"You'll go too far one day," I mutter.

"I already have."

I look at him sharply.

Oni is an outcast, and he's one because of *me*.

When he waves his hand, cinnamon scented dark magic shimmers in the air between us, and my breath catches. I weave my fingers through it, catching at the threads. It sings to me, but I no longer can sing back.

I burn inside at the loss.

Out of the magic, bursts a song that burns the same as me about an ex's loss and jealous love. The moody hip-hop *anti-love* anthem rips through me. It's not exactly the rock love song that Oni usually serenades me with.

*My possessive guy who I love.*

I tap my foot. "The Prince of Fire has spent too

317

much time in the human world. He's totally wrecked you with all this modern *human* strangeness, which he brings back from his travels."

Is Oni making a point with his choice of song?

Oni blinks at me with pretend innocence. "You're no better. You're always peering at the advancements of the non-magical. And Sol, my flame baby…"

I snort. "Disrespectful."

Oni waves his hand dismissively. "The prince loves it. Anyway, love, my flame baby's obsessed with music."

"*Uh-huh.*" I glance at the ropes, working out whether I can untangle them and let the cage down gently. "Do we need to talk about anything?"

"What do you suggest? What's our favorite sexual positions? Who should play me in a movie of my life? How am I so devilishly handsome?" He waggles his eyebrows.

"What about why you're blasting the glade with a song that makes it sound like I ripped your heart from your chest and then ate it?"

He pats at his chest. "Didn't you?"

My own chest aches like he's thrust his claws through *my* heart. "*Ha-ha.* Have fun playing with the Shadow Demons."

I spin on my heel away from him.

"*Wait,*" he calls, and the pain that threads his voice with anguish makes me screw shut my eyes, "you say you love me but then we can't be together. That's not how it should be. Your blood beats through mine. Even when we're apart, I feel you...*I need you.* By demon tradition, we're Soul Bonded..."

"It doesn't matter." My eyes snap open, and I turn back to him, stalking closer. All I want to do is kiss him again, and it hurts that I can't. It wasn't fair to accept his first kiss. "On the Tree of Life, I won't bind us, when my sister has already forced it on you."

"My love is real," Oni hisses.

His fangs elongate from his sharp white canines. I shiver with desire to lick over each one, as I once used to, lying on his chest high in the branches of the trees. His gentle bites in our Soul Bond were a claiming.

*But that was the illusion because my sister was the one to claim him.*

When our love was fresh, and Oni and I were first exploring the forest together like wild things, I didn't realize that he was breaking the rules of his own Emperor, Anwealda, by venturing into the forest.

*By loving a witch.*

When he disappeared, I was frightened to begin with because there were many terrifying creatures in the forest that could have hurt or killed Oni. Desperate, I searched for him for weeks...months...*years.*

I never gave up hope.

I never gave up on him.

*I never gave up...*

I begged Ecstasy to help me, despite her hatred for demons. Our sisterly love for each other has never dimmed; I've forgiven her for her role in the Bacchanalia. After all, she was only following Bacchus' will. And she's my only family.

I was still shocked, when she finally agreed. I was even more shocked, when she dragged Oni to me in chains from the Emperor's dungeons.

She made a deal with the Emperor that bound Oni to me by a Personal Guard spell. He was now an outcast to the underworld, the bodyguard servant to witches, and mine by Bacchant magics.

How could I hold him to his Soul Bond and as my lover, when he was held to me by a *spell*?

*When he wasn't free?*

"How about we chat about this, when you've got me out of this cage? That's unless you've suddenly developed a kink I don't know about…?" Oni winks. "If that's the case, love, you know I have almost no limits, at least with you. Shall we test it out?"

Why is he always so dangerously tempting? He loves playing with fire as much as I do.

I reach for my scythe, which leans against the tree next to the cage; I only placed it down earlier to examine the cage. The scythe shakes and glows, welcoming my touch.

It craves me, as much as I need it: *The Infernal Scythe.*

I shudder, as its ancient magic creeps around my fingers, drawing them around its shaft. Like an addict, I shudder at the taste of its magic.

*That's right... Join with me... Live and seek savage death...*

My leaf brown eyes fade to milky white, as I snatch the scythe.

Bacchus didn't leave me without a job in the Tree of Life. Instead, I was granted the role of Guardian to the forest. My sister's magic connected me to the ancient Infernal Scythe, transforming me into an Infernal: a reaper with the power to kill both demons and gods.

I thought that I was feared as a Chaos Witch but that was child's play. Now, I can reap the Souls of the most powerful beings in this forest. And by reap, I mean *kill*.

Blotting out the sun and traveling to alternate universes doesn't sound so bad now.

Yet I only devour with the scythe the wickedest Souls: *killers*. They're those who escape the deepest dungeons of the underworlds and flee to the forest to stir up the spirits here. I maintain the peace for all the worlds. I'm the balance, rather than the chaos.

*Or are they the same thing...?*

Hollow as I am, the scythe's borrowed magic fills me up with dark whispers. Hewn from the Tree of Life, it gleams with malicious magic, tipped at the bottom with a sharp steel point. The huge curving blade, which is fastened to the shaft by chains, is sharpened on both sides (all the better to fight with). The blade glints with silver and is deformed as if with gaping mouths like the souls that it's devoured.

It's shaking, desperate to devour more.

This morning, the Infernal Scythe called me to it. I've been on the hunt ever since.

Two demon souls, a bonded couple, escaped from the demon underworld. They were traitors, who were executed for the murder of the Emperor's own son.

It's no wonder Anwealda is a cold prick, when his kid was assassinated.

*They'll be hell to pay if I don't catch these Souls.*

In fact, worse than hell. Demons and gods hate each other. It's a war that's rumbled on for millennium. Yet the Demon Emperor allows Bacchus' cult to live in the heart of the forest's shadows, as long as I reap for the demons as well.

*On Hecate's tit, why was I distracted from my patrol...?*

My eyes narrow on Oni, before I swing my scythe and slash through the ropes. Oni yelps, as the cage smashes to the glade floor with a *clang.*

"A little rougher next time," Oni peers up at me, "my balls aren't totally crushed. I won't be able to reach the high notes of a castrato."

"Now don't you wish that you weren't naked?" I smirk.

He makes the universal sign with his hand for *fifty-fifty*.

"Shuffle back," I say.

He edges to the back of the cage, and I swing the scythe again. The sharpened edge of the blade sparks against the cage's door, breaking the enchantment.

The door swings open.

I rest the scythe over my shoulder because I allow myself a certain quotient of smug a day, and this is mine.

Oni crawls out of the cage, before pushing himself to his feet and rolling his broad shoulders with a hiss of satisfaction.

*He's so tall.*

I raise my chin to look at him, and the familiarity of needing to look up at him, tugs a smile to my lips. "Do you want to talk about our love life or do you want to hunt?"

He flashes a hint of fang, before darting closer and wrapping his strong arms around my waist. His breath is hot against my cheek, and my skin prickles at his tightly coiled danger that always somehow also means *safety*.

"Thank you," Oni breathes. His fingers dance lightly across my lower back; his claws draw light circles. Then he pulls back, and his dark gaze is serious. "I'll forever protect you, love. Who are we hunting?"

My breath hitches.

I protect the Eternal Forest, and Oni protects me. It's like the rainbow after the rain. I know it's true. Yet I wish that I could be sure it's because of the Soul Bond and not because he's my Personal Guard.

"Two fire demons," I reply. "The ones who killed the Emperor's son."

Oni's expression darkens, and he stalks to the other side of the grove, lowering his horns aggressively. "We couldn't be reaping a worthier pair of criminals. Those bastards conspired to let the Shadow Demons into the underworld. They became known as the Shadow Traitors. They planned to do it on the day of the funeral, when the kingdoms were distracted by grief. Who uses someone's kid like a chess piece?"

"A demon." I tap my fingers on the scythe's shaft.

Oni snorts. "Gods are just the same. You don't even know half the screwed-up..." He peers at me. "What's the consequence if we don't catch them?"

I love that he never hesitates over the *we*.

"Does it matter? We have three days and nights as normal to make the reap." I struggle to meet his gaze. Anwealda was too *graphic* on this point. Oni merely continues to look at me steadily. "He always hurts me through you."

Oni stiffens but then shrugs. "Good, then it means he's not hurting *you*."

"He'll take your horns," I whisper.

A demons' horns are their weapon, pride, and manhood. For them to be broken or taken is the ultimate shame.

If you wish to hurt a demon, hurt their horns. If you wish to break them, break their horns. And if you wish to *destroy* them, then *take* their horns.

Oni's expression is solemn. "Then we better hunt those bastards, right?" All of a sudden, his eyes light up. "Summer! Baby, did they hurt you?" Oni crouches beside a giant iron hammer which glistens with runes. He cradles it to his chest like a lover. Then he kisses along its ash handle. "Naughty men taking you away from me."

*Witching heavens, is he about to hump it...?*

I refuse to daydream about Oni fucking the hammer.

Stop it, I said *refuse, refuse, refuse...*

Oh, all right then.

*Too late.*

When I laugh, Oni shoots me a too knowing sideways glance. Then he attempts to stand and swing the hammer in his hand in as *demonly* a fashion as possible.

"Look at my terrified face," I deadpan. "The horror of the demon and his mighty hammer."

Oni points at me with Summer (his magical hammer…and broomsticks, how he did sulk, when I nicknamed him *Thor*), "Don't be jealous. Summer may come before Autumn, but I always make sure that my lovers are equally satisfied."

I groan. "That's truly bad, even for you."

He prowls closer. "I promise that it wouldn't be."

"And I promise—"

"Down," he hisses.

Instinct bred of centuries fighting together kick in, and I duck.

Oni swings the hammer over my head, and something *screeches*.

It's a hideous wail. The hairs along the back of my neck rise, and my fingers tighten, until my knuckles are white around the shaft of the scythe.

*Devour…devour…devour…*

I am Infernal.

The scythe calls to me, thirsting.

*The Shadow Traitors are here.*

*They* hunted *us*. No Soul has ever sought out the Infernal before.

For the first time, it shudders through me that these truly are the demons who in life, tried to topple their own underworld. They're not the average killer that I reap. *What do they want now?*

Flames flicker across my skin; I close my eyes

against the intense heat. Oni hollers. I twirl around him, and my eyes snap open.

The souls of the Shadow Traitors are ghastly orbs, which blaze like flickering suns. Unlike less dangerous spirits, which are hunted by normal reapers, these are misshapen. Arms and legs bulge in and out; horns stick from the top of the orbs and malevolent black eyes watch me from their centers.

Why did they escape to the forest? Are they planning to conspire with the Shadow Demons here?

I bite my lip. *I won't let them.*

My scythe howls in fury at the presence of the Souls who were once lovers in a murderous pact. Are they still?

The scythe heats in my palms. I swing it over my head in a practiced rhythm, and it *swooshes* through the air. One of the orbs flares brighter; the face of the male demon pushes itself free from the orb for one horrifying moment.

The light blinds me.

*Don't let me miss.*

This is what I trained to do for over a thousand years. I've fought and reaped escaped Souls for centuries. I've never failed a mission.

Why does it feel different this time?

Oni's claws and horns elongate, glowing. He growls, and his savagery rumbles through me.

I hook the scythe, catching the male fire demon

before he can escape, and then pull down, slicing him in two.

It's the *female* fire demon who screams.

*Devour…devour…devour.*

I howl to the skies, as the gaping mouths of the scythe open and *devour* the orb. The shaft vibrates with a stinging dark magic, but I don't let go because if I do, I feel like the world will shake to pieces.

Perhaps, it will.

My eyes narrow, and my shoulders straighten.

*Now, to reap the female demon…*

All of a sudden, the season of the forest changes, however, and a blizzard sweeps through the glade. I stumble backward, as a snowstorm gusts, driving snow into my eyes in a white shroud. The ghostly wail of the mourning Shadow Traitor echoes through the snow.

Why are the seasons changing so violently? Even for these unpredictable woods, it's unusual. What's triggered it?

"*Now* I wish that I wasn't naked." Oni braces me with an arm around my waist.

Unexpectedly, something soft…the softest fur in all the Realms…whirls out of the white, sinuously flying on the wind, before winding around my neck.

I breathe in deeply; the aroma of sweet apple blossoms coils through me.

Oni senses the new magical — *trickster* — presence and growls, but I sooth my hand down his arm.

"It's my Kit," I whisper because I'd know my kitsune fox-spirit blindfolded, after centuries with him living at my side. "Now isn't the time for cuddling, nine-tails, I'm on an Infernal mission, and I can't fail."

Kit clings tighter around me like a scarf, draping his nine golden tails down between my tits. He's a gorgeous fox shifter, who's mischievous but heartbreakingly loyal.

He'd never follow me, *unless*...

My gaze darts out into the blanket of white. Where's the second She-Soul? Has she escaped deeper into the forest?

Kit's golden eyes swirl, mesmerizing through the storm. "Has Kit broken the rules? Is Kit in trouble?"

Sweet Hecate, I wish that I could kick the ass of the witch who captured Kit as a cub, Hestia. She restrained his magic and raised him to make the fox-spirit believe that he had no more freedom than a pet.

Now as a gorgeous man and shifter, at times of panic, he slips back into that thinking. I refuse to bind either Oni or him like that.

I stroke over Kit's silky head, and he huffs. "No rules with me, remember? You're wild. But it's dangerous out here."

*Horns sticking out of deformed orbs...ghastly wailing...blazing fire...*

Then I think of Kit and the way that his soft tails brush against my skin. I pale, before glancing back at Oni.

Oni nods. "I'll check out if the She-Soul is still in the glade. Nice day for it."

He draws back from me, and is swallowed by the white.

My hands are sweaty on the scythe.

Why does it feel like Oni will disappear on me again? That I'll lose him for good this time.

*My heart would shatter.*

Kit rubs his ear against me. "Kit eats danger for breakfast: *munch, munch.* All eaten. No more danger." I stifle a laugh. "But it's safer out here than in TOF. That's what this intrepid kitsune came to tell you."

I stiffen.

TOF is our name for the Tree of Life. It's my home, shelter, *everything.* I'm the tree's Guardian. No one threatens it and survives.

I shake, and the Infernal Scythe glows with dark, dangerous magic. "Who dares to bring danger to *my* forest...*my* tree?"

Kit's eyes blaze. "*Loki.*"

## LOVE DRAGON SHIFTERS? HOW ABOUT ADORABLE DEMON FAMILIARS?

The handsome shifter with molten silver eyes vibrated on the edge of bursting into his dragon form and burning down Evermore Farm. He smartly clasped his hands behind his back like he was restraining himself. His magic coiled out of him, however, in fluttering silver streaks towards me.

*It was spellbinding.*

I still took a step back because Starlight, who'd abandoned me, had been equally gorgeous and mesmerizing.

Yet he'd also been deadly underneath it like a tiger...*or a dragon.* Both could rip out your heart, use it as a chew toy, and spit it out in a bloody puddle. *Then* make you embarrassingly howl out "Wrecking Ball."

I shuddered. I couldn't live through that again and I knew that Satan wouldn't survive it.

The shifter's magic licked across my cheek like it couldn't resist the temptation (Satan had invented a special potion to make my skin silky soft), dragging at the magic deep inside me and entwining with it.

Okay, that was *way* too intimate.

*What'd happened to magical personal space?*

Satan, my demon kitten familiar, hissed. He subtly

winded his magic around me, at the same time as stinging the shifter's.

Satan's magic cocooned me in the ultimate cock block.

*Having a demanding cat alone was perfect for that.*

The shifter grimaced and withdrew his magic with a shrug of his shoulders, although he eyed me with a wary respect like the power that he'd sensed had been *mine.*

*That was right, Alpha jerk dragon: fear the scary all-powerful witch.*

Satan shot the shifter a smug look from his place perched on my shoulder.

"My apologies," the shifter said, grudgingly, "dragon instincts, you know?"

I turned on my heel. I needed to get back to the opening, before the Witch Inspector turned up.

"Don't let those instincts hit you on your dragon ass on the way out," I called over my shoulder.

"Wait," he called with an edge of desperation that surprised me. I hesitated. Psycho dragons were not on my To Do List today. I sighed, before turning back to him. "I suppose my invitation was lost in the post...?"

He strained to look past me at the buzz of other villagers in front of my cottage.

The yard was so crowded that the familiars had to scurry between legs, swoop in the skies, or hop on the guests' startled shoulders. It looked like almost the entire village had turned out.

Why did the shifter care that he hadn't been invited? Wasn't he the recluse, whose sole reason to march over here was to complain?

But if that was true, why was he trying to hide crushing disappointment mixed with wary hope beneath that haughty mask of his?

*Crack my broomstick, was he hoping that I'd invite him to join us?*

And if so, he had the worst manners that I'd come across and I worked with demon familiars.

Of course, he *should've* received an invite.

I raised an eyebrow at Satan, who instantly plastered on his innocent face.

The problem with having a magical familiar like Satan was that he always knew more than me (and I was witch enough to admit that), and he was always scheming.

On the other hand, it was his most adorable feature.

Satan looked the dragon shifter up and down. "*You're old and posh. It's like this, see, you probably don't even have a computer. I bet you only have antiques and stuff. So, how could you receive the email for this event?*"

The shifter flushed, flustered. "I admit that I possess a quantity of antiques, however, I also own a computer. On the other hand, I'm not old...I mean, not in dragon years... I'm the younger son; it's my brother who's the Duke. I'm merely the Earl..." *A witching earl was my next-door neighbor?* Then his mouth snapped shut, and his eyes narrowed at Satan. "How can I hear that kitten?"

He spat out *kitten* like it meant *snake*. Except, some of my favorite familiars were snakes. Perhaps, I should've said *dung beetle*.

*So, not a cat lover then.*

Satan's fur fluffed up in outrage, at the same time as my own hackles rose.

*Sweet Hecate, if a man didn't love cats then he was dead inside.*

Starlight had adored Satan, and he'd been a vampire. Except, the truth was that vampires were Fallen Angels, so Satan had taken full advantage of sleeping on Starlight's wings, treating them like movable feathery beds.

To be honest, I think it was the only reason that Satan had wanted me to bond with Starlight.

I stroked Satan's head. "You can hear Satan because he *wants* you to. Some witches don't grant their familiars that freedom, but let's just say that Satan can choose who he talks to, where he goes, and what time he wakes me up in the mornings." Satan snickered. "That last one is up for negotiation though if it's abused."

*Wow, did Satan abuse it.*

Exhibit A, this morning: *Rise and shine, my witch. It's 3 a.m. and my stomach's awake and demanding tuna.*

The shifter blinked. "You let him tell people lies…?"

Satan winked. *"And insult them."*

"Sounds right," I agreed. "But as I told you, there's no *let* about it. Since we're total strangers here, I'll explain that I'm Astra of the House of Demons, but even though my mum's notorious for controlling demon familiars, I'm more for…"

*"Being controlled by them?"* Satan purred.

"Unhelpful," I whispered.

"You and the cat parrot on your shoulder are strange." The shifter cocked his head, and dark hair tumbled across his eyes like he was trying to work me out.

*Good luck on that.*

It was more fun playing with this earl dragon than I'd expected.

Morgan had never thought that I'd break away from the family business, and no one amongst the covens had guessed that a witch of the House of Demons would choose to work with the rejects of the familiar world.

*Doing the unexpected was working for me so far.*

I smiled sweetly, enjoying the flash of confusion

on my neighbor's face. "Why don't you join us? We have these delicious cocktails that are enchanted to taste like your choice of flavor on each sip, and the village caterers have laid on a feast." My eyes lit up. "You may even find a familiar you'd like to rehome." At the shifter's horrified expression, Satan chuckled. "A panther, perhaps," I muttered.

"What was that?" The shifter demanded.

"Nothing," I singsonged.

The shifter *harrumphed*, before leaping over the remains of the fence and okay, that was impressive.

In no way was I noticing his bunched muscles or athletic legs.

*Of course not.*

"*Lay off, I'm the mini-panther around here,*" Satan complained.

I rolled my eyes. "Obviously."

"*Don't patronize the Great Satan but do stroke him.*"

I lifted Satan off my shoulder and cradled him in my arms, so that I could get in a full-on belly stroke.

The shifter raised an elegant eyebrow. "He has you well trained, Astra."

Satan purred. "*Aye, it took years of hard work, but the results speak for themselves.*"

When I dumped Satan in a ball of disgruntled fluff amongst the daffodils, it was the shifter's turn to laugh.

I was shocked at how musical his laugh was. I could get used to that.

*But well trained my witchy ass...*

When the shifter marched closer, his spicy scent of myrrh wound around me, wrapping me in its warmth. "Who am I to turn down such hospitality? Wait, I know..." He held out his hand. "I'm Earl Sinclair, at your service. Although, my friends call me Sin because..." His smile was dangerous. "...Perhaps, it's more fun if you discover that for yourself."

"Goodie, games. My favorite." *Unintentional innuendo alert.* Why were his eyes darkening like that? Time for desperate backpedaling. "You know, like non-sinful online gaming, Cluedo, or poker. Don't try and beat me at card games because this face has no tells."

"*Uh-huh.*" Sin's butterfly long black lashes were criminally unfair. Men shouldn't be allowed to have lashes like that without mascara. "I'm reading you just fine right now."

*Mr Boastful Dragon.*

When his hand rested on the hilt of a curved scabbard, which was strapped to his side, my eyes widened. "You brought a weapon over to complain about the noise? *Oh no, my new terrifying witch neighbor and her shelter for wild familiars, I'd better strap on my sword.*"

He blinked. "Was that meant to be an impression

of me? I most certainly do not sound like a cowardly prince with a stick up my behind. I need my sword…"

"You have a sword fetish?"

His jaw clenched. "It's ceremonial. At least, for me. Dragons from my Court…warriors from it…fight with these, but I don't any longer."

"And is that a ceremonial gun in your pocket, or are you just pleased to see me?"

Sin looked trapped. "I don't have a gun."

I blushed at the same time as him. *Don't look down at his crotch.*

*Stupid innuendo mouth…*

Satan glanced between Sin and me, before deliberately breaking the tension. *"Satan and Sin sounds like a fine duo."* Satan preened. *"Like a crime fighting team. Help, the world's in peril because of the evil chickens."* Satan was caught up in a war with the chickens (entirely normal, non-magical ones that I kept for their eggs). Last week, he'd tried to make friends with them, expecting them to talk back but instead, they'd chased him. One of the few rules I had was that he mustn't use magic against non-magical animals. *"Who shall we call?"*

"Ghostbusters?" I hazarded.

Satan puffed out his chest. *"Satan and Sin, that's who. You do want to be saved from the terrorist chickens, right?"*

"Why not Sin and Satan?" Sin drawled. "After all, *I'm* the earl."

Satan waved his tail at him in his version of a rude gesture.

But the fact that he was Earl Sinclair *was* a problem.

Witches had a complex relationship with dragon bluebloods. Being aristocracy meant that they were the leaders of their people or in positions of power.

Sin's magic must be powerful.

Covens either fought, screwed, or had an uneasy truce with shifters. I should keep up with that sort of thing but Mum had always moaned that with me, if something wasn't about familiars or books, it went in one ear and then out the other.

*Nothing had changed.*

To be honest, I was regretting that now. Were witches at war with dragons still?

# ABOUT THE AUTHOR

ROSEMARY A JOHNS is a USA Today bestselling and award-winning romance and fantasy author, music fanatic, and paranormal anti-hero addict. She writes sexy shifters and immortals, swoonworthy book boyfriends, and epic battles.

Winner of the Silver Award in the National Wishing Shelf Book Awards. Finalist in the IAN Book of the Year Awards. Runner-up in the Best Fantasy Book of the Year, Reality Bites Book Awards. Honorable Mention in the Readers' Favorite Book Awards. Short-listed in the International Rubery Book Awards.

Rosemary is also a traditionally published short story writer. She studied history at Oxford University and ran her own theater company. She's always been a rebel…

**Thanks for leaving a review. You're awesome!**

Want to read more and stay up to date on Rosemary's newest releases? **Sign up for her \*VIP\* Rebel Newsletter and get FREE novellas!**

**Have you read all the series in the Rebel Verse by Rosemary A Johns?**
Rebel Academy
Rebel Werewolves
Rebel Gods
Shadowmates
Rebel Demons
Rebel: House of Fae
Rebel Angels
Rebel Vampires
Rebel Legends
**Have you read all the series in the Oxford Verse?**
Biting Mr. Darcy
Hexing Merlin
A Familiar Murder
A Familiar Curse
A Familiar Hex
A Familiar Brew
A Familiar Ghost

A Familiar Spell

A Familiar Yule

**Have you read Rosemary A Johns' Contemporary Romance?**

Elite

**Read More from Rosemary A Johns**

Website

Facebook

Instagram

TikTok

Bookbub

Twitter: @RosemaryAJohns

**Become a Rebel here today by joining Rosemary's Rebels Group on Facebook!**

# APPENDIX ONE: ELEMENTALS

Prince Breeze, Demon of Air, Demon Shifter, eldest
brother
Prince Roman, Demon of Earth, Demon Shifter
Prince Sol, Demon of Fire, dragon Demon Shifter
Prince Caspian, Demon of Water, Demon Shifter,
youngest brother


Kingdom of Air
Kingdom of Earth
Kingdom of Fire
Kingdom of Water
Elemental Palace, Emperor Anwealda's court

# APPENDIX TWO: DEMONS

Oni, demon, Guardian, Sol's best friend
Anwealda, Demon Emperor, ruler of the underworld
Oran, Lord Oakthorn, Demon of Misrule
Duke Oakthorn, Oran's father and Iago's Guardian
Iago, Demon of Memories
Shadow Demons
Shadow Traitors, fire demons
Alpha, winged wolf

# APPENDIX THREE: HUMANS

Blue, Skye's twin

Skye, Blue's twin

Maxton, the twins' best friend in The Hill

Lana, Duchess in The Hill

Mrs. Ward, leader of human Soul Bonds and
housekeeper in Elemental Palace

Printed in Great Britain
by Amazon

81440923R00212